AD ONE DEAD CRITIC

A KATE CAVANAUGH CULINARY MYSTERY

Cathie John

JOURNEY PRESS

Journals of Kate Cavanaugh:
ADD ONE DEAD CRITIC

Copyright ©1997 by Cathie Celestri and John Celestri
All Rights Reserved

JOURNEY PRESS
is an imprint of
CC Comics / CC Publishing
P.O. Box 542 Loveland, OH 45140-542
(513) 248-4170

Back cover photograph by David Koetzle

Logo designed by Steve Del Gardo

ISBN 0-9634183-4-3

Printed in the United States by:
Morris Publishing
3212 East Highway 30
Kearney, NE 68847
1-800-650-7888

The authors wish to thank the following:

Bruce and Phyllis Martin, Carol Miracle, and Matt Hellrung for their gifts of time and energy, helpful criticisms, and enthusiasm. Lisa Bauer, Connie Wade, Jon Cheek, Robin Mace, and the rest of the Tri-State Siblings Chapter of Sisters in Crime for their generous support.

To Debbie Pettit for her unique perspectives, and Lorraine Gibbs for her sharp eye.

Special thanks to:
Captain Will McQueen, Assistant Chief of the Indian Hill Police Department and Lieutenant Thomas Smith of the Indian Hill Police Department, Cincinnati, Ohio, and Rick Combs, Chief of Police, Village of Glendale, Ohio. Despite what Kate Cavanaugh thinks, they're all great cops.

And to Dr. Elyse Lower and Dr. Karen Columbus. Without them, we would never have come to this point in our journey.

Dedicated to the
over 2.6 million breast cancer survivors
in the United States.

ADD
ONE
DEAD
CRITIC

The first deadly killer I ever confronted face-to-face was a lump I found hiding in my breast. The mystery was: How did it get in there? And how the hell do I kill it before *it* kills *me?*

My personal cancer-fighting Sherlock Holmes was an oncologist working out of the Barrett Center in Cincinnati. With her keen analytical eye guiding my treatments, the murderous monster growing inside of me was arrested and destroyed.

That was over six years ago.

The experience awakened my dormant sense of humor -- it was either laugh or go crazy. And when I finally licked that terrible disease, I found the experience had also taught me a lot about myself and life.

I'm still learning.

LIFE'S LESSON #2007
I found out that dead men can tell tales.

Six days ago ... Friday, December 15th

CHAPTER ONE ....

I read in the morning edition of *The Cincinnati Enquirer* that my friend Preston Schneider, restaurant and fine arts critic of *Cincy Life* magazine, was found dead the previous night, slumped over the organ in the sanctuary of the First Community Church of Clairmont. No cause of death was listed.

I imagined how he must have felt when he breathed his last without an audience. Knowing him, he probably had written and rehearsed his final lines many times.

When I'm on my deathbed, I hope to have something worthwhile for my parting words. A Porky Piggish "Th-Th-That's all, folks!" won't cut it. I also hope that someone will be there to hear them.

That's why I could visualize Preston being frustrated at dying without someone around to record his final observations. He always needed to voice his opinions -- profound and otherwise -- and I was sure that he had some kind of statement to make about facing death.

Those who knew Preston in elementary school told me that he grew up "a fat little wise guy with his mouth wide open." Apparently, he was either stuffing in food or tossing out sarcastic remarks.

By the time I met him, Preston had developed these

childhood interests into a career. He'd let nothing stop him from giving others a piece of his mind -- "even if he was buried six feet under!" a victim of his once screamed. "And then, that arrogant bastard would be shouting outside the Pearly Gates, insisting that some incompetent angel forgot to write down his reservation!"

It wasn't the thought of Preston trying to speak from beyond the grave that gave me shivers. I could feel the Snow Witch's breath in the air. The Snow Witch from the North was Dad's name for winter -- and she was on her way. Occasionally, by this time, she would have already been here, bringing an unwanted gift of slush that turned the seven hills of this old riverboat city into a giant 200 square mile roller coaster and bumper car ride. The old witch was late. Still, the warm temperatures were retreating south as she approached. That morning was a sunny 34 degrees. My teeth chattered in as wide a grin as I could manage for the camera that stared at me while I posed in a white, gauzy, summer dress. I vowed to have my head examined. At forty-three years of age, you'd think I'd have more sense.

Click! "Just a few more, Kate," said Siegfried Doppler, the gangly, square-shouldered art director for *Cincy Life* magazine. Wearing an over-stuffed, brown ski vest, he looked like a giant pop-tart-on-a-stick leaping around me, as he snapped eight by ten glossies.

I lounged, shivering, on a flamboyant orange, pink, and lime green quilt at the edge of the pond on my twenty acre farm. When I agreed to model for the magazine's special section on summer picnic cuisine, I didn't know that he scheduled photo shootings six months ahead of publication. I raised an awful stink.

"Oh, don't worry," Siegfried said. "It'll be over in one, two, three." He didn't tell me he meant hours. Siegfried spent at least one of them trying to fold and drape my bony six-foot-three-inch body and long blond braid into an elegant pose around the picnic basket. I planned to strangle him once my hands thawed.

The late Preston Schneider had asked me to put together "a

3

picnic menu, as only Kate Cavanaugh, Cincinnati's queen of theme party consultants, can. How about a Caribbean picnic for two?" I've always been a sucker for free publicity -- and he knew it. Mr. Schneider had the knack for persuading people to do what he wanted. But not anymore. Or so I thought.

The bottle of Gewurztraminer was perfectly chilled. So was I, clear through to the bone. I was imagining a thin coat of ice forming over the colorfully displayed picnic setting of Jamaican "Jerk" Chicken, Heart of Palm and Avocado Salad, and Rum Pecan Cake.

Click!Click!Click! "One more, Kate." Siegfried smiled his bonded grin and moved in for a closeup of my shivering knees and the grilled chicken. *Click!* "Now, give me that bright, warm smile everyone associates with Kate Cavanaugh. Pretend it's June."

Right. Those two dinky pieces of sod he had placed around me, and that potted plant behind my head, didn't bring to mind a summer's day. I tried to imagine the vivid purple and yellow Japanese irises I had planted around the pond. But all I could see were the cold, spindly, dead sticks of the lilac and butterfly bushes.

The male model hired to be my "date" called in sick that morning. So, there I was -- as usual -- "stood up".

"But with food like this, who cares?" Siegfried said, as he munched on a stolen drumstick. "If I postpone this shoot, I'm dead. The forecast's for snow from tomorrow 'til New Year's."

I gritted my teeth and we carried on. Only now it was a pathetic picnic for one.

My mind's eye shifted to that morning's newspaper report. Preston's tuxedoed body was discovered at about ten-thirty p.m. by Terry Poole, the church's Choir Director, and a childhood friend of mine. However, since the article failed to mention the cause of death, and knowing that Preston's ample belly was the direct result of his love of fine dining and hatred of strenuous exercise, it wasn't much of a stretch for me to conclude he probably died of heart failure.

Preston was only fifty-three years old, and a lot of men his

4

age die when they mix neglect of health with stressful careers. However, Preston Schneider was the type of person who gave stress to others. But not to me. And, contrary to catering industry gossip, our relationship was always business, not personal. He happened to like what I offered the public and thought I had great taste in the way I organized and catered parties. If only Mother were as supportive -- but then, she'd have to admit I was an adult.

I don't know why, but Mother is never happier than when she can find fault -- in anything. "Kathleen, the reason you're not married at your age," Mother said on my fortieth birthday, "is because you probably picked up some mysterious gypsy curse while hitch-hiking through Iran when you were in your hippie phase."

My mother, Tink Cavanaugh, has a tendency to blame me for all the "not normal" events that happen in my life. "I hope you won't embarrass me" rolls off her lips as automatically as "Bless you" when someone sneezes. As matriarch of the family and fortune, she's constantly worried I'll bring scandal to the Cavanaugh name, which in Cincinnati is synonymous with chili franchises. But she won't give me credit for my successes. According to Mother, they come as a result of her "parental guidance" -- not my abilities.

It drives me crazy. Her idea of a perfect daughter -- or even an acceptable one -- hasn't been created. A parent like this either crushes a child's psyche or pounds it into steel. Verbal bullets now bounce off me, but still leave black and blue marks on my insides.

Knowing what it's like to be on the receiving end, I try not to jump on others for having faults of their own. I also know what it's like to be an oddball -- being so tall in the seventh grade that I almost had to duck to walk into my classroom puts me in that category. These experiences are what made it possible for me to be friendly with Preston Schneider.

"Earth to Kate! Earth to Kate!" Siegfried's snapping fingers brought me out of my trance and back to the cold.

"Show us your pearly whites." Siegfried directed me with

5

his hand. "Tilt your head to the left. Great! Your blond hair and blue eyes say *summer!*"

"And what do my blue knees say?" I could barely hear myself over the knocking sound.

"Oh, c'mon, Kate. It's not that cold."

"Are you kidding? Do you realize how many hours it'll take your magazine's computer artist to airbrush out the puffs of breath coming from my mouth?"

"None of it'll show. Just smile." Siegfried raised his camera.

I took a deep breath and exhaled an enormous cloud of white steam that obscured my face just as Siegfried *clicked!*

"Please, Kate. Just pick up the bottle of wine and look as though you were admiring its vintage."

I flashed my most sincere grin and did as he asked. With a grip that was ready to throw. He must have read my eyes, because he ducked as soon as he snapped the picture.

VROOM!

"Who is that?" My head snapped around at the unmistakable sound of a rumbling Harley-Davidson.

"I don't know." Siegfried stopped in mid-*click!*

Zooming around the banks of the pond, zipping under the leafless birches and past the towering white pines was the biggest Harley I'd ever seen. Any larger and it would've qualified as a mini van.

And it was rocketing straight at me, on target to leave tire marks right between my eyes.

The rider, dressed in a bulky black leather outfit with chrome zippers and wearing a bright red helmet with matching scarf, brought the motorcycle to a skidding halt no more than ten feet from my blanket.

The biker flicked off the engine's power and popped off her helmet. That little red headed party girl hadn't changed in almost twenty years. Even her haircut was the same -- short with

6

stubborn little cowlicks here and there.

Immediately, I was engulfed in remembered smells -- the spicy sandalwood and warm coconut oil of the beaches of India, the cheap scotch and cigarette smoke of that bar in Greece.

"Cherry!" My heart raced as I scrambled to my feet, stepping on the rum cake and sending chicken wings and drumsticks splashing into the pond. I reached my friend's side in a step and a half, and wrapped my arms around her -- which was awkward to do. With her standing just over five feet tall, her head was somewhere around my belly button, and in danger of being twisted off by my exuberant embrace.

"I was just in the neighborhood and thought I'd drop by." Cherry hugged back and we both jumped as a ball of fur raced between our legs and dove into the pond. Mr. Boo-Kat, my Welsh Terrier, was on a mission to save the "Jerk" Chicken from drowning.

I could feel rock hard muscles through Cherry's down-filled jacket, as she squeezed another hug. She craned her neck to look at me. Close up, she had added twenty years of new trails to her rugged, road warrior face. "How's the weather up there, Katie?"

I was surprised by a sudden stab of pain. Buried memories of thirteen year old boys calling me "giraffe face" flashed through my mind. But these were immediately replaced by the happy memories of Cherry and I lounging on the beaches of Goa on the western coast of India without a care in the world -- or a stitch of clothing on.

"Katie?" Cherry waved her hand in front of my unfocused eyes. "How are you?"

"Freezing!" The adrenaline rush caused by her arrival had subsided and I grabbed my long coat.

Cherry looked at the picnic basket, then at my gauzy summer dress, stepped back and cocked her head. "I know you have your own sense of style that goes against the grain -- but isn't this carrying it a bit far?" She turned and struck a Marilyn Monroe pose for Siegfreid, who had been capturing our reunion on film.

I introduced them with a few quick words, and then bombarded Cherry with questions. "How did you find me? What have you been doing all these years? Why didn't you keep in touch?"

"Glad to see you, too, Katie." Cherry looked at the picnic basket full of food, then at me with a silent "May I?" on her face.

"Go right ahead." I turned to Siegfreid. "I think we're done, right?"

"Just one more -- Oh, never mind. We're done." Siegfreid began packing up his camera equipment.

As I broke down the food display, Mr. Boo-Kat rolled around on the picnic blanket, trying to dry off from his unsuccessful rescue of a chicken wing from the pond. Cherry got down on her knees, wrapped him in the blanket, and started toweling him with one hand, while munching on a drumstick with the other.

"I'm on my way to New Orleans," Cherry finally answered. Our conversations always went in fits and starts. *"MMMM! This is good!"* she said with her mouth full. "Jamaican, right? You were always such a foodie -- and now you're what? A caterer?"

"She's the most talented creator of international cuisine parties in the Greater Cincinnati-Tristate area!" Siegfreid tossed his two cents into our conversation. "Whatever the dining experience you want for your affair, by the end of the evening you'll swear you and your guests have been transported into that corner of the world."

"Well," Cherry looked at me, "now I see what you've done with all those recipes you kept writing down in your little journal. Is he your publicity agent?" She pointed to Siegfreid with a drumstick bone now completely stripped of meat.

"No," I said, and explained about the magazine shoot her arrival had just brought to an end. "But you still haven't answered all my questions."

"Well," Cherry drawled, as she delicately picked up another

8

chicken leg. "Remember Klaus in India?"

How could I forget him? He was one of the few people I met on my travels who actually kept in touch. "You mean Klaus the German, who dressed like a Maharaja -- all in silks and satins, topped off with a jeweled turban?"

"Yes."

"The guy who always had a pet flying squirrel on his shoulder?"

"That's the one. He's sort of a main branch of the grapevine." Cherry continued. "In fact, he may actually *be* the grapevine. He's got addresses and even telephone numbers of hundreds of people he met on the road. He knows where we all are -- and if he doesn't, he knows who does."

"That's amazing. It's been a few years since we've exchanged letters. Is he still in England?"

"Yep. He's now writing romance novels out of his flat in London."

"Does he still keep that mangy squirrel for a pet?"

"Nope. His dog ate it." Cherry licked her fingers after finishing off her second piece of chicken. "Anyway, I've wanted to see you for years. But you know how it is -- you get busy with something -- or you're roaming around on a different part of the planet....."

"I know -- I'm just as bad."

"Sorry about not getting back together again in Greece, as we planned." Cherry examined her half-eaten chicken wing. "There was this guy in Palermo, Italy .... and then when I finally did show up back in Athens, you were gone. But hey, here I am. Better late than never."

"So, you were on your way to New Orleans," I said, trying to get Cherry back on track.

"Right. This year, I spent spring and summer in Rhode Island -- you know I'm always on the beach -- but every winter, for the past ten years, I zip down to New Orleans from wherever I am. I

9

just love that Big Easy. I've got friends there and I visit with them right through Mardi Gras." Cherry's eyes had a faraway look -- she'd gone on a little journey in her mind. She blinked. "So, anyway, I figured I'd take a side trip and visit the best traveling partner I've ever had. The plan was to get here by mid-October, but things happened."

"Like what?" Siegfreid had stopped packing and jumped into the conversation.

"I got held up by the police," Cherry said.

"Which type was it?" I poked her with my finger. "City cop or State Trooper? Did your eyes meet across the intimate lunch counter of some exotic, out of the way truck stop?"

Cherry winked in response. "You know a lady never kisses and tells."

"I don't understand what you gals are talking about." Siegfreid frowned at both of us.

"She has a thing for men in uniform," I said. "Especially cops."

"I don't go looking for romantic flings --" Cherry continued my thought. "They just happen."

"Okay, I get the picture." Siegfreid turned to me and gave a look that said, *and I bet you were a wild one, too!*

"Anyway," Cherry continued, "I got side-tracked for a couple of months. But when the fireworks fizzled out, and I found myself standing at his kitchen sink in pink fuzzy slippers, I knew it was time to go."

I shook my head and smiled. She would never change. I wondered how she knew to come to the pond. "Did you stop off at the farmhouse?"

"Yep." Cherry wriggled her finger for me to lean down. She stretched up on tip toes and whispered into my ear. "That hunky assistant of yours said you wouldn't mind my bringing this pain-in-the-ass photo-session to an early end."

A single laugh burst out of my mouth and Cherry grinned

with me at the private joke. A mystified Siegfreid stared at us from about twenty feet away. "Are you packed and ready to leave?" I called out to him, changing the subject. "We're going in for lunch. You're invited to join us if you wish."

"No. But thanks anyway. I've got to get back to the magazine office and start developing these pictures for layout."

Cherry was on her Harley, waiting for me to climb aboard. Hunching down, I secured myself with an arm around her waist, while holding onto the picnic basket loaded with the food and dishes I'd brought for the shoot. My old traveling companion turned around in her seat and looked up, studying me with her green eyes.

"You know, I forgot how tall you were. Must give you one hell of an edge in doing business. When you talk, people listen."

This time, I didn't hear the voices of thirteen year old boys calling me names -- just the compliment from a friend.

Cherry kick-started her bike, and we took off around the pond, rumbling along my farm's gravel road. The cold, crisp breeze slapped against my face and whipped through my hair -- but it didn't bother me. The ride brought back memories of freedom. As a twenty year old, I dodged the trap Mother planned for me -- a marriage with the "right young man", with the "right family connections", with "great bloodlines", full of "potential for making beautiful babies." I was one of her purebred poodles being readied for breeding.

Mother was born a Vasherhann -- a Cincinnati blue blood -- a family with old money roots in soap manufacturing. Her family tree was firmly planted in conservative attitudes, and so she could never understand my wanderlust. Her idea of adventure was a shopping spree in New York -- not thumbing a ride through Spain.

But I escaped. For two exciting years I followed my nose in whichever direction I pleased -- from Paris to Tangier, Athens to Bombay. When I returned, it was because I wanted to. I'd proved to myself that I was a survivor, had journals overflowing with memories, and had an idea of what I wanted to do with the rest of my life.

"Looks like you've got company," said Cherry. We were fast approaching the parking area, just outside the farmhouse. There were several vans and other cars. But it was Mother's white Mercedes that sparked anxious anticipation within me.

Years ago, after hearing about some of my adventures, Mother was horrified at what my friends and I did to survive. She flatly stated "I hope I never meet any of your vagabond friends. I'd just die."

Of course, none of her social circle could possibly have had any skeletons in their closets.

But we both knew Preston Schneider. I wondered if she'd heard of his death. Now there was a man who probably had closets full of skeletons.

Officially, I call my home Trail's End Farm. But this farm is not the usual cow and chicken type. No cows. No chickens. In fact, it's not really a farm at all. I just refer to it as such because fifteen years ago it was part of the last working family farm in the area.

The widower farmer's kids wanted no part of that life, so when he died, they chopped up the acreage into lots and made, what was at that time, a ton of money selling it.

I managed to come up with enough money on my own -- I didn't run to Dad for help -- to purchase twenty acres and the original clapboard farmhouse. Over the years, I replanted the fields with trees and added a couple of wings to the house. I'm now living on prime real estate just inside the northern border of Clairmont, the CEO suburb east of Cincinnati. It's out of this little plot of Heaven that I run my business.

The parking area was full of activity. Chuck, my meat supplier's delivery man, was busy unloading fresh geese and other meats from his van. *Bang! Bang! Bang!* Robert Boone, my combination groundskeeper-butler-handyman, was hammering loose shingles on the roof of the rambling, white clapboard building. His teenaged daughter Julie Ann balanced herself on the top step of a ladder, stringing the miles of Christmas lights that would soon outline the black shutters and gingerbread trim of the house. My indispensable housekeeper Phoebe Jo, wife and mother of the Boone family, was hanging a huge green wreath with a red bow on the black double front doors. My twenty-five year old assistant, Tony Zampella -- also known as Tony-Z -- ran in and out of the back door, to and from my 'Round the World catering van, carrying crates of vegetables. Off to the side of the house, by the giant Douglas firs, was a third van, which belonged to Queen City Costumes.

The next day was Mother's annual Christmas luncheon, and like every year, the cream of Clairmont would arrive to see and be seen, to mingle with those there, and verbally mangle those who were no longer on the A-list. And, like every year, a new chapter would be added to the mystery.

The mystery was as to when Mother would compliment me face-to-face for the success of her catered affairs. Oh, I didn't really need it for my ego or feeling of self-worth. Anymore. I constantly got positive feedback from the guests. My reputation in the industry was solid. And I heard from friends that Mother constantly bragged to others about me.

But she'd never personally given me that glowing praise. Always a "nice, but" and then a list of what could have been better. Realistically or not.

Every year, the affair became more and more involved. This particular luncheon was going to be the most elaborate yet and involved juggling many things. It's Mother's unspoken challenge to see how many balls I could keep in the air. I love it.

"You call this an authentic period costume?" Mother's angry high-pitched voice cut through the crisp air.

Cherry pulled into a parking spot and I quickly hopped off the back before she turned off the bike. "Stay here a minute," I said to her, "I better see if I need to call 911."

13

I followed the sound of Mother's wrath towards the Queen City Costume van. There I found Mother confronting a large ruddy-cheeked man. His back was up against the side of the vehicle, and he was looking very perplexed. The van's rear doors were open, and a rolling rack full of English Victorian costumes was waiting to be unloaded. Mother held a high-necked gentleman's coat right up under the man's nose and pointed to an offense on its lapel.

"You call this authentic?" Mother accented each word with a tap of her freshly manicured finger on the costume's lapel. "The clothing during that period was made with woolens and cottons which were muted in tones and rough to the touch. This material has some shine to it. It is obviously polyester!"

"But lady, I didn't make this stuff. I'm just the delivery man." The perturbed driver shrugged his shoulders with his hands extended in a pleading motion.

"Then a word to the wise, young man. Obviously, your employer is not one to be trusted. These were supposed to be authentic period costumes, but it appears that lower quality items are being passed for higher ones. That's not what was agreed to. Be careful. Your employer may try to put something over on *you*."

"What're you doing, Mother?" I could already guess the answer. "And why?"

Mother's perfectly coiffured silver hair stayed rigidly in place as her head snapped around to greet me. "Hello, darling." The rest of her cashmere clothed body turned to face me. "Just doing your job for you."

"And what does that mean?" I said, looking down at her and feeling my adrenaline begin to pump.

"Here!" Mother shoved the costume under my nose -- or as close as she could possibly reach without stretching her arm.

"What?" I said. "And don't repeat that silliness about polyester."

"You, of all people, should understand that I want quality. *This* is not it." Mother repeated her lapel tapping.

I folded my arms. "You also are a stickler for spending wisely. They don't make rental costumes out of those old-fashioned woolens and cottons. Would you have preferred that I had these outfits custom made for the four hours that the serving staff and carolers will be wearing them tomorrow?"

Mother stopped her irritating tapping. I could see her calculator mind at work. An interior button was pushed. Outrage vanished from her face. "That'll do." She tossed the costume over her shoulder into the hands of the driver. "Carry on." Relief washed across the poor man's face and he went back to unloading the rest of the suits and dresses.

"Come!" Mother grabbed my coat sleeve and almost pulled it off my arm as she dragged me towards the front doors of the house. "Why did you run off this morning to do that silly magazine picture taking and abdicate your responsibility? This party faces disaster."

"Mother, you're overreacting."

"Hardly." She stopped in front of the huge wreath Phoebe Jo had just hung up and pointed. "First -- *that's* not big enough." Then without waiting for me to answer, Mother pushed through the door and marched into the foyer. Phoebe Jo and Julie Ann had put out a lot of energy the last few days and had done a great job of decorating the house. The theme for the luncheon was a Charles Dickens Christmas and I felt that Bob Cratchit, Tiny Tim, and Ebenezer Scrooge would feel at home.

"This is awful." Mother halted at the staircase and began her list. "Look at this."

I looked in the direction of her point. Pine roping and garlands wound up the bannister. Burgundy and gold plaid bows were strategically tied onto the balusters. "What's the problem?"

"You should have known that real pine wouldn't last long. It doesn't look fresh. The pine needles are drooping."

"I agree my supplier goofed and didn't send the absolute freshest material, but the needles are only slightly droopy. Besides,

15

by the time the roping and garlands arrived, I didn't have time to replace them."

Mother flicked her hand in disgust and continued her march.

"Mother -- first, you complain that the clothing's not authentic enough. Then, you complain about the condition of the natural decorations. Stop and consider. Don't you think that pine needles drooped during Charles Dickens' Christmas parties?"

"Disaster, disaster," she muttered under her breath as she led the way to the Great Room. Phoebe Jo had done a beautiful job of decorating the mantle of the huge stone fireplace with evergreen and holly boughs. Little birds perched in the greenery beside clusters of berries and pine cones. Red and white poinsettias and wreaths of holly adorned each window. In one corner, a fir tree heavy with cranberry roping and old-fashioned sparkling glass ornaments reached towards the cathedral ceiling.

"Calm down," I said to her, and to myself. I could feel my adrenaline and blood pressure steadily rush and rise.

"How can I be calm when there are booby traps all over this house ready to sabotage the most important party of the social season?" Needless to say, Mother tends to exaggerate.

"Where?" I said, as we stepped into the center of the room.

"Right here." Mother lifted the edge of one of the ivory damask tablecloths covering the seven round tables already set with Spode china, Waterford crystal, and centerpieces of miniature snow-covered Christmas trees and brass lanterns with votive candles inside. She waited for my reaction.

"What were you expecting?" I said. "The centerpiece to blow up or what?"

"These tablecloths are too long. I'll demonstrate." She sat down on one of the rented metal chairs -- *with* padded seats I may add. "Couldn't you have gotten better seating? Oh, never mind -- watch what happens when I get up." The tablecloth moved slightly, but the settings remained in place. "See?"

"What?" I was beginning to regress to my teenage years of frustrated no-win discussions with Mother.

"Don't you realize that if someone gets up too quickly, there's a good chance the edge of the cloth might catch on a leg and be dragged off the table, knocking over glasses of wine and who knows what?"

"I very much doubt that anyone will accidentally do anything of the sort. Besides, those centerpieces are heavy enough to hold down --"

"Speaking of which," Mother accented her manicured forefinger straight up to the ceiling. "Those table decorations are too big and chintzy looking. And these wine glasses are not big enough. They've got little flaws in the crystal. *And water spots.* Who checked in all this rented stuff? Your assistant Tony the Z? It's tacky."

"Mother. It's top of the line rental," I said through firmly clenched teeth. My lid was beginning to blow. "Besides, Tony-Z is an excellent assistant. He is my right arm and you know it."

"But you should have been here, checking everything in -- not at some silly magazine shoot. You know how important this is to me. Everything must be just right. It must be the very essence of a Christmas party that Dickens himself would have given. The sights, the sounds, the smells -- which reminds me. It doesn't smell right in here. Not piney enough. Not -- Excuse me, there." Mother looked past my right elbow -- she's not tall enough to see over my shoulder. "Deliveries are in the back of the house."

Who was she talking to? Mother quickly moved past me, with a look of dismay as though the person had just committed sacrilege by walking upon holy ground.

It was Cherry carrying a Victorian costume -- a woman servant's dress. "The driver said this one fell off the rack, so I told him I'd bring it in for him. He's gone now."

"Deliveries are in the back." Mother began shooing Cherry out the door. "Kate," she continued over her shoulder at me, "you

17

must put up a sign out front explaining where the tradespeople are to leave their parcels and such."

"Stop," I said, feeling terribly embarrassed. "This is a friend of mine."

Automatically, the Cavanaugh smile clicked into place. Mother switched from a gruff keeper of the castle gate, getting ready to hurl rocks and boiling oil onto an attacking mob, to a cordial hostess at her only daughter's first wedding reception. "Hello. I don't think I've had the pleasure."

"Well," said Cherry, taking the offered hand, "I'm sure we'll make up for lost time." Mother's smile appeared to momentarily flick off into a grimace. Cherry's handshake might have been too surprisingly powerful for her majesty.

"Let me take that." I reached to take the costume from my friend. "Sorry you were put to work."

"No problem. I may be a visitor, but I'm not going to sponge off you. I'll do my share of the housework."

Mother sneaked a quick side glance at me. I knew the quizzical look meant, *What have we here?*

"Mother, this is my old friend, Cherry Jublanski. Cherry, this is my mother, Patricia Cavanaugh."

"Please, call me Tink."

"Okay, Tink -- but my name is Jubilee." Cherry met my surprise expression with a smile.

"You mean," Mother folded her hands together in front of her, "it's Jubilee Jublanski?"

"Don't tell me it's --" I began.

"Yep. Cherry Jubilee."

"That does have a certain ring to it." Mother had her polite, attentive face on.

"Exactly what I thought," said Cherry. She was noticing Mother begin to squirm a bit. I stood back to watch the situation develop. "After Katie and I split up in Greece," Mother's face immediately registered horror, "I continued wandering around the

18

middle East for another year. Then, when that business with the Shah of Iran blew up, I decided it was time to return to the States.

"You know that Katie and I had to do a lot of things to survive in our travels -- but it was easier to make ends meet over there. When I arrived in the U. S. of A., I got quite a shock -- I had to work all day to keep the simplest of life styles. And the work was hard!

"Employment agencies didn't want me because I didn't have a resume. So I got into waitressing, but you know that's a dead end job."

Mother's expression turned blank.

"So, I turned to construction work. I lucked out there, 'cause I've always been into weight training," Cherry took off her black leather jacket, rolled up a sleeve and flexed her biceps. "I could take the taunts because the pay was so good. But it was still hard work -- all day long.

"Then, one day, I decided, hey -- I'm still young. I've got a good body. Why not use it?"

Mother's jaw dropped. She looked at her watch. "Excuse me -- I do have an appointment with --"

"Wait," Cherry reached out her hand, "I'm almost finished." Mother began inching towards the front doors. "So anyway, one day I saw a sign outside this lunch place called The Wild Horse Tavern. It said, 'Wanted: Exotic Dancers.' I thought-- I'm a dancer, and I've been to exotic places. I qualify. I made two hundred bucks the first day. In only two hours."

"That's quite interesting," Mother said through her frozen smile. "Nice meeting you. Goodbye, Kate. See you tomorrow." She turned and hurried out the door.

Cherry called out after her. "I liked my stage name so I kept it."

Thirty seconds later, I learned that Preston Schneider didn't die of a heart attack.

He'd been murdered.

JAMAICAN "JERK" CHICKEN

6 whole chicken legs
1 Tbsp. ground allspice
1 Tbsp. hot pepper flakes
   (or cayenne pepper sauce)

3/4 cup vinegar
1/2 cup orange juice
1/4 cup each olive oil,
   soy sauce

1 Tbsp. granulated sugar
1 tsp. each salt, black pepper
1/2 tsp. each nutmeg, cinnamon

juice of 1 lime
1 onion, finely chopped
4 green onions, chopped

2 cloves garlic, minced

chopped, seeded jalapenos or
other fresh, hot peppers -opt.

Combine allspice, hot pepper flakes, sugar, salt and pepper, nutmeg, cinnamon and minced garlic in large glass bowl. Whisk in vinegar, orange juice, olive oil, soy sauce, lime juice, chopped onions and chopped hot peppers, if using. Add chicken legs (skinned, if desired) and refrigerate, covered, for at least 8 hours or overnight, turning occasionally.

Grill over medium-hot coals or at medium setting, turning often, until juices run clear (25-30 minutes).

Bring reserved marinade to a boil, let simmer for 2-3 minutes. Serve as dipping sauce.

CHAPTER TWO ....

I know that Mother can be a real pain in the neck -- but who am I to cast stones? I give my staff as hard a time when I want things to be just so. Almost. I'm just a little more reasonable in my demands. Oh, let's face it -- if I had a daughter, she'd probably have the same problems with me as I have with Mother dearest.

This is not to say that Mother didn't deserve to get a dose of her own medicine. She had attempted to make Cherry feel uncomfortable by treating her as a lowly servant -- an untouchable. Instead, I enjoyed the spectacle of her squirming in unspoken terror at actually meeting one of my so-called "vagabond friends." In fact, I was giving in to a slightly sadistic impulse by doing so and watching how long it would go on.

But my conscience wouldn't allow me to let Mother leave on that note.

"Mother," I shouted as I trotted out after her. "I'll see you at the Christmas concert tonight?"

She stopped just as she reached her Mercedes, and called back to me. "Haven't you heard? Poor Preston's dead. Murdered."

"Murdered?" I almost stumbled over my own big feet as I stopped in surprise. "In the church? I read about it in the paper this

21

morning, but it didn't mention homicide. I just assumed it was a heart attack or some such ---"

"Oh, no, no, no." Mother's chunky gold charm bracelet clanked as she waved her hand to correct me. "The dear man was found knocked unconscious by a blunt instrument. He died at the hospital an hour later. Terrible, terrible. And on top of that, the police have blocked off the entire sanctuary as a crime scene -- so, of course, the concert has been canceled. Or at least postponed."

"But that's horrible. Who would want to kill him?" As soon as I said that, I realized how dumb the question was. Mother gave me the answer I already knew.

"Darling, if anyone in this city had enemies, it was our Preston."

"Do the police have any clues?"

"I called up Pastor Luebens this morning as soon as I read it in the paper, and he told me that the police have not released any information. So I asked him...." Mother continued on, but my mind began to drift.

I looked down from my position, floating high above the church's massive pipe organ -- my head almost touching the sanctuary's ceiling. Preston Schneider was seated at the keyboard. His fingers raced across the black and whites, and Bach's Toccata and Fugue in D Minor burst out of the enormous pipes.

I could see the preparations that had been made for the Christmas concert. Huge poinsettia arrangements, Douglas firs strung with tiny twinkling white lights, and multi-colored silk banners filled the gathering place, promising a joyful celebration service, all of it anchored by the centerpiece -- the enormous pipe organ.

I moved in closer. As I did so, a faceless figure slipped out from behind one of the banners. Preston poured himself into his music, his chest and shoulders rising and falling, breathing as though running a marathon. He was oblivious to all but the resonating notes that filled the sanctuary.

A hand swung a blunt object.

Preston's face crashed down upon the organ's keyboards, his cold, gray eyes locked open in shock.

The image was immediately replaced by the sad smile of Demetrius -- another friend who had met a violent end.

"Kathleen?"

I jumped at the sound of my name. It was Mother. She was peering up into my face with a great deal of concern on her own. "You okay? You don't look like you're all here."

I nodded. "I'm fine."

An icy chill shot through my bones. "*Brrr!* All of a sudden, this coat doesn't feel warm enough. I've got to go inside and change." I reached down and grabbed Mother's hands. "Don't worry about me or tomorrow's luncheon. Everything's under control."

Mother looked up into my eyes with great intensity, as though attempting to break into my private screening room. "You're always doing that. I wish I could see what's going on in that overactive mind of yours." She let go of my hands and got into the driver's seat of her car. "Get some rest."

"Don't worry, I will."

"Right," she said, and drove away. She knew I was lying. I never got any real sleep before one of her affairs -- and now that this murder had happened, I was sure not to get my customary three hour beauty sleep.

"Katie?" The sound of Cherry's voice made me feel suddenly weary. The luncheon, Preston's murder, and now an unexpected guest from the past. There were too many things for me to juggle. I needed to get away to process all that had happened -- but I smiled at my friend.

"C'mon," I put my arm around her shoulder, "let's get you settled." We walked back towards the house, passed under the towering oak tree, climbed the flagstone steps, and entered through the front doors.

"I guess this is a bad time for me to show up, huh?" Cherry put down the two beaten up canvas knapsacks she had unloaded from her Harley.

"Whatever gave you that idea?" I said, squeezing her arm.

"I've always been good at sizing up situations. But seriously, Katie. You look like you've just lost your best friend."

I sighed. "Preston wasn't my best friend -- but he was a good one."

CRASH! "STUPID IDIOT!" The sounds of disaster and Tony-Z's profanity came echoing through the hallway from my kitchen. Cherry lurched forward and took several running steps, then stopped when she realized that I didn't seem concerned.

I caught up with Cherry and led the way through the swinging door and into my commercial-sized kitchen. We were temporarily blinded by the harsh December sunlight pouring through the huge south window and reflecting off the white walls and the stainless steel equipment.

"Dumb! Dumb! Dumb!" my kitchen assistant Tony-Z said, slapping his forehead with the palm of his hand, eyes clenched shut, his lanky chocolate brown hair bouncing with each slap. He was standing at the end of the long stainless steel counter in the middle of the room -- the plucked carcass of a twelve pound goose lay sprawled at his feet. Tony-Z was almost six feet tall, with broad shoulders tapering to a narrow waist. He had piercing black eyes, a strong, finely chiseled chin with a permanent five o'clock shadow. I could see Cherry out of the corner of my eye react to this sight with a combination of amusement and lust.

"Hello, Miss Kate," Phoebe Jo called out in her Kentucky drawl. She stood at the prep table in the far corner of the kitchen, wiping her hands on her white cotton apron. Her long, frizzy light brown ponytail peaked out from under a bright red bandana. "How was the photo shoot this morning?" She picked up a peeler and continued scraping mountains of potatoes and carrots, dropping them into large white plastic buckets of water.

"Glad it's over," I said. "Now, what's going on here, Tony? Need some help?"

Tony-Z bent down and picked up the metal roasting pan from the floor. "Naw, I'm okay -- just moving too fast. I was running back and forth unloading the vegetables from the van, and I banged into the counter. Scared the goose right out of the pan."

"Yeah, right -- gave it goosebumps?" I said.

Tony-Z grabbed the bird and headed for the kitchen sink. "But not to worry. As Julia Child says: 'Just brush it off. Your guests will never know'."

I clapped my hands together. "Okay. I see everything's under control in here. Cherry, let's get you to your room." We started out the door, "Oh, I'm sorry." I spun around on my heel. "Phoebe Jo, this is my friend Cherry Jublansk -- uh, Jubilee."

The two exchanged waves. "Oooh, just like one of them fancy desserts you have us make, Miss Kate." Phoebe Jo said.

"And just as hot," my friend added with a loud laugh.

"Whoa! Check out those moustaches," Cherry said, pointing to the pictures on the wall as we climbed the steps of the front oak staircase. "Who are they?"

"The Chili Kings," I answered with pride. "From Great-great-grandpa to Dad. They're the founders of the family Crown Chili Parlor fortune."

Mentioning the beginnings of the family business made me think about the first review Preston did of one of my catered affairs. He was skeptical -- who could blame him. I mean who would expect the Crown Chili Heiress to know the difference between pinto beans and haricot vert?

I was already starting to miss the old windbag. But something told me I hadn't heard the last from him.

A half-hour later, I was back in the kitchen -- having

changed into my favorite knock-around outfit of jeans and UC Bearcat sweatshirt -- and was grazing on leftovers from the Caribbean picnic.

I'd taken Cherry on a short tour of the various wings of the farmhouse. As I said, I'd been adding to the original house for years. Besides the commercial kitchen for my catering business, I had a small gym with a half-court basketball area built.

One of the ways Dad had helped me deal with the oddity of standing six feet three inches tall was to turn that apparent female liability into an asset. I turned out to be a halfway decent basketball player for the Clairmont High School Cougars, and playing a half-court game still keeps me in shape. But mostly it's a release from the stress of catering to the whims of Clairmont's rich and powerful.

I always seem to need that release at two o'clock in the morning, after one of those nerve-wracking events. There weren't any twenty-four hour gyms in Clairmont -- so I built one.

After the tour, I showed Cherry to one of the guest rooms, and pointed to where all the towels and linens were kept. She wanted a shower to clean off the dirt of the road. I told her to join us in the kitchen afterward.

"That was terrible news about your friend, Miss Kate." Phoebe Jo had finished peeling the vegetables and had moved on to chopping up prunes and apricots for the goose stuffing.

"Yeah," Tony-Z said as he carried in fifty-pound bags of pastry flour. "I knew a guy once in my old neighborhood in Price Hill who tried to skip out of paying off on a bet. The bookie sent two guys to collect his pinkie. Did Preston play the horses and lose a lot?"

"Ha!" I couldn't help the sarcastic laugh that automatically answered that idea. "Preston? Gamble? He hated the mere thought. The closest he came to it was when he was an altar boy and helped with his parish's bingo nights."

"Damn shame that writer fella getting killed like that." Robert Boone, Phoebe Jo's gangly husband, came loping in through

26

the kitchen's back door. He was wearing old, dusty brown coveralls and a leather utility belt loaded with tools and keys that clanged with every step. "He was a little on the prissy side, but that's not a hanging offense."

"He wasn't hanged," Tony-Z said as he spread walnuts out on the counter in front of him. He raised a rolling pin over his shoulder and smashed it down on the nuts. *Crack!* "Just like that. His head was split open."

I shuddered.

"Oh, Tony." Phoebe Jo shook her head. "It wasn't split open. The Channel 9 News at Noon said that he died from a head wound that caused internal bleeding."

"Whatever." Tony-Z pulverized more nuts and looked at me. "Only your friend and the killer know what really happened."

Once again, I realized that most of the people in the Tri-State restaurant industry could be suspects. I knew them all. Maybe even the killer. Maybe he -- she? -- was on Mother's guest list for tomorrow. You could probably run into at least a couple of Preston's enemies at any one of Clairmont's gatherings.

This was crazy. I found myself starting to make a mental list of anyone I thought might have a motive for murder. I couldn't help it. The two that immediately came to mind were Martin Wolfenden and Frank Meyer.

Frank and Wolfie were old school buddies. Frank became a hotshot financial consultant and was looking for a high-profile, high-potential investment. Wolfie was the talented chef. Together they had birthed a trendy little bistro in Mount Adams, called Papillon. Wolfie and Preston had hated each other's guts for years. Preston badmouthed Papillon from the day it opened until it went belly up in less than six months. Frank lost tons of money, and Wolfie hadn't found a steady job since. That was over a year ago, and I never heard the word "forgive" pass through either of their lips when they mentioned Preston's name.

But then, maybe it was a random mugging. No, the church

wasn't in an area prone to that. In fact, the local police force -- the Clairmont Rangers, as they were affectionately known -- patrolled the area continually. Clairmont spent the money to protect its wealthy voters with an almost personal security guard ratio of one officer for every one hundred households. It was routine for them to check in on residents known to be ill, or if they hadn't seen any activity around the house for a couple of days.

I mentally slapped myself. I was getting off the track. Preparation for Mother's luncheon was the number one priority, and the responsibility loomed over me like a huge hungry monster.

"Tony!" He snapped to attention at my drill sergeant's delivery.

"Yes, Ma'am?"

"Have all the supplies been checked in and put away?"

"Yep."

I pulled out my menu plan and called a staff meeting -- for all three of us. "I need a status report. Prime Rib and Roast Goose?"

"We've got four geese," Tony said. "They're cleaned and ready for stuffing. The beef is seasoned and ready for roasting tomorrow."

"Start chopping the fruit and bread for the stuffing. Now, roasted garlic potatoes and vegetables?"

"Taters are peeled," Phoebe Jo said. "And the garlic's chopped. I've also peeled the carrots."

"Don't forget to grate the orange rind." I rubbed my temple where it was beginning to throb. "I need to make sponge cake and pastry cream for the Trifle." I checked off the Christmas pudding with Hard Sauce. "At least this is made. Oh, Tony -- did you chop up the walnuts already?"

"Yeah. You saw me doing it."

I sighed. "Indulge me. My brain's gone into overload." For a tough kid from Price Hill, Tony had turned out to be a pretty good assistant. Excellent in fact. He came to my attention when he

28

won a *Cincy Life* magazine sponsored dessert competition. Preston and I were judges and we both recognized his self-taught, natural flair for baking. That was seven years ago. Today, I could trust him with any job in the kitchen.

"Phoebe Jo." I turned to my housekeeper. "When you're done, start prepping the fruit for the trifle, and then pipe out the chocolate stars."

"Yes, Miss Kate." Phoebe Jo beamed. I usually saved the artistic jobs for myself, but time was short. I started cracking eggs and separating the yolks from the whites for the sponge cake. Mother's huge hungry monster had fifty gaping mouths and, as usual, I questioned the wisdom of taking on Mother's challenge.

The kitchen hummed and buzzed as we each worked at our stations. Fifteen minutes later, the cake was in the oven and I began what, to me, was the most enjoyable task of the day.

I mixed together the ingredients for my pastry cream in a large sauce pan on the stove, and soon was caught up in a tranquil, meditative state as I slowly stirred and heated the mixture. Gradually, it thickened into a perfectly silky and sensuous cream. I was one with the cream.

"Hey, Kate!" Tony shouted. "Remember when Preston first started writing his restaurant reviews?"

I tore myself away from the spiritual moment and looked at Tony, who continued. "He said the culinary scene in Cincinnati consisted of one astronomically expensive five star restaurant and a couple hundred chili parlors."

I laughed and then yanked the pot off the burner just as it was about to scorch on the bottom. I stirred vanilla and chunks of butter into my still perfect pastry cream, then poured it into another pan and covered it with plastic wrap.

The cake still had about twenty-five minutes to go in the oven, so I took a breather. "Tony, you were only about five years old when Preston started his column."

"Yeah, but that was a classic review. Everyone knows about

29

that one."

Twenty years ago, Preston's opinion of the local restaurant scene was almost true. He wanted to be noticed, so making obnoxious statements seemed the easiest road to that end. Preston took it to extremes never seen before in Cincinnati, which, in turn, made him a hot columnist for the just starting *Cincy Life* magazine. I think he might have become trapped in that style. I don't know -- maybe he started out using his childhood tendency to sarcastically mouth off and created the print persona of the Critic from Hell with the intention of softening after a little while. But it sold magazines. In unguarded moments, I'd seen a lonely, bitter Preston -- a round, sad little man looking for friends, but finding none. I think he decided to take revenge against the world and become the character he had fabricated for his column.

I once asked him, "Why are you so harsh?"

"Me? Harsh?" Preston laughed. "I'm just being truthful. Absolutely truthful. As a member of the Press, with an exhaustive knowledge of the culinary and creative arts, I consider it my responsibility to act as a protector of the unsuspecting public. The little people who spend their hard-earned money deserve the very best -- better than what is being offered them. I help keep up standards -- sometimes I think I'm the only one who notices the mediocre trash these hucksters are dishing out."

"Does that include my family's chili parlors?"

Preston smiled. "At least your grandfather did the best he could with what he had. He was no phony and he gave the people what they wanted. I, personally, think the stuff tastes horrendous, but I admit Crown Chili is a quality operation."

Then he said a strange thing. "But I am a searchlight, shining into dark corners. If those creatures can't stand the light, let them go scurrying back into their lairs. I make no apologies for the truth."

There were a few restaurants he liked, but he destroyed countless dreams with his column. Not just dreams of restaurateurs,

30

but also those of local musicians and actors. If the police were stuck for a killer's motive, all they needed to do was read old copies of *Cincy Life.*

CHAPTER THREE ....

"Wow!" Cherry said, standing in the kitchen's doorway. "This house is humongous! And Katie, your gym is amazing!" It was getting on to about four o'clock by the time she joined us. "I couldn't resist playing around with your Soloflex machine. I've been getting a bit flabby these past few months."

I couldn't see an ounce of fat on Cherry's muscular little body. "What flab?"

"Look." she flexed her right biceps and grabbed the underside of her arm and gave it a shake. "See? It's soft and wobbly."

"I wish my arms wobbled like that," Tony commented under his breath. His eyes were like saucers as he gazed at Cherry. She wore a stretchy leopard print top and skin tight black leggings. Her short red hair was plastered against her head, still wet from her shower.

"As long as I'm visiting," Cherry replied, walking over to the sink where Tony was washing salad greens, "I can offer my services as your personal trainer."

I saw Tony's olive complexion change into a deep red blush

as Cherry came up beside him. She still had it -- that ability to attract tough macho men and transform them into shy little puppies.

"I'm sure there'll be plenty of time for that," I said, amused. "But right now, Tony, you've got tons of cleanup to do."

"Yeah, I'll get to it."

"Okay, Katie," Cherry winked. "If you won't let me flirt with your help, then give me something to do that'll keep me out of trouble."

I pointed to a stool beside me at the prep counter. "Sit here, and pull the outer leaves off these brussels sprouts."

Cherry's smile clicked into a grimace. "But there's *thousands* of them."

"Don't worry, honey." Phoebe Jo dropped a trimmed brussels sprout into a big stainless steel bowl. "Half of them are done, already."

"Stop whining." I handed Cherry a paring knife. She sat down on the stool, heaved a big sigh, picked a sprout out of the bowl and examined it. "So what's this I hear about a murder?" She slowly pulled off a leaf as if the tiny vegetable was a bomb about to blow off her hand with the first wrong move.

I began cutting little x's into the stem ends of the brussels sprouts and gave her the *Reader's Digest* version.

Cherry finished peeling a second one and threw it into the bowl. "Wasn't there anything likable about the guy?"

"If you could get past Preston's aggressively defensive behavior, he was a bright, entertaining man. He was a great tenor -- sang everything from arias to show tunes. He made me laugh with what he called his personalized theme songs."

"What?" Cherry wrinkled her brow.

"He said every time he met someone, a song would automatically come to mind, and that would become the person's theme song. For example, mine was *Around the World in Eighty Days*."

Cherry chose a third sprout. "Interesting. I wonder what he

33

would have heard if he met me?"

"GOODNESS, GRACIOUS, *GREAT BALLS O' FIRE!*"
Tony gyrated in the middle of the kitchen, playing air piano.

"Good Lord." Robert sauntered into the room. "That poor
boy is having a conniption. Phoebe Jo, call 911. Are you sick,
boy?"

"I'm surprised at you, Robert." Phoebe Jo said. "You, of
all people, should recognize a Jerry Lee Lewis imitation. You used
to do that as part of our act."

"What act?" Cherry spun around on her stool to face
Phoebe Jo.

"Back in the mid-1960s, Robert and I were a singing duo."

Robert pulled out a harmonica from his back pocket and
played a few chords. "We called ourselves ..."

"The Boones! Of course!" Cherry slapped a hand on her
knee. "I've got your album. I loved the way you guys harmonized
together. It was so unique."

"Must have been too unique." Robert replied. "You're one
of the few who bought our album."

"But you guys were so great."

"Yeah, well -- we appreciate that, Miss -- eh --"

"Cherry," Tony said.

"Jubilee," Phoebe Jo added.

Robert scratched his beard. "Hmm. Catchy."

"So, why did you stop?" Cherry jumped off her stool and
leaned back against the counter.

"We worked real hard," Phoebe Jo said, "trying to build a
career in the Country Music industry. Toured everywhere. Sang in
every bar that would have us."

"Paid more'n our share of dues." Robert blew a chord on
his mouth organ.

"But after twenty-five years living out of a suitcase,"
Phoebe Jo continued, "and with four year-old Julie Ann needing
schooling -- we started realizing that we might not make it to the big

time."

"The clincher was when Garth and those young New Country types took over the scene." Robert tapped his harmonica on the palm of his hand. "The writing on the wall was clear. Time to change careers."

"And we're real happy here." Phoebe Jo smiled at me.

"Could you do just a few bars of *Silver Threads and Golden Needles?*" Cherry folded her hands in a plea. "That's one of my all-time favorites."

The Boones exchanged surprised looks. Phoebe Jo shrugged her shoulders. "Sure."

Just as they started to sing, the kitchen phone rang, and I went to pick it up. "'Round the World Catering. Kate Cavanaugh speaking."

"Ms. Cavanaugh, this is William Sanoma of the law firm Sanoma, Richards, and Kent."

"Yes?" Now what?

"We are representing Mr. Preston Schneider's estate. There are a number of important matters I must discuss with you."

"Me? Why?"

"My client left a communication to be given to you, but I would rather conduct this business face to face. Can you come into my office tomorrow morning? It's urgent."

Oh, great -- just what I need -- another ball to keep in the air. "Tomorrow's impossible. I have a luncheon for fifty guests to supervise. It'll have to wait until Monday morning."

"I'm sorry to insist, Ms. Cavanaugh, but I must speak with you tomorrow. There is a timing constraint."

I ran through the next day's schedule in my mind. "Well -- uh -- the best time -- if you can come here, the only time I could talk to you would be around three-thirty. The guests will still be here, but my assistant can take over at that point."

"I'll be there."

"Do you know how to get ..." *Click!* The phone went dead.

CHAPTER FOUR ....

"Is Julie Ann still outside, stringing up lights?" I asked Phoebe Jo. "Go call her, dinner's almost ready." It was six o'clock and we had moved to the smaller family kitchen. I sprinkled the last of the feta cheese over the top of the Greek salad in the large glass bowl and gave it a final toss.

"Oh, Katie," Cherry said, her eyes wide. "I haven't had a meal like this since we were on Mykonos."

"I made it specially for you." I pulled a pan of Afghan flatbread out of the oven and set it on top of the stove.

"Sorry I'm late." Julie Ann Boone came running into the kitchen, her long, straight brown hair done up in a braid copycatting mine. "Do you need help, Kate?"

"Yeah, you can turn over those kebabs on the grill." I watched her as she reached for the metal skewers. "No! It's hot. Use a mitt." Julie Ann's face turned pink. She gave me a flustered, helpless look, and jabbed at her eyeglasses with a finger, pushing them back up onto the bridge of her nose. Julie Ann was a terrific, intelligent, fourteen year-old kid -- a computer whiz -- high school honors student. But lost when it came to finding her way around a kitchen.

I handed her a mitt and pointed to the furthest skewer. "Start turning at that end, because they've been cooking the longest."

"Okay." Julie Ann smiled, nodded, and focused all her attention on the task.

"How many wine glasses should I put out? Is Tony here?" Robert was opening a bottle of Chardonnay.

"No, he's gone home," I said. Phoebe Jo was setting the oak farmhouse table in the windowed alcove. Cherry was busy dishing out the salad. I put a basket full of flatbread on the table, told everybody to line up with their plates by the stove, and I gave each one a skewer loaded with chunks of grilled marinated lamb, green pepper, and onion.

When all were served, we sat around the table. Mr. Boo-Kat positioned himself at my feet knowing that I was sometimes a little sloppy and there was sure to be more than a morsel or two landing right in front of his nose.

"I got a strange phone call today," I said as I wrapped a piece of soft, warm bread around the kebab and pulled out the metal skewer. I spooned Tzatziki sauce on top of the meat, rolled it back up and took a bite.

"You mean heavy breathing kind of strange?" Cherry arched an eyebrow as she took a mouthful of Greek salad.

"No. It was Preston Schneider's attorney. He's coming to see me tomorrow. Said Preston left a message -- some sort of important instructions for me."

Julie Ann froze in mid-action, Tzatziki sauce dribbling off her spoon and onto the table. "You mean one of those *To be opened in the event of my death* envelopes? Wow, that's exciting. Maybe he knew he was going to be killed and he's going to tell you who did it."

"I don't think so."

37

"Well, what else would he want to tell you?"

"I don't know -- I'll find out tomorrow -- but it is puzzling."

"That's it." Julie Ann flung her arms out in excitement. "Mr. Schneider was always playing with puzzles -- making them up -- you know, trying to stump everyone." She swung around to face Cherry. "He had a daily syndicated newspaper feature where you had to solve his cryptogram." She turned back to me. "I bet this is some final game of his."

"I can't think about that now. Let's just wait and find out." I could see disappointment in Julie Ann's eyes at my not wanting to play this game of "what if?"

"You know, Katie," Cherry interrupted, "this isn't the first time you've been involved in someone's mysterious death."

Julie Ann's eyes widened. "Really?"

Phoebe Jo frowned slightly as she glanced at Robert and then back at me. "I don't remember you telling us that one, Miss Kate."

One of the many stories I haven't told anyone. I gazed out the bay window at the barren plots of land that were my flower and vegetable gardens in the summer. I often wondered what it would be like if some of my old traveling companions showed up all these years later. I didn't realize it would mean revealing more of my strange past -- more than I was comfortable with -- to the people who were now a part of my world. As the memory of that particular event in my life took shape, I wondered if it might eventually give me an insight into who killed Preston. After all, people all over the world kill or are killed for essentially the same reasons.

"Tell the story, Kate." An excited Julie Ann almost jumped out of her seat.

"Well...." I sighed and settled back into my chair. "Cherry and I were on Mykonos -- one of the Greek islands -- and had run out of money. We knew we had to head back to the mainland to find jobs, so we boarded the ferry boat and headed for Athens.

"It was common knowledge that fast money -- and a lot of it -- could be made working in bars as hostesses to the American servicemen. Back in the mid-1970s, there was a huge military base in a suburb of Athens. At night the bars were filled with young, lonely American guys anxious to meet English-speaking women.

"These bars were owned and operated by Greeks of questionable reputation, but they were shrewd business people. They knew that a couple of reasonably attractive American women, with fun-loving personalities, could make them a lot of money. It was easy to convince the owners of the Glyfada Pub that we could increase their business, but they weren't too thrilled with the way we dressed."

"What was wrong with the way you dressed?" Phoebe Jo got up to bring some more kebabs to the table.

Cherry laughed. "We looked like something out of *Arabian Nights*. We had spent the last year traveling through India and Nepal, so all we owned were these strange Tibetan dresses, mirrored and tasseled cotton blouses, and frayed jeans."

I nodded. "We didn't match up with their ideas of the perfect, desirable bar hostess, so they took us next door to the dress shop and bought us each a couple of skimpy cocktail dresses. I was kind of hard to fit."

"Ha!" Cherry slapped her hand down on the table. "Hard to fit? What was full-length on me only came to her knees -- and that was if she could squeeze into it at all."

"Those bar owners knew a six-foot-three inch blond would be a draw," I continued, "so they paid extra to have a couple of dresses altered for me.

"We were expected just to talk to the guys and offer distraction -- if they wanted to talk to us, they had to buy us a drink. We would get a percentage as part of our pay. We weren't supposed to get any more involved than that. Instead, we turned every night we were there into a wild, noisy party. The first night, the owners were upset 'cause we didn't do what they told us to do. But when they saw how many guys showed up the second night, they decided to go along with our party plans. To the owners' amazement, the Glyfada Pub soon became the most popular bar in the area."

I looked at Cherry. "Didn't we exceed the occupancy limits of the room?"

"Yep," Cherry replied. "Every night we worked."

"They sold a lot of booze," I continued, "and we drank a lot, too. The more we drank, the more money we made. As I said, the customers were expected to buy us drinks -- they had to if they wanted to spend time with us. As the night wore on and things got wilder, our drinks began to taste of just plain ginger ale. We'd joke with the servicemen. We'd say 'Do you know how much you're paying for me to sit here and drink ginger ale?' They paid twice the usual price -- they didn't care."

"Those owners were always trying to rip us off," Cherry added. "What they didn't know was that every time someone bought us a drink, we'd put a pen mark on our wrists, so no matter how crazy things got, we'd know how much they were supposed to pay us at the end of the night. There was always an argument, but we always won."

Julie Ann drummed her fingers on the table. "Okay. So? Who got killed?"

I continued. "There was a man who came in on a regular basis, but was given very special attention. Demetrius was the bar's only Greek customer -- an expensively dressed older man in his late fifties. I remember the first night he came in he caused great excitement to the owners, who knew him as a wealthy and very visible Athens businessman. We never did find out what brought him to that particular bar in the first place. Greeks didn't frequent the neighborhood unless they were owners of local businesses. They didn't come for the entertainment. It seemed he was looking to buy himself a nice young American girl to be his trophy."

"And he chose Katie," Cherry said in a high pitched voice. "Made me kind of jealous at first -- I mean there they were, sitting in a private booth at the back of the bar, and the owner's wife would serve Katie these frothy pink drinks in stemware. They probably soaked him for four times the usual price."

"He chose me," I said, rolling my eyes to the ceiling, "because I was -- in his words -- 'an Amazon goddess.'" Cherry laughed. I stretched my long arm across the table and gave her a punch. "The owners asked me to indulge him and string him along -- keep him coming back.

"I would entertain him with stories of my childhood -- mostly made up -- tales of our traveling adventures -- mostly exaggerated -- and listen to his complaints about his business and life in Athens. He had made a lot of money in what he called the import/export business -- something to do with tiles and carpeting. We always wondered what exactly he was trading in -- it sounded kind of shady.

"A few weeks later we read about him on the front page of the newspaper. He had killed a reporter who was investigating him and then turned the gun on himself. The newspaper was still unable to prove anything, but they reported their suspicions that he was dealing in more than carpeting and tiles."

Cherry said, "Weapons and drugs were more likely to have made him a millionaire than floor coverings."

I said, "The article mentioned that he hung around a lot in the American suburb and they figured he was doing some wheeling and dealing there. His regular visits to the Glyfada Pub were not mentioned. The owners were ticked off that they lost out on the free publicity."

Julie Ann stared at me, mouth opened and glasses perched on the end of her nose. She blinked and pushed her glasses back into place. "Wow. You should write a book."

"I'd buy a copy." Phoebe Jo nodded vigorously.

Cherry pointed at me. "You were always writing that journal -- you probably have a few novels by now. Do you still do that?"

"No," I lied.

TZATZIKI SAUCE

16 ozs. plain yogurt
1 cucumber, peeled and finely chopped
2 tsp. lemon juice, or to taste
1 or 2 garlic cloves, minced
1 Tbsp. chopped fresh mint
Salt and pepper, to taste

Whisk all ingredients together and chill for one hour.
Serve with lamb or chicken kebabs wrapped in pita or flatbread.

* * * * * *

GREEK SALAD DRESSING

1 c. olive oil
1/3 c. white vinegar
3 cloves garlic
1 tsp. oregano
dash of Worcestershire sauce
1/4 lb. Feta cheese
4 tsp. Parmesan cheese
Salt and pepper to taste

Combine all ingredients in blender or food processor.
Toss together with a salad of romaine lettuce, slices of cucumber and sweet onion, chunks of tomato and Kalamata olives.

Saturday, December 16th

CHAPTER FIVE ....

I peered at the red digital numbers on my clock radio as I climbed out of bed and padded across the Persian carpet in my bare feet. Stumbling in the darkness, I kicked something soft and warm. It growled, got up, and scooted under my four-poster bed. "Sorry, Boo." My dog's been sleeping in the same spot for the past four years, but I always trip over him on my nightly prowls. It was two-thirty in the morning and I couldn't get to sleep.

Stepping out into the hall, I followed the trail of glowing night-lights past the closed door of the guest room where Cherry slept and the opened doors of the other two unoccupied bedrooms. I stopped at the top of the main staircase and looked down the hall that led to the Boones' living quarters. All was quiet in the house. But inside of me my brain buzzed like a hornet's nest full of anxious thoughts and questions. I proceeded down the stairs, past the gallery of Chili Kings and headed to the back of the house and into the family kitchen.

Who killed Preston? And why? Did either Martin Wolfenden or Frank Meyer have anything to do with his death? Why did I agree, once again, to cater Mother's stupid, impossibly elaborate party? Won't I ever learn? Hadn't I got past seeking her approval yet? What does that lawyer have to tell me? What was Preston trying to drag me into?

I cut myself a piggy-sized chunk of the rum pecan cake, put it in a cereal bowl, pulled out a tub of Starbuck's Javachip ice cream from the freezer, and piled five scoops on top. I wrapped up the remaining little slice of cake, put the tub back into the freezer, and padded upstairs to my room.

My gluttonous little terrier crawled out from under the bed to see what I had. I turned on a lamp. "No. You can't have any." I glared at him, sat down on the loveseat by the window, pulled my legs up underneath me, and began trying to fill the anxious pit in my stomach. Boo-Kat sat down, inches from my knees, and fixed his intense dark brown eyes on my bowl. I ignored him.

What I couldn't ignore were the conflicting emotions that Cherry's surprise visit stirred up in me. Over the years, I had created a pretty nice world here on my farm, built up a successful business, and earned the praises of my peers. But none of that could ease my loneliness and the feeling of being very different from everyone around me. Seeing Cherry again roused up an old spirit that had been sleeping inside of me for a long time -- that part of me which wanted to pack a knapsack and hit the road without any itinerary. Wanderlust was in the Cavanaugh genetic code passed down through the lineage of Chili Kings.

For three generations, the Cavanaugh men were merchant seamen, traveling the world as ship's cooks. But Dad broke that chain -- he was more earthbound. He had the business mind to turn a simple recipe which was handed down through the generations into a food empire. It seemed the family wanderlust condition skipped a generation and resurfaced in me. It was just my bad luck to inherit these two opposite dispositions. No wonder my insides felt like they were being pulled apart.

I scraped up the last bits of cake and ice cream, licked the spoon, and wondered why I still felt so empty. Mr. Boo-Kat looked horrified as I set the empty bowl down on the table beside me. I realized that pouring myself into my business didn't fill up that hole, but a life on the road wouldn't do it either. I had my share of Cherry-like flings -- there were even some proposals -- but I didn't love any of them.

Reminiscing about our summer in Athens and the tragic story of Demetrius made me curious to look in my journal and see what I had written. I went to the walk-in closet, rummaged around behind some old clothes, and pulled out a large cardboard box. Inside were stacks of books and papers, old photos, and trinkets from my travels. I found the tattered blue notebook and quickly leafed through it until I found the right entry.

SEPTEMBER 5th

This evening, Demetrius came into the bar in an extremely upset and agitated mood. He told me he couldn't come to visit me anymore, that someone had been digging into his private affairs and watching him. They had been snooping around his business and seemed intent on collecting evidence which would destroy his reputation and status in the city.

"It's now or never," he said to me, and if I wanted happiness, adventure, and to not have any worries about money ever again, this was my chance. "Pack your bags and come with me, tonight."

I said no. He tried to convince me otherwise, but I stuck to my decision. The owners watched us closely when they heard the intense conversation and frantic tone of his voice. They were very upset with me when he eventually gave up and stormed out of the bar, rejected and furious.

I closed the old, dog-eared journal. It had been years since I'd reviewed it, and I realized it wasn't Demetrius' death that would give me insights into Preston's murder. I needed to look at the killing of the newspaper reporter -- he was dead because he was trying to find the truth and got too close to it. Preston was like that. Whenever I questioned him about the fairness of his reviews, he'd answer, "Fairness? I'm looking for the truth."

Maybe that's what got him killed.

I put the book in the drawer of my nightstand and went to the bathroom. I'd been wearing my plastic boob all day and could feel the inevitable rash flaring up again. Cortisone cream usually took care of it. I pulled down the neck of my nightshirt and rubbed the cream into the bony hollow the surgeon had left six years ago. For the thousandth time, I wondered if I should have had the reconstructive surgery after my breast cancer, but then I thought of all the women who were now testifying that their silicone implants were killing them. Or at least making them very ill. I'd rather deal with a little rash. A lot of the time, especially when I was working in the kitchen, I'd go without wearing it, but I put it on for the morning's photo shoot and forgot to take it off.

Funny that Demetrius used to fantasize about me being an Amazon. Now that I had lost a breast, I really was one.

Wanting to get my three hours of sleep in, I turned off the light and crawled into bed. Sleep seemed impossible. I counted slowly from one to ten over and over and over again. The sheer tediousness of it soon sent me off to dreamland.

I sat at the end of a long mahogany dining table. Before me was a huge silver serving tray with an ornately engraved lid. A sharp, cabbagey smell wafted from underneath the cover as I lifted it, revealing a mountain of brussels sprouts. There were hundreds of them, all perfectly green and shiny.

Their outer leaves began to slowly unfurl.

Pop! A tiny gray eye blinked from under a leaf and stared up at me. Another eye popped open -- the sprout looked like a replica of Preston's head. *Pop! Pop! Pop!* Hundreds of tiny Preston heads began shouting in high falsettos, "Who killed me? Who killed me?"

CHAPTER SIX ....

His expression had a touch of surprise as I opened my front door. "Ms. Cavanaugh?" said the tall, gorgeous man flashing a police badge. He was about six-foot-five, and I could tell he was used to speaking with women a lot shorter than me. His eyes readjusted their line of vision to meet mine. "Ms. Kate Cavanaugh? I'm Officer Matt Skinner of the Clairmont Police Department."

Or, as the local citizens prefer to call them, Clairmont Rangers. I was taken off-guard, because Rangers usually wear green uniforms, and this one was wearing a suit. A nicely tailored one at that. "Yes?" I replied, looking into his eyes and getting lost in their deep chocolate pools. I felt an unfamiliar, but decidedly pleasant, crick in my neck from looking up at this man. A very handsome man -- just about my age, I guessed.

"Sorry to bother you this early on a Saturday, but I'm investigating the murder of a Mr. Preston Schneider. Perhaps you've read or heard about it."

Wow! This knight in shining armor was on the trail to see

that justice was done. "Yes, I have."

"May I come in? I have a few questions to ask you." Matt the Knight's entire body language smiled -- I know that's not physically possible, but that's how it seemed to me.

"Sure." I opened the door wider and breathed in the warm woodsy scent of his aftershave as he passed by and stepped into the foyer. Where had he been all my life? "Now, what can I do for you?" I tried to keep my mind clean.

Officer Skinner looked at his surroundings and appeared to be taking mental notes. Then he focused on me. "Did you know Mr. Schneider?"

"Yes."

"What kind of relationship did you have with him?"

"A professional one."

"Not a social one?"

I frowned and shrugged my shoulders. "Well, in my business, socializing is part and parcel of what I do."

"And what is that?" Officer Skinner smiled.

I smiled back. "I'm a caterer."

"Hmmm. Parties -- weddings, birthdays, etcetera?"

I nodded and wondered where he was going with this line of questioning -- and how I could get to ask him to come back for some socializing.

Matt the Knight took a second look around at the Christmas decorations and pointed towards the Great Room where the dining and buffet tables had been set up. "Looks like you're having an event today." He pulled out a notebook. "The reason I'm here is because Mr. Schneider had one of your business cards in his pocket."

"And?" I said pleasantly. So what? I'd blanketed all of Clairmont with those things.

"Well, your company name on the card was underlined with several pen strokes, and the message 'See Kate!' was written on it. So it seemed he was planning to call you. Have you had any recent dealings with Mr. Schneider?"

"No," I said, mentally differentiating between Preston and his lawyer, who was coming to see me that afternoon. "But he was going to attend my Mother's Christmas party here today." I bit my tongue and kept from blurting out, "Do you wanna come?"

"Well..." Officer Skinner reached into his pocket and pulled out a single white card and handed it to me. His nails were trimmed and very clean. No wedding band. "If you do remember anything unusual he might have said to you, please give me a call."

Stupid me. The whole idea of Preston's lawyer coming was strange, so I recounted the previous day's telephone exchange, and ended with "and you can meet him here yourself." There. I said it.

He checked his notebook. I checked his cute little earlobes. "I don't think I can make it," he said, "I've got a few more people to see. Thanks for the information. I'll contact Mr. Schneider's lawyer as soon as I can."

I ran my finger along the edge of his card. "Do you have any hot suspects?" My plan was to prolong this little encounter as long as I could. The hell with Mother's party.

Officer Skinner reached for the door knob. "Sorry, but I can't tell you anything, other than we are following every possible lead. That's why I stopped by here."

I wanted to offer him ham and eggs, coffee and donuts, or whatever else cops ate for breakfast at eight o'clock in the morning. But he was out the door before I could finish mentally making up my menu.

Damn.

CHAPTER SEVEN ....

"Kathleen!" I heard Mother's shrill voice coming from the foyer. I was in the kitchen and had just finished arranging a crudite platter of ripple cut carrot slices, Belgian endive leaves, red pepper strips, and thin slices of white turnip rolled up into trumpets.

"Kathleen!" Mother burst through the swinging doors. She was dressed in a black velvet pantsuit, the vest sparkling with gold embroidery. "Where is everyone? The place is dead. There are no greeters at the front door. I thought we were going to have carolers. Where are they? The guests will be here any second."

I held my hand up like a traffic cop. "Stop. Slow down. We have another hour before the party starts, and you know that none of your friends like to be the first, so they'll all be late." I pointed to the tray. "Do you want me to add cherry tomatoes and broccoli flowers?"

Mother followed my finger and sniffed. "Wh? -- who? -- sfut! I don't care." She shook her head and marched back out, her heels clicking on the linoleum tiles. "I have to check on the Great

51

Room." The door swung shut. I sighed. "Darling," the door opened and Mother poked her head back in, "nobody eats cherry tomatoes." She twirled and disappeared.

"Okay," I said to no one in particular, and assumed Mother meant "yes" to the broccoli flowers. I, myself, thought the tray needed more red, but she was the client, so I added the broccoli, picked up the tray, and exited the kitchen. In the foyer I came face to face with the four carolers hired from the First Community Church of Clairmont's choir wearing costumes which made them look like they walked straight out of Charles Dickens' Christmas Carol. I half-expected to turn around and see Tiny Tim. Instead, I was greeted by Mother.

I said, "Don't they look great?"

"I suppose." Mother squinted. "What are they supposed to be doing?"

"The carolers, Mother." I gave her an exasperated look. "They will be standing outside the front steps singing while the guests arrive, and provide musical entertainment inside while luncheon is being served."

The Cavanaugh smile quickly appeared on Mother's lips and she nodded to the quartet. "Lovely."

"You can relax or warm up, if you want," I said, turning to the carolers. "Showtime isn't for another forty-five minutes." They wandered off. "Mother, I'll be right back, this tray is getting real heavy. Let me go set it down on the hors d'oeuvre table."

It was just sixty seconds from the time I left her standing in the foyer, walked across the Great Room, set down the platter, and returned. I couldn't imagine what kind of disaster took place in such a brief moment to account for the look of shock and horror on Mother's face.

As I approached her, I heard a loud throaty groan coming from above and behind me. Hearing that, and seeing Mother's expression, I figured Marley's Ghost must have been coming down the stairs. Wrong. Standing in the upper walkway, overlooking the foyer, was a disheveled figure in lime green leggings and an oversized, ratty, black T-shirt, yawning and stretching her arms to the ceiling, red hair tousled and cowlicked.

It was Cherry Jubilee -- Mother's idea of someone sent by the devil himself to torment her.

Mother looked at me with panic in her eyes. "Do *something*."

I ran up the stairs, taking three steps at a time, gently grabbed a befuddled Cherry by the arm, and led her back to her room. "When's breakfast?" Cherry yawned in my face.

"Never mind breakfast." I had forgotten that her body clock was always on nightclub time. "Get dressed and come down for lunch. Do you have something partyish?"

Cherry's eyes lit up. "Always ready for a party."

"Good. When you're dressed, come down and find me. I'll probably be in the big kitchen." When I left, she was heading for the shower. I checked my watch -- it was only half an hour before guests were scheduled to start arriving -- and I remembered that I, too, needed to look presentable. The sneakers I wore for standing and doing kitchen work didn't look so lovely with my burgundy raw silk pants and tunic. I went to my room and slipped into a pair of black patent leather skimmers. Ready.

Well, almost. I needed a moment to calm myself and get centered. I sat down on the bay window seat and looked out across the expanse of lawn, pine trees, and meadow in front of my house.

Purple-gray clouds moved across the sky. They hung low and heavy over the farm, suffocating any festive feelings I'd been able to muster up within myself. My stomach tightened as I remembered why Preston would not be coming. I wondered if the guests, all of whom knew Preston well, were going to behave as if nothing had happened? It was going to be very difficult to paste on a smile and socialize, while thinking at the same time I might be standing face to face with the killer.

An old, beat-up, green Jaguar turned off the road and made

its way, crunching up the gravel lane, towards the house. It was Martin Wolfenden's car. Like an Agatha Christie novel, the suspects were beginning to gather. It wasn't surprising that Wolfie was the first to arrive -- he probably wanted to snoop in the kitchen. All chefs are that way.

He ignored the large parking signs directing visitors onto the lawn and pulled into the last spot right beside the house. Typical.

I breathed deeply, reluctantly left my bedroom and went downstairs. Wolfie was just coming through the double front doors and flung his arms out to greet me. "Katie, you look gorgeous."

He looked pretty good himself, dressed in a nicely tailored charcoal gray suit, bright red vest, and a green tie with a prancing reindeer design. Wolfie walked toward me with his Jimmy Cagney strut. He stood a little over five and a half feet tall, and was just shy of his fortieth birthday. "What's cooking?"

"My goose, if this affair isn't successful." I stooped down and gave him a friendly hug, and -- as usual -- he didn't know when to let go. I unwrapped his arms from around my waist and hoped my reaction didn't look strange, because I certainly didn't feel normal. It was very bizarre. Suddenly, I was aware of the possibility that I might not know the people around me as well as I thought I did.

I pulled him by the hand into the kitchen, where we were greeted by the heady aroma of roast goose, prime rib, and garlic that filled the room. Tony pulled his head out of the oven and let the door slam shut. "Hey, Wolfie."

"Tony, my man." The two roosters shook hands in the middle of the kitchen. "Just wanted to get a preview." Wolfie walked to the stove, lifted a pot lid and sniffed. "Hmm." He then systematically uncovered each pot and sniffed the contents, eyes closed, nostrils doing an impression of a vacuum cleaner. Completing his inspection, he scanned the room. I thought I saw a wistfulness in his eyes.

"Do you want to help?" I blurted out without thinking.

Tony-Z glared at me.

For a moment it looked as though Wolfie's eyes were going to jump out of his sockets with excitement. Then, his ego regained control. "Well, if you guys need help. Sure." He took off his jacket, hung it on a hook by the back door, and grabbed a white cotton apron.

"Kathleen." Mother was calling again. "Gotta go. Tony, give him something to do." As I pushed through the doors, I realized I might have started a time bomb ticking.

"There you are, Darling. Uncle Cliff is here." Mother was standing in the pillared archway leading into the Great Room. The tall, cheerful, impeccably dressed man standing next to her was my favorite relative, Mother's younger brother Clifford T. Vasherhann. He was a flamboyant, but highly respected, defense attorney and a constant source of material for the local gossip column. I gave him a hug and looked past him towards the front door. "No date? Uncle Cliff, are you feeling okay?"

He winked. "Never better, K.C." Then he leaned towards me and said in a loud stage whisper, "Your mother's never forgiven me for that second divorce. She gets edgy around my girl friends, so I didn't bring one -- sort of a Christmas gift to her."

Mother was holding her lips together so tightly they almost disappeared. She looked up at me and down her nose at the same time -- an almost impossible thing for someone of her small stature to do. "I don't think you have enough punch." She pointed to the single bowl of iced cranberry-cider punch on the hors d'oeuvre table. Mother is so helpful.

"I have some Wassail warming on the stove. Now that your guests are arriving, I'll put it out." One of the hired servers dressed in a high-necked Victorian jacket came into the Great Room. I called him over and gave him instructions to set out the Wassail in a warming pan. Out of the corner of my eye, I saw Siegfreid Doppler dressed in a bright red jacket and snappy green and red plaid bow tie, taking a photo of the Christmas tree. The editor at *Cincy Life* magazine had received Mother's permission to use pictures from this year's luncheon as part of next year's special Christmas Party issue.

"Joy to the world, the Lord is come...." Places everyone. The quartet was outside singing in perfect, exuberant four part harmony. Robert, dressed in a Victorian butler's outfit and wearing his most sober, dignified expression, was stationed at the front door, ready to open it for each arriving guest. Mother, Uncle Cliff, and I stood in anticipation, a mini receiving line, waiting for the arrival of the "cream of Clairmont society". Seigfried's camera was poised to capture the entire afternoon's festivities -- and maybe a few future mug shots.

Ding! Dong! The suspects began filing in.

CHAPTER EIGHT ....

"Those S.O.B. writers should all be shot!" Mabel Crank, owner of the minor league Cincinnati Twisters hockey team puffed on her cigarillo, sending little dots and dashes of smoke out the side of her mouth. I watched her apple doll face scrunch up in a look of disgust.

"Damn reporters are nothing but a bunch of leeches -- the whole lot of them." Charles Hassenbacher, president/owner of Hassenbacher Brewery, rubbed his beet red face and patted the few strands of hair on his head into place.

These two, along with Walter "King" Yankovitch of Yankie Pineapple, Incorporated and Richard James Wagner, President of Wagner Savings & Loan, were gathered in my library, which I had designated as the smoking lounge.

"Now, now, Chuck, don't get your blood all in a boil," said Wagner, his voice a soothing baritone. He dragged lightly on his rosewood briar pipe, the aroma from his tobacco acting as a sweet cover-up of the pungent cigars being waved around by the others.

"You know that publishers are in business to make money, and gossip is what the public is buying. As a business owner, you should understand and appreciate that. Besides, there's a concept in this country called Freedom of the Press." He stood by the window as straight as an arrow. I marveled at how the sunlight glistened off his perfectly groomed white hair.

"But, James," said King Yankovitch, "they take it too far. Those ink stained Peeping Toms think nothing of dragging our names through the mud. They go too far."

"At times." James Wagner nodded and looked out the window.

"Bah!" Mabel Crank jabbed her cigarillo into an ashtray and immediately lit up another one.

Yankovitch turned to me, his usually jowly face shaking with indignation. "Kate, how would you feel if every time you opened a newspaper or watched television, you found your momentary lapses in judgment were being put under a microscope and scrutinized? Nobody wants to report on your good deeds."

Mabel Crank didn't give me the chance to answer. "Good deeds aren't entertaining." She popped a mini cheese ball into her mouth and reached for another one from the tray I had just brought in.

Charles Hassenbacher took a gulp of punch. "Some of those mud slingers haven't even got the courage to sign their own names to the exaggerations and half-truths printed about us."

"Yeah," King said, waving his cigar in the air. "Remember that piece of trash printed last year that everyone was buying? Made the *Enquirer's* Best Sellers List. What was it's title?"

"*False Fronts,*" Charles replied through clenched teeth. "My son Tom's political aspirations were killed by that book. He made a little mistake and got caught with that congressman's wife at the Red Roof Inn. The boy's always been a little too arrogant for his own good, but someone went to a lot of trouble to get those pictures. If I ever get my hands on that writer, I'll kill him -- her -- whoever it is."

"Tom wasn't the only one hurt by that book." James Wagner rejoined the conversation. "There were attacks on half a dozen other people, but all we know about the author is the pseudonym Wagging Tongue. Pretty brave, eh?"

I looked at these four heavy hitters of the Cincinnati business community. They were Mother's friends -- or rather, acquaintances. Friendship entails opening up to a person and allowing that person to see the real you. Like most members of Clairmont society, Mother's circle didn't let non-family members in on their personal affairs, and jealously guarded their privacy. To the outside world, every problem was under control and life was "marvelous, Darling".

Some of the information I knew about them was what they allowed their personal secretaries to meagerly dispense to the public. The rest was from what I read in the newspapers. Both sources put their own spin on things, so you had to take what they said with a hefty serving of salt.

Charles Hassenbacher had for years been trying to use his family's fortune to buy his children's way into politics. He envisioned himself as being another Joe Kennedy, backing his four sons Thomas, Carl, John, and Henry in bids for local political office. Unfortunately, each of the boys had a tendency to shoot himself in the foot, and Charles was probably doomed to being a frustrated patriarch.

Richard James Wagner -- known to all as James, so as not to be confused with his father, or be called Junior -- was president of Wagner Savings and Loan, one of Cincinnati's oldest, and most solid, family-owned financial institutions. The bank and family have been community-minded with a pristine reputation since just after the Civil War. Everyone connected with this family guarded their reputation from all sticks and stones, real or imagined, which must have been very easy -- they weren't exactly rebels. From my personal dealings with the Wagners, both professionally and socially,

I concluded they were the most boring clan of rich folk I'd ever met.

Ah, Mabel Crank -- the sportswriters' favorite dartboard. She had the unfortunate tendency to mistime her most innocent off-handed comment and have it land on the next day's front page headline. The latest was her cry to heaven "Why me?" when a well-liked referee suffered a stroke during the second period of the hockey season's Home Opener Day at the Cincy Gardens. She wanted the game to go on, but the league president saw fit to cancel it, to be replayed later. Unfortunately, she was in the middle of a live TV interview from her customary seat in the stands when the official dropped to the ice, and her tongue spoke before her brain could stop it. She was a prime candidate for sensitivity training.

There was antagonism between her and Preston Schneider. Preston said she made Cincinnati a laughing stock with her big mouth, and one of the reasons Mabel hated him was because he made fun of the quality of hot dogs she sold at the games.

Walter "King" Yankovitch was probably the master of keeping his name out of the news. In a way, his success at being invisible inflamed the passions of reporters to dig in search of information about him. King was an extremely secretive, but successful, business man buying companies, developing them over a period of years, and then selling at an enormous profit. A big time wheeler-dealer, he contributed to both political parties, and had been seen at fundraisers seated with the President of the United States. He used Yankie Pineapple, Incorporated as the holding company for all his acquisitions.

The combination of cigar smoke and negative energy was beginning to make me ill. I set the tray of hors d'oeuvres down on the mahogany and leather card table in the middle of the room. "Help yourselves -- I need to circulate. We'll be sitting down to eat in fifteen minutes." I received a couple of nodding acknowledgements and a weak smile from Mabel that erupted into a spasmodic coughing fit.

I left the room, gasping for oxygen. Every year, after Mother's Christmas luncheon, the library had to be aired out. It would be a couple of weeks before I could enjoy staying in there for any length of time.

As irritating as those old crows were, I couldn't see them getting worked up to the point of losing control and actually murdering someone. Even though Charles Hassenbacher was furious that his son's philandering had been exposed, I doubted he'd make good on his threat. Dealing with the press came with the territory they had staked out. The only thing that would incite more passionate anger was if those "damn reporters" ignored them completely.

"Hello, there." The lounge lizard quality of Frank Meyer's voice, as always, put me on edge. He had the irritating habit of sneaking up from behind, which was very difficult to do considering he was as tall as me. Frank was reasonably good looking, very successful, and my age. So, as Mother would say, what was wrong with him? Well, for one thing, he was in love with himself. I wanted someone who would make room for me.

"So, Kate. It's been a while since we've talked." Frank offered me one of the two Scotches he had in hand.

I shook my head. "I'm on duty." He was blocking my way and knew I was too polite to push past and ignore him. "You're right, Frank, it has been a while. Taken over any new companies lately?"

His head reared back and he laughed. I could see right up his hairy nose. "That's what I like about you, Kate. You have such a sense of humor."

I felt like Mother. My facial muscles had instinctively switched to the Cavanaugh smile position.

"You know," Frank stepped forward, I took one step back, "I was wondering what your plans were for this New Year's Eve."

My brain's lying lobe began manufacturing excuses. I was about to start transferring those stories to my lips when Frank's cellular phone rang.

"Excuse me," Frank said, and flipped open his communicator.

In the meantime, I beamed myself to another part of the house.

CHAPTER NINE ....

"Terry! Marilyn!" I hugged my two friends. "I'm so glad you could come."

"Sorry we're late," said Terry Poole. I welcomed him, his wife Marilyn, and their two boys, twelve-year-old Daniel and nine-year-old Jason, into the foyer.

"No. You're not late at all," I replied as Robert began taking coats.

I lingered for a moment at the front door before shutting it. I was aware that the Snow Witch was getting closer by the hour. The temperature was dropping, the purple-gray clouds moving across the sky had come together into a solid gray mass blocking out the sun. The wind was picking up, sending old dead oak leaves crackling across the front yard and bouncing off the split rails of the fences lining the private road that led up to the house. I shivered and closed the door. Breathing in the comforting smells of wood burning in the fireplace, pine boughs, and roasted goose, I felt safe in my sanctuary.

"We're just about to start serving," I said.

"Great!" shouted Daniel. "I'm starved, Aunt Kate."

"Any hot dogs?" asked Joshua.

Daniel poked his younger brother in the ribs. "She doesn't make kid stuff like that. She makes chili." Joshua punched back.

"Boys, boys," Marilyn called out in a surprisingly strong voice. Well, strong for Marilyn. She was a soft-spoken, gentle soul. The two siblings stopped. "Don't you have anything to say to your hostess?"

"Oh, yeah." Daniel pulled out a little box wrapped up in bright red paper and a gold bow. "Merry Christmas, Aunt Kate."

"Ohhh! For me? Cool!" I took the present and gave both squirming brothers a hug. "Thanks. Merry Christmas. There's something under the tree for you -- but you'll have to wait until after lunch. Today's menu might not include ballpark food, but I know you boys like drumsticks, so ..." The two didn't wait for me to finish. They ran into the Great Room and up to the still empty buffet tables, jockeying for position to be the first one in line. Marilyn rolled her eyes to the ceiling, excused herself, and went to supervise her pups.

At first glance, Terry was his usual, perfectly groomed self. But it seemed there was something out of place, and I couldn't put my finger on what it was. Even though his mouth smiled, his light blue eyes didn't -- they had a distant, tired expression. Having known him my entire life, I didn't need to beat around the bush. "How are you coping?"

"I'll be okay, but it stirs up a lot of demons." He lowered his eyes and his brow furrowed. I reached out and rested my hand on his arm. He continued in a soft voice. "Seeing Preston's body lying there ... I was thirteen again, walking into my parents' bedroom and finding my mother..." Terry cleared his throat and looked up. "It's tough, but I'll be fine. Thanks for asking, Kate." Then, with a brighter tone in his voice, he said, "I better go see what my family's up to."

Terry left, and I stood alone in the foyer. I had always wondered how he must have felt when he discovered his mother shot to death. When it happened, I had been too young to understand the depth of his anger and fear. But maybe now, having gone through my battle with breast cancer, I had a better idea of what it was like to struggle with such powerful emotions.

Terry and Marilyn had helped me then. They were the only ones who would let me talk plainly and honestly about how I felt. Mother didn't want to hear from me on the days when I was convinced I was dying. Brushing me off with a "You'll be fine, Darling" was far from being supportive. In fact, it felt downright uncaring. Terry and Marilyn filled the void.

Now it was my turn to be there for them. I had a sense that Terry's problems were just beginning -- and not just with his childhood demons.

"Kathleen!" A shrill voice cut through the din of chattering, laughter, and carol singing that filled the house.

I closed my eyes and counted... eight... nine... ten. "Yes, Mother."

"Kathleen!" She shouted again as she came wheeling around the pillared archway of the Great Room and plowed into me. "There you are. Come here and look at what you've done to me."

Now what? Did someone get caught up in a table cloth and fall and break their leg? Did the Christmas tree crash down into the punch bowl? Did the brussels sprouts explode?

Mother pulled me into the Great Room and pointed a long, shiny Chanel red fingernail at the room full of guests. "There," she whispered loudly.

I followed the aim of her point and shook my head. "What? Give me a clue. I don't see anything wrong."

"She's half-naked."

I squinted and searched the crowd, looking for Lady Godiva. Bingo. I should have guessed. What a combination -- Uncle Cliff and Cherry. I had to admit, her dress looked more like underwear, but all the important parts were covered. Barely.

Uncle Cliff bent down so Cherry could whisper something in his ear. He burst into his boisterous laugh that carried all the way across the room.

"Looks like Uncle Cliff's having a good time."

Mother stood at my side like a stone statue, her cold blue eyes frozen in panic.

"Let's go join the party," I said, pulling on her arm. She resisted, then gave in and switched on a half-hearted smile when she realized people were watching.

Cherry was wearing a slinky black number with spaghetti straps that showed off her taut body and her slightly pumped biceps. As we got closer, I recognized something I'd forgotten about, but had been with her the day she had it put on the back of her left shoulder -- a small tattoo of two red cherries on stems with green leaves.

Uncle Cliff saw us approaching and I could see his face was flushed. "You've got a real spitfire friend here, K.C."

Cherry finished sipping her punch. "Hey, girl. I've been looking all over for you. When do we eat? I'm starving." She looked at my uncle. "Fortunately, Cliffie here has been entertaining me with the dirt on some of your guests."

I sneaked a peek at Mother. Her forced smile had turned into a painful grimace. I was sure she would be making an emergency visit to her dentist to check for cracks in her pearly whites.

"You're just gonna have to hold your tongue. We're here, Eleanor -- let's have a good time." We all turned at the sound of the booming Texas drawl to see the Battling Sloanes, Patrick and his huge wife, filling the archway with their enormous bulk.

"Eleanor, darling." Mother fled to her bridge partner's side and gave her a hug.

"Hello, Tink. Gorgeous setting." Eleanor kissed the air beside Mother's ear.

"Thanks for inviting us," Patrick said, flashing a big cowboy grin. He stuffed his hands into his pockets and wandered off into the crowd. "What's a boy got to do to get a drink around here?" he called out to Robert, who was tending bar.

I checked my watch. Serving time. "Kate!" I felt someone tugging at my sleeve. It was Julie Ann, dressed in her Victorian server's costume and looking almost cute, except for the frantic expression in her eyes.

"Kate, you gotta come -- quick," she whispered and pulled me towards the door. "Those two are gonna kill each other!"

CHAPTER TEN ....

I slammed through the swinging doors and into the kitchen.

"Tony? Wolfie? What's going on in here?" The two were nose to nose in the middle of the room.

Tony responded without taking his eyes off the older chef. "He's trying to tell me what to do. I was watching the clock like you told me to, Kate. I knew it was almost serving time, so I started carving up a couple of the geese."

Wolfie threw up his hands in exasperation. "But Kate, he didn't let them sit long enough."

Tony looked at me and shrugged. "I didn't have time. Even putting the forks inside the cavities ... they took longer to roast than we counted on."

"They have to sit for fifteen minutes so the juices settle back into the meat. It's gonna be tough." Wolfie folded his arms in an I Know Better Than You pose.

Tony shot him a look of disdain. "Ha! The goose is so greasy, a little less fat will be good for the guests. We got to get it out. Right, Kate?"

I went over to the platter and pushed on the roasted skin. A trickle of juice ran out. I picked up a little piece of meat Tony had already sliced and took a bite. Delicious. And he was right -- we were behind schedule. "Tony, carry on with what you were doing. Wolfie, if you want to help, we need some of the prime rib carved right away. Time to hustle, guys."

I started pulling pans out of the warmer and loading them onto a trolley. I motioned to Phoebe Jo, who had just walked in. "Take these out to the buffet table and start setting up."

The next fifteen minutes were enough to send anyone's blood pressure soaring. I yelled out commands that choreographed my small kitchen staff's movements. It was like a precision drill team routine that I was spontaneously making up as we went along -- goose carving, rib slicing, gravy making, rolls baking in the oven. Metal pans clanged as they were tossed. A rush of adrenaline pumped through me as I rescued the Yorkshire pudding from burning. The smell of hot grease and baked bread filled the kitchen. I loved it.

My Victorian serving staffers were running back and forth, carrying out the food as fast as we could get it ready. Things were moving faster than I could keep track of. I knew I was forgetting something, but I couldn't take the time to figure out what. I was caught up in a tornado of activity, whirling from one end of the kitchen to another, everything, but the task I was focused on, a blur.

Suddenly, it all came to a halt. The last trolley was wheeled out of the kitchen and I leaned back against the door of the walk-in refrigerator. "Yes!" I felt like I had just played a full-court game and had scored the winning basket at the buzzer.

I walked over to the warming oven to turn it off and noticed a pan still on the rack. I grabbed a towel, wrapped it around the edge of the pan and pulled it out. Brussels sprouts swimming in a sauce of browned butter and lemon juice. "Julie Ann." I waved the teenager over. "Here, take this out."

She looked around frantically. "Where're my mitts?"

"Just use the towel."

Julie Ann hesitated, then gingerly picked up the pan. "Oh, it works." She marched out, head up and braid swinging from side to side.

Seeing the brussels sprouts made me think of Preston. He probably would have been back here enjoying the last minute flurry, and making sure I didn't mess up. "Hey, Wolfie, did you hear about Preston Schneider?"

Martin Wolfenden was standing by the kitchen window, sipping a glass of wine, and gazing out at who-knows-what. It seemed he didn't hear me. "Chef Wolfenden?" He slowly turned his attention to me. "Did you hear what happened to Preston?"

"Yeah." Wolfie gulped down the last of his wine. "I'll go out there and carve."

I watched in stunned silence as he set down his wine glass, strode past me, and out the door.

Tony said, "That was damn strange." He had been stacking dishes in the washer and pulled on the metal door. It shut with a clang, and the washer automatically started its cycle.

I agreed. It wasn't like Wolfie to give a monotone answer like that and leave the room. I knew there was bad blood between him and Preston because of the Papillon bankruptcy. I wondered what Martin was doing last Thursday night. Did the blood get so bad between them that Wolfie spilt some of Preston's? I liked Wolfie. I didn't want to think him capable of that, but I also knew him as a passionate man who could lose his temper.

I told Tony, "You did a good job, no matter what Wolfie said."

"Well, if it's okay by you, I'm going to keep my distance from that guy and stay in here and finish cleaning up."

I poured a couple of glasses of Cabernet, handed one to Tony, and we clinked a silent toast to each other. I took a sip and said, "Don't stay in here all afternoon. Come out, take a bow, and enjoy yourself. You're due some praise."

Tony nodded and smiled.

I started to leave, then halfway out the door I stopped and looked back at my assistant. "But first, change into a clean chef's jacket. That one's a greasy, disgusting mess."

He snapped me a salute.

A streak of black and tan came bounding down the stairs and zig-zagged around my legs as I made my way across to the Great Room. "Boo-Kat!" I yelled. "Come here!" I could tell he was up to mischief by the way he ran. He had something in his mouth. I reached out to grab it. Missed. He darted away and disappeared into the Great Room. A wave of loud laughter rippled through the crowd and followed him as he made a victory lap around the perimeter of the room, one of my not-so-beautiful bras dangling from his mouth. I'm gonna kill that dumb dog.

He'd already made a fool of me, so I didn't bother chasing the little terror. I waited by the entrance, arms outstretched, ready to grab him, knowing he was going to try and dodge me again. Boo-Kat hurtled towards me, aiming to run between my legs and take another lap.

I stamped my foot. He came to a startled halt. I grabbed him and left the room to the sounds of cheers and applause.

CHAPTER ELEVEN ....

Five minutes later, I was back in the Great Room checking the buffet line, making the rounds, and answering questions about my pet's underwear fetish. To Mabel Crank at table number one: "Yes, he has been fixed." To Patrick Sloane seated at table number two: "No, he has never had a date."

I was very happy with the way the buffet table decorations turned out. As the guests lined up and waited for their slices of roast goose with fruit and nut stuffing, or prime rib of beef with roasted garlic potatoes and Yorkshire pudding, they were busy admiring my collection of antique Santa Claus figurines. We had displayed them along the length of the table with each grouping surrounded by sprigs of holly and pine boughs.

In the center of the table was our pièce de résistance. Julie Ann, Phoebe Jo, and I had spent countless hours over the past few weeks designing and creating a mini Dickens Village out of gingerbread. Bob Cratchit's and Ebenezer Scrooge's houses flanked an old stone church. Lights twinkled through the windows made of hard candy, and drifts of royal icing snow had been piped onto the rooftops and window sills. The scene was completed by miniature pine trees and little porcelain figurines of carolers and Dickens characters. Moving further down the table, guests were served brussels sprouts in brown butter, orange glazed carrots, and green salad with warm bacon dressing. At another table were three huge glass footed bowls brimming with English Trifle, and two Christmas Puddings on silver trays with a silver bowl full of hard sauce between them.

I had to admit, it was a beautiful feast.

Going from table to table, I caught little snippets of conversation. Some guests were discussing the new stadium plans, the proposed tax levy, and the latest shenanigans of City Council. But the predominate topic was the murder of Preston Schneider.

I stopped at table number five.

"I didn't know we were going to have a fashion show," remarked Holly Berry-Wagner, giving me a cool, polite smile. "That was an unusual idea, using your dog as a model."

"Oh," I said in a casual tone, looking down at her, "just one of those spontaneous touches I'm known for."

"Actually, a fashion show would be a good idea for your next party, Kate. You know I used to model for Tink's annual Garden Club Gala." Holly smiled, showing off the results of years of expensive dental work.

Her husband of twenty-five years, Nate Wagner, James' younger brother, surprised me with a rare display of talkativeness. "You're looking nice, Kate."

I almost fell backwards. Thin, pale Nate was the most introverted man I'd ever met. It must have been the rum in the Wassail that loosened his tongue. I thanked him for the compliment.

Nate's tongue ran wild. "It's almost the end of the year, Kate. Start gathering up your receipts. Best to get a head start on these things." As president of the accounting firm of Wagner and Pincus, Nate had been handling my family's personal finances for years.

Holly wiped her shiny pink lips delicately with a white cloth napkin. "You've done your usual splendid job. The food is delicious."

James Wagner toasted me with his wine glass. "Yes, Kate. Top notch." The other four guests at the table nodded and smiled at me.

Holly reached out and patted my hand. "I must have your recipe for the stuffing."

I couldn't imagine her stuffing anything -- I was sure the woman never cooked. She was a true product of Clairmont breeding, passively allowing everything in her life to be done for her. That even included an arranged marriage into the right Clairmont family, the very thing I had escaped. Oh, the matriarchs and patriarchs would deny it, but there were ways of controlling who their children came into contact with.

Just then, Mother arrived. Playing perfect hostess, she greeted everyone with a radiant smile and linked her arm in mine. "And how are we all doing at table number five?"

They all made the appropriate noises.

Mother looked up at me. "It's not the same without Preston, is it, dear." Without giving me a chance to respond, she turned to the guests. "Why, I was going to have him seated at this very table." Something from across the room stole her attention. I followed her gaze. Eleanor Sloane was waving her Texas-sized arm in the air. Flashes of light danced off her bejeweled fingers.

"Enjoy yourselves. I must go." And Mother did.

James Wagner said, "Sad business, Preston being killed. And in church. Terrible evidence of what society has become. We need people like Preston -- men and women who will uphold the highest of standards."

Replies of "Yes, yes" and "Awful" came from around the table. I was surprised, and I'm sure Preston would have been, too, at the outpouring of sympathy.

Holly shook her head slowly. "I saw him only hours before he was killed. I might have been one of the last people to see him alive." She looked up at me. "I was at the dress rehearsal on Thursday night. I'm in the choir. You should have heard Preston's solo -- his singing brought tears to my eyes."

I felt a sudden compulsion and asked, "Did you notice anything strange about him that night?"

"No." Holly frowned. "He was his normal perfectionist self. But there did seem to be some antagonism between him and the choir director, Terry Poole."

I said, "Terry? Antagonistic? He gets along with everyone."

"I know. Come to think of it, that was pretty strange. It wasn't anything they said, they barely spoke. But the way they looked at each other...and just the tension in the air...I wondered how we were going to get through the rehearsal. You'd swear they wanted to kill one other."

James clicked his tongue. "Holly, you're blowing things way out of proportion. I was there for a while, and I didn't sense any antagonism."

I felt a surge of anger. How could Holly say such things? There was no evidence, just some vague feeling on her part. Preston was murdered, and there she was, fabricating a story that implicated a man who had helped me through one of the darkest chapters in my life.

Holly turned quiet and started poking at her Yorkshire Pudding.

I asked, "James, are you in the choir, too?"

He waved his hand, dismissing the whole idea. "Me? No, no. Can't carry a tune. Don't even sing in the shower. I was sitting in on a finance meeting downstairs. I'm a church elder, you know. Stopped in at the sanctuary afterwards to hear the music and went home before the rehearsal ended."

"So you didn't witness the same thing Holly did?"

James shook his head. It amazed me how people can see

things so differently.

Nate had been sipping his wassail throughout the conversation. "Maybe Preston had another life we didn't know about." He studied his empty glass. "He did have a pretty rough past, didn't he?"

"He grew up very poor." I replied.

James arched his eyebrows in a look of surprise.

"Oh, yes," I continued. "Preston bragged that he was a kid from Over-the-Rhine who made good. But he would never talk about growing up there, except to mention that he lived with his parents over the tiny grocery store they owned. He would clam up if I tried to dig any further."

An awkward silence followed.

"Well," I said, "I need to check on the food and make sure things are going smoothly."

Holly pushed back her chair from the table. "I'm coming, too. I have to try your desserts."

We parted company at the buffet line. I stepped behind the table to check in with the servers, and Holly took her place on the short line of guests behind Patrick Sloane. Everything seemed to be moving along very nicely. There was still plenty of food for those coming up for seconds -- and in Eleanor Sloane's case, thirds. Guests, other than Holly, were already beginning to dig into the desserts. I heard Cherry's laugh. Wolfie had pulled two forks out of the roast goose he was carving and waved them at me. *That's* what I'd forgotten about back in the kitchen.

I also kept forgetting that Cherry was visiting. With all that was going on, I hadn't had a chance to reconnect with her. I hoped she was having a good time. I noticed that Patrick Sloane was having a good time watching her chest as she laughed.

I also noticed that Holly Berry-Wagner was throwing visual darts at his back.

CHRISTMAS WASSAIL

1 gallon apple cider, or natural apple juice
1 quart cranberry cocktail
3/4 cup white sugar
3 (3 inch) cinnamon sticks
3 (1 inch chunks) fresh, peeled ginger
1 Tbsp. whole allspice
1 1/2 tsp. nutmeg
2 oranges, unpeeled, cut in wedges
1 Tbsp. whole cloves
2 to 2 1/2 cups dark rum

Combine apple cider and cranberry cocktail in large saucepan. Add orange wedges (studded with whole cloves), sugar, cinnamon sticks, ginger, nutmeg and whole allspice. Bring mixture to a boil, stirring constantly, until sugar dissolves. Reduce heat, cover and simmer for 10 minutes.

Stir in rum. Cover and heat through. Strain into a large serving bowl or warming pan. Float freshly-cut orange slices in Wassail and serve hot in cups.

(If a fruitier, less spicy flavor is preferred, add more cranberry cocktail.)

CHAPTER TWELVE ....

"How's the entertainment at table number two?" I asked Cherry, as she loaded a plate with Christmas pudding and trifle.

"Katie, this is the best damn party I've been to for a long time. You're one hell of a chef." She licked some pastry cream off her finger.

"Thank you, I was hoping you were having fun. Are your tablemates behaving themselves?" I was following Cherry back to where she was sitting.

"Your Uncle Cliffie's a hoot! He has his own Harley and he says he's planning on taking a few weeks off in the spring and wants to meet me in New Orleans."

I laughed. Great. That's all I need. Mother would never let me out of the doghouse for introducing those two. "Give me lots of warning if there are any wedding plans."

"And those Sloanes. What a riot. It's like watching an old rerun of Dallas. First Eleanor tells Patrick he's drinking too much. Then, good ol' boy Patrick throws down a double Scotch and tells her to go stick her nose in someone else's life. Everybody else at the table's embarrassed. They all start making dumb jokes and laughing real loud, pretending not to notice."

Cherry and I arrived at her table. Since some of the guests had gone off to mingle and there was an empty chair, I decided to take a ringside seat.

Patrick Sloane was looking a little flushed, but I was sure he had control of himself. He wouldn't be Executive Vice President of Sales for the food conglomerate Rodger's if he couldn't handle his liquor in public.

Eleanor Sloane spilled out all over -- her chair and the top of her emerald green taffeta dress. "You always look so refreshed and relaxed, Kate. I would be a wreck if I had to do all the work needed to put on a party like this."

"I'll crash after you've all left. But don't tell anyone, it'll destroy the myth."

"Yep," Patrick winked at me and lifted a glass. "The Chili Princess does it again." Then he winked at Cherry.

Eleanor smiled at me and jabbed her meaty elbow into her husband's flabby side. "Preston Schneider would have given you a good review for this one, Kate."

Patrick rubbed his rib cage. "Last thing I heard Preston say on Thursday night was that he was looking forward to this party."

I sat forward in my chair. "You saw him Thursday night? Where?"

"At the choir's dress rehearsal."

"Clairmont Community Church? I didn't know you were in the choir."

"Yep. Eleanor wanted me to go to church, but I was always falling asleep. So I joined the choir. Figured that would keep me awake."

"So? Did Preston seem okay to you? Was he acting normal?"

"Yeah, I guess. But I never considered that guy normal to

79

begin with."

Eleanor glared at her husband. "I liked him."

"You would," he answered. "The man was a pain in the butt. Always complaining about things. Terry Poole knows what he's doing. Knows how to run his choir. But that dress rehearsal was murder -- pun intended. Just because Preston was the soloist, he was acting like the star of the show. Preston kept wanting to go over and over this one line. I couldn't see what he was getting at. But I could see in Terry's eyes that he was getting more and more pissed off at him."

This was frustrating. Three people had been at the same place, at the same time, and were giving me three different accounts. What really happened?

I wanted to pump Patrick for more details, but the man had an intense, faraway look in his eyes. He seemed to be staring at something over my shoulder and across the room. I turned to look, but there wasn't anything unusual going on. All I saw was a group of people hanging around the Christmas tree watching the kids shake the presents.

"Excuse me ladies." Patrick looked at his watch, then pushed his chair back from the table and got up. "I'll be back."

Eleanor's pencil-thin eyebrows pulled together in a frown. She gulped down her mouthful of trifle and twisted her neckless head around to look at him. "Where are you going?"

Patrick bent close to her and said in a low, measured tone. "If you *must* know, I have to go to the can. There, feel better?"

I choked back a laugh and watched as he ambled across the room.

Eleanor's eyes were following him. "You may not believe it, girls, but I really love that cowboy." She turned and leaned across the table towards Cherry and me, her bosom almost tipping it over. "I'll tell you gals a little secret -- I get real excited after one of our little scraps."

Cherry and I stayed quiet.

"Kate," Eleanor continued, "I hope I see the day you find someone. It's just not right -- an attractive young woman like you without somebody. You need a special person to share your life with -- the good times and the bad. Patrick and I know each other so completely, there are no secrets between us".

There went Eleanor. Off again on one of her romance novel preachings. For the next ten minutes, she filled the air with pink, flowery clichés about prince charmings and happily-ever-afters.

"That's not to say Patrick and I don't have our bumpy roads, as you can probably see for yourself. But we work things out." She spooned a mouthful of Christmas pudding. "Now take Thursday night for example."

Cherry's eyes were at half mast. "Eleanor, Kate. You'll have to excuse me -- I need to walk around." She got to her feet and smoothed the wrinkles out of her skin-tight dress. "I can feel all this rich eating and drinking settling on my hips."

Eleanor's eyebrow arched. She snorted. "What hips?"

Cherry and I wriggled our fingers at each other. "Catch you later," I said. It was now just Eleanor and me. "What about Thursday night?"

The two of us leaned closer, as though we didn't want anybody else to hear. "Well," Eleanor began, "Patrick always hangs around the church after choir practice, chewing the fat with some of the other guys. So, I'm used to him coming in late. But this time he really had me riled up. He was two hours late. Lord, how I lit in to him when he finally came through that door. I went on and on about how worried I'd been, and he had no right to put me through that. I told him he was an inconsiderate lout for not calling me and telling me he'd be late. I used words that would have made my old prospecting granddad blush.

"But when I finally, noticed the look on his face, I knew something terrible had happened. He said, 'Preston's been attacked.' That put the brakes on my mouth. Patrick said he was driving home after practice, but then he realized he had picked up the wrong scarf. It was the same color as his, but it didn't have his monogram. He went back to church to see if his scarf was still there.

"When he entered the sanctuary, where they had held the dress rehearsal, he found Terry Poole standing over Preston Schneider and he was holding one of those big, brass candlesticks."

I stared at her, trying to visualize the scene.

"You know," she continued, "like the ones they have on the communion table."

It had been years since I'd gone to church, but I nodded anyway.

Eleanor took another bite of Christmas pudding. "Patrick said that Terry looked real scared and kind of panicky. Preston was still alive, but in some kind of coma or something. He told me Preston looked real bad -- his head had a big dent in it, but he wasn't bleeding. This is delicious pudding, Kate." My stomach churned as I watched her scrape up the last bit of hard sauce and lick her spoon.

I said, "So, what'd they do? Call 911?"

"Yep. Patrick stayed with Preston, while Terry called from his office and then came back. They just sat there, waiting for the police. I can't imagine what that must have been like. I wonder if Preston made any noises?"

"Noises?"

"Yeah -- like wheezes and gurglings. Have you ever been in a situation like that, Kate?"

Thoughts from the past flashed through my mind. "I've seen dead bodies, but I never witnessed someone dying." It was my turn to ask a question. "Did they talk about anything while they waited?"

Eleanor thought for a second. "Terry explained to Patrick how he had just found Preston lying there when he came up from his office to turn off the lights."

"Anything else?"

She scrunched up her face trying to remember. "No-o. That

was it." She paused, leaned closer, and whispered. "Patrick thinks Terry did it."

"Oh, come on! Based on what? Do you actually believe Terry Poole is capable of assaulting someone?" My blood was beginning to boil. "And in the church, for crying out loud. That would be stupid!"

Eleanor sat back in surprise. "What's so special about Terry Poole? He's human, too. And anyone is capable of killing if pushed hard enough."

I looked her in the eye and tried to telepathically transmit my sense of logic into her brain. "I think it would take more than a difficult choir rehearsal to push Terry to that point."

As Eleanor meditated on that little insight, I began to look around the room for an excuse to put an end to this conversation without appearing unfriendly and impolite.

I caught a glimpse of fur flashing past the entrance to the Great Room. A high-pitched, manic *Rap! Rap! Rap!* echoed through the hallway. Boo-Kat to the rescue. But how did he get out? I had closed him up in the small family kitchen, thinking that would keep him out of trouble.

I jumped up. "Sorry, Eleanor. Boo's loose. We'll have to talk later." She waved a startled goodbye.

Out in the hallway, I found the two Poole brothers trying to round up Boo-Kat and not even getting close. All three were scrambling back and forth and screeching "Get him!" "Grab him before Aunt Kate finds out!" *"Rap! Rap! Rap!"*

Daniel and Joshua saw me and froze, eyes wide. Boo-Kat raced up the main staircase. At once, Daniel, the older of the two, spoke up. "Ooh, sorry, Aunt Kate. We thought he'd stay with us."

"Yeah," said Joshua, "we heard him whining and figured he was lonely." He gave me his best sad dog look. "We just wanted to play with him."

"That's okay," I said. The sound of furious scratching and whimpering came down from the upper landing and caught my attention. From my position in the foyer I could see Boo-Kat standing intently outside the closed door of one the guest bedrooms. His little tail was almost a blur as it wagged. The door opened and out stepped Holly Berry-Wagner.

Followed by Patrick Sloane.

ENGLISH TRIFLE

1 small sponge or angel food cake (or 2 pkgs. ladyfingers)
2-12 oz. pkgs. frozen strawberries (or fresh)
2-12 oz. pkgs. frozen raspberries (1 pkg for sauce)
1/3 c. good quality, medium-dry sherry

Pastry cream: 3 Tbsp. cornstarch, dissolved in 1/4 c. milk
                1/2 cup sugar
                1/4 tsp. salt
                2 3/4 c. milk
                3 egg yolks
                3 Tbsp. butter
                1 tsp. vanilla

Mix sugar, dissolved cornstarch and salt in heavy saucepan. Gradually stir in remaining milk and heat to boiling over medium heat, stirring constantly. Boil 1 minute. Stir half of the hot mixture gradually into egg yolks and add back to saucepan with rest of hot mixture. Boil and stir 1 more minute; remove from heat. Stir in butter and vanilla. Cover and refrigerate until thoroughly chilled.

Raspberry sauce: 1-12 oz. pkg. frozen raspberries
                    1/3 c. confectioners' sugar
Purée thawed raspberries in blender or food processor. Add confectioners' sugar and process until smooth. Strain the sauce to remove the seeds.

Assembly: Halve ladyfingers, or slice cake thinly and place one-half in bottom of 8 or 12 cup glass trifle bowl. Spread with half of the raspberry sauce and sprinkle with sherry. Arrange half of the raspberries and strawberries over top of cake and spoon one-third of the pastry cream over fruit. Repeat layers, ending with pastry cream. Cover and chill for four hours or overnight. Just before serving, top with whipped cream and toasted, slivered almonds, fresh berries (if available) or chocolate decorations.

Chocolate decorations: Line baking sheet with waxed paper. Melt 2 ozs. semi-sweet chocolate, spoon into pastry bag and pipe designs (stars, flowers) onto paper. Refrigerate 15 minutes or until firm. Remove from paper with thin knife. Alternately, spread melted chocolate 1/16th to 1/8th inch thick onto waxed paper. Refrigerate until almost set. Cut out shapes with small cookie cutters or canapé cutters and refrigerate again until completely set. Gently break shapes apart, peel away waxed paper, handling chocolate as little as possible.

CHAPTER THIRTEEN ....

I ducked under the landing, out of sight, and waited for Holly and Patrick to come down and rejoin the party. I wished I hadn't seen what I saw, but I did. I wasn't really surprised. Now the look I had seen Holly give Patrick when he was ogling Cherry made sense. I wasn't even disappointed. The episode fed my cynicism about Mother's friends -- not a side of me that needed nourishment. I always believed I was given a special ability to perceive and discern what was really going on under the surface.

If I reported this to Mother, she would automatically come up with some above-board reason for them to be in my guest bedroom. It could never be to satisfy some illicit urge. Emotional survival was dependent on denial in Mother's world. So much for Eleanor's rosy picture of her marriage that she had just painted for me. Patrick and Holly were smearing turpentine all over it. And this was the world they all wanted me to become part of? No wonder I never met anyone I could relate to.

I heard a single set of footsteps come down the main

staircase, followed by the *clickclickclick* of Boo-Kat's nails on the hardwood. I stepped into the foyer. "There you are, Boo." My little terrier raced ahead of Holly and jumped into my arms.

"I saw him go upstairs, Kate, and I thought I'd help you and stop him before he did something else to embarrass you."

A likely story. I'm not the one who should be embarrassed. "Thanks, I'll shut him up in the kitchen."

The sound of a door opening and closing came from above. We both looked up and watched Patrick start to descend the staircase. Holly blushed, seemed to lose some of her usual cool composure, and said, "I -- I must get back to Nate," as she ran off to the Great Room.

Yeah, you better, I thought.

"C'mon, Kate," Marilyn called to me, "get into this picture with us."

I walked over to table number seven, where the Poole family was seated, and stood between Terry and Marilyn.

"No, Aunt Kate. Here. Between *us*." Daniel and Jason made room for me to squeeze in. Siegfried Doppler was doing his usual hopping around and snapping of photos from different angles. He said, "You're gonna have to bend down, Kate -- your head is getting cut off." I bent down a little. He motioned me with his hand to go further.

"I can't, my back is killing me."

"Aw, then get down on your knees."

I groaned. It was a long way down, but I did as he said, which brought me face to face with the two Poole boys. I wrapped my arms around them and squeezed them in tight against me. They stuck out their tongues like they were being choked.

"Perfect." Siegfreid took the picture. Daniel and Jason wriggled out of my death grip and began chasing each other around the table.

"Sorry about the boys, Kate," Marilyn said. "I know they're getting a little wild."

"Oh, let them have fun. We'll be handing out presents to all the kids soon -- that should get their attention." I got up off my knees and pulled an empty chair up to the table and sat down. "I hope you're enjoying yourselves."

"Yes," Marilyn replied with a gentle smile, "it's a nice party." A little wrinkle appeared in her otherwise unlined brow. "But we've noticed people have been a little uncomfortable around us."

Terry brought his chair in closer and leaned his elbows on the table. "I've tried to avoid bringing this up, but I can't help it ... I have to know. What are people saying about Thursday night?"

I didn't want to get into that, but he asked. "Well, they're saying that there was some antagonism between you and Preston during the rehearsal. But," I shrugged, "so?"

"Preston was being difficult. It's not unusual for the soloist to have strong opinions about how a piece is to be performed. He *was* taking up a lot of time, though, and I had a lot of other music to rehearse, so I might have been a little short with him." I could see tension in the way Terry held his body and rubbed his forehead. I waited a few seconds. He said, "So they think I did it. Right?"

"A couple of people mentioned that possibility, but they didn't have anything to base it on."

Terry looked at me with tired eyes. "I can't believe this is happening. Why would they suspect me without having any reason to?"

Marilyn put her arm around her husband. "They've known Terry for years, but they'll still turn on him in an instant. That's what so hard for us to deal with. I'm worried, Kate."

I believed Terry was innocent and wished there was a way to stop the gossip. But until I received the superpower to shut people's mouths, all I had to offer was my friendship and support.

I addressed both of them. "It's just mindless gossip. Try not to worry. Terry, you used to tell me, when I was fighting cancer, that worrying wasn't going to add one more day to my life and, in fact, would destroy any days I had."

I reached out with both hands and took theirs. "I'm here for both of you."

Terry and Marilyn each gave my hand a squeeze. "Kate, that means a lot to us," Terry said. "I told the police that I thought it must have been a robbery attempt. I was working late in my office after the dress rehearsal, and then went up to turn off the lights in the sanctuary. That's how I found Preston lying on the floor by the organ. There was no one around, but the doors to the church hadn't been locked yet, so anyone could've come in off the street looking for something to steal."

"Ho! Ho! Ho! Merry Christmas! Merry Christmas!" Santa Claus made his entrance, ringing his bell and gathering up the children as he headed for the Christmas tree. The Kentucky accent was the only thing that gave away the fact it was Robert Boone underneath those whiskers and pillows.

Jason and Daniel came running up to our table and pulled on Terry and Marilyn. "C'mon, Mom! Dad! It's time for the presents!"

The other adults and children were congregating around the tree, so we joined them and watched as Santa Boone made a big show of handing out Christmas socks full of treats. I was standing beside the fireplace. It crackled and radiated a warmth that I realized my body was desperately craving. The afternoon's gossip about violence, murder, and suspicion, plus the apparent hanky panky upstairs, had drained me of any festive feelings I might have had, and left me cold.

I moved closer to the fireplace and felt my shoulders relax. I took in a deep breath, enjoying the fragrance of the pine boughs draped across the mantel. The little ones crowding around Robert Claus bounced with excitement as he searched under and around the tree, finding a present for each one. Out the front window the first flakes of snow were starting to fall -- The Snow Witch had finally arrived.

I looked across the room and caught sight of Mother in the midst of an exuberant conversation with three of her friends. She laughed at something one of them said, and I think it was the happiest I had seen her in a long time. Mother tilted her head to one side and allowed her face to crease in a genuine smile. She was really quite pretty, I thought, when she let go and enjoyed herself. I personally took some credit for Mother's good mood, knowing she would never acknowledge I had anything to do with it. But it still felt good to see her so happy. On the surface, Mother's luncheon was a success.

"There you are, Kate."

My shoulders tensed back up. I acknowledged Frank Meyer with a monotone, "Hello." Once again, he had sneaked up on me. He wasn't an unattractive man -- it was his personality that needed a face-lift. As a young boy, Frank had a vicious streak he expressed by capturing frogs down by the Little Miami River and then stepping on them, popping their little bodies like water balloons. That aspect of his personality never changed, only now he showed it when he engineered unfriendly buy-outs of medium-sized companies. He dissects them, sells off their valuable assets, and leaves the remaining corporate bodies like so many lifeless bits of road kill. That's what made me shiver, plus the fact that his mother and my mother were still scheming like a couple of old matchmakers to bring us together.

Frank moved in close against me and I could smell the Scotch on his breath. It was so strong, my eyes watered as he whispered in my ear, "I hear you like to unwind after one of these parties of yours by shooting a few hoops in your gym."

So?

He propped himself up against the mantel. "When are we going one-on-one? Remember, I was a starting forward for the Bearcats back in the good old days."

Oh, great. This is his subtle approach. "That was twenty years ago, Frank."

"Yeah, but I'm still in pretty good shape. And you," Frank scanned my body from head to toe, "you look like you're in fantastic shape. Aw c'mon, it'll be fun."

I could see his eyes focused on the mirage of our sweaty bodies rolling around on my gym's parquet floor. He must have seen an It Ain't Gonna Happen look on my face, because he switched topics. "So ..." He suddenly seemed interested in studying the little birds and berries that Phoebe Jo had positioned here and there amongst the pine boughs on the mantel. "Have you been hearing all the talk about Preston?"

I nodded.

Frank straightened a little chickadee that had fallen over. "People are talking about Terry Poole, too. Some incriminating stuff."

The hairs on the back of my neck immediately stood up. I didn't want to hear anymore backstabbing gossip about Terry -- it offended me. But then I realized if I was going to be of any help to him, I'd better know what rumors were flying around.

"Frank, I've heard at least four different versions of what happened that night. Are you going to give me a fifth?"

"Well," Frank said, puffing his chest up a little, "I'm the only one who can give you the truth about Preston and Terry." He leaned closer to me, his flat gray eyes squinting. "Call it insider information."

Already, I didn't like what I was about to hear.

Frank said, "Patrick Sloane told me that when he came back into the church to look for his scarf, he found Terry standing over Preston and holding a brass candlestick in his hand. Apparently Terry was quite nervous."

"I've heard that. Wouldn't *you* be upset if you found a friend lying on the floor unconscious?"

"Well, I wouldn't exactly call them friends. Didn't you know that Preston and Terry hated each other?"

"Oh, are you talking about the way they treated each other

Thursday night? Is that the hatred you're referring to? Arguing over his solo?" I shook my head. "Preston was a perfectionist -- you know that -- everyone knows that."

Frank scrunched his eyes. "Nah." Then raising an eyebrow, he said, "But, there is talk that Preston crushed Terry's chances of having a singing career. Add to that our dear Pastor Luebens forcing Terry to accept Preston as soloist for the Christmas concert -- Preston was going to make a large donation to the church to help balance the year's budget -- and you've got more than a little friction."

"How do you know? I've never heard any of this."

Frank shrugged. "I'm on the church's finance committee. So is James Wagner. He's always telling us stories about the time he and Preston were on the opera board together, and how he witnessed firsthand the ongoing feud between Preston and Terry. It wasn't a very public feud, but, essentially, Preston ruined any chances Terry had of having an operatic career in this city."

For half a minute I was dumbfounded. I didn't know what to say. I thought I had a close friendship with Terry, but I guessed I had revealed more of myself to him than he had to me. Not only was Frank a slimebucket, but now he was telling me I didn't know my own friends, Preston included. "That still doesn't add up to a motive for murder."

Frank shrugged again. "Who else could have done it? You have any better ideas?"

I felt sick.

CHAPTER FOURTEEN ....

"Tink," said James Wagner, "your party was wonderful. I enjoyed myself immensely, but it's time for me to go, I'm meeting someone at the Symphony tonight."

Mother's eyes widened a little. "A date?"

"Oh, no, nothing like that. Just entertaining a business associate from out of town."

The three of us were standing by the Christmas tree. Kids were racing back and forth, playing with their presents. Their screeches and giggles contributed to the overall buildup of noise that would soon reach a deafening critical mass. I was beginning to feel frayed at the edges, and I looked forward to the luncheon's inevitable end.

"Kate," James said, extending his hand, "your culinary talents are remarkable."

I shook his hand, smiled back, and was about to say something equally inane when Robert, still dressed as Santa Claus, approached us with a strange looking man following him.

94

"Kate, this gentleman says he has an appointment with you. I told him you were in the middle of a big affair, but he insisted and said you had scheduled this meeting, yourself."

"That's okay, Robert." I turned my attention to the visitor. "You must be Preston's lawyer." I stuck out my hand to greet him. "Mister ...?"

"Sanoma," he answered, shaking my hand with a cold, dry grip. "William T. Sanoma. Good of you to see me in the midst of your..." He glanced quickly around the room as if searching for a word, "...party," and gave me a smile that brought to mind a pirate's skull and crossbones flag.

"I think it would be best if we went into my library." Mother and James were frowning at me, and I could see they were anxiously waiting for my explanation as to what business I had with a murdered man's lawyer. But they would just have to wait. "This way, Mister Sanoma." I lead the way out of the room and down the hall, sensing that if those two weren't following me, certainly their eyes were.

The library was blue with smoke, and despite the Surgeon General's warning, I went inside anyway and opened the window directly opposite the door to create a cross current. Mister Sanoma seemed to enjoy breathing in the gaseous mixture of cigar and pipe smoke. He placed his large attache case on the mahogany and leather card table, opened it up, and pulled out a large manila envelope.

Striking an old-fashioned orator's pose -- one hand behind his back -- the cadaverous-looking lawyer quickly came to the reason for our meeting. "Preston Schneider presented this envelope to me twelve months ago, instructing me to hold it in my vault for safekeeping. He said he had some kind of premonition that he would come to an untimely end and made quite intricate plans for the event. As you probably know, Mr. Schneider had no living relatives. He said you were the person to carry out his final wishes."

Preston knew he was making people angry enough to

actually want to kill him? I was numb. "What could he possibly want *me* to do?"

Mr. Sanoma pointed a long, bony finger at the envelope. I undid the metal clasp and looked inside. There were some papers and a set of keys. I pulled out the keys first and held them up. There were three of them, different shapes and sizes, attached to a long gold chain. "What are these for?"

"One opens the front door of Mr. Schneider's home, the small one opens a file drawer in his home office, and the third one unlocks his wine cellar.

"What am I supposed to do with these things?"

"You need to read the letter, Madam," Mr. Sanoma said, tilting his head towards the envelope in my hand. "It's rather lengthy, but I can tell you the gist of it. Mr. Schneider has set aside an appropriate amount of money from his estate so you can cater his wake."

"What?" I dropped the keys. Mother and James Wagner poked their heads into the room.

"Is everything all right, Kathleen?" Mother asked, staring at the lawyer.

I stooped to pick up the keys.

"Do you need help, Kate?" James Wagner said.

I waved them out of the room. "I'm fine, everything's okay." Both Mother and James hesitated a moment.

"Well," said James, "I'm off. Once again, it was a grand party, Kate."

Mother didn't seem to want to leave. "I'd be happy to stay, if you want me to."

"No, that won't be necessary, I'll catch up with you later." Mr. Sanoma and I stood for a moment, waiting. Eventually, it sunk into Mother's brain that she wasn't needed there, and, looking slightly dejected, she turned and left the room.

I fingered the keys in one hand. "Why do I need these?"

"The wake is to be held at Mr. Schneider's house. It is by

invitation only, and I have the list of guests that he wanted to be there."

A guest list for a wake? What kind of last bizarre fling had Preston planned? "How many people is this for?"

"Twenty-five -- if they all attend. He also had some very specific ideas for the food and presentation."

"Ha! He would." That was Preston -- control freak to the end.

A cold wind blew through the window and slammed the door shut. I wanted to read the letter while the lawyer was there and, reluctantly, decided it would be best to stay in the still smoky library where we had some privacy. As I walked across the room to shut the window, I asked Mr. Sanoma, "Would you care for some dessert?"

"What?" The lawyer seemed quite startled at my offer. "Oh, no, thank you." He closed up his briefcase and appeared ready to leave.

"If you have the time, I'd like you to stay while I read this letter. I'd be happy to bring you some Trifle or Christmas pudding." I saw his expression begin to soften. It appeared his guard was momentarily lowered, so I sweetened the offer a little more. "How about a brandy to go with it?"

I thought I saw a faint pink tinge his chalky complexion, and a shy smile lift the corners of his mouth. "Oh, thank you," he said, "that sounds very nice."

"Have a seat," I told him, and hurried off before he had a chance to reconsider. A couple of minutes later, Mr. Sanoma was enjoying a helping of both desserts and a snifter of brandy, while I sat at my desk and plowed through Preston's verbose and obsessively-detailed document. At the end of the typed instructions, in what appeared to be Preston's hand writing, I read:

"My Dear Kate, You are the only person in the city I trust and believe respects me enough to fulfill my final wishes right down to the last detail. Thank you, Preston."

I sat back in my chair, speechless for a moment. The

logistics of carrying out his wishes were overwhelming. "When does this have to take place?" I asked.

The lawyer was holding the snifter of brandy up to his beak nose, his nostrils flared with pleasure. "Tuesday," he responded without opening his eyes. "This is excellent brandy."

Damn. I couldn't believe Preston had dumped this on me. What a manipulator. If I said no, then I was, in essence, refusing his last request. I couldn't live with myself if I did that. And he knew it. "But how did he know he was going to be killed?"

Mr. Sanoma had taken a sip of brandy and was holding it in his mouth, appearing to savor it for a few seconds. He swallowed, then responded. "Mr. Schneider never revealed that to me. All I can say, at this point, is that I have more communications from him. However, his instructions were to reveal them at the wake."

More communications? How much more can there be? I looked at the papers in my hand and shook my head. Preston had already spelled out the menu he wanted for his wake, right down to the minute he wanted each course served. I wondered what difference it would make to a dead man. I could understand his desire for particular favorite dishes -- he had even included some recipes. And I could almost understand why he wanted a gypsy violinist strolling about playing schmaltzy Hungarian love songs. But why would he care whether the cabbage rolls were served at twelve-forty-five or one o'clock?

Preston had been a good friend -- but a very weird one.

I checked on Mr. Sanoma. He still had half a glass of brandy, so I pulled out the phone book and looked up the number of Rigós Hungarian Restaurant in Madeira. "I'm just going to make a quick phone call to get this thing rolling." Mr. Sanoma nodded and sunk further into the leather armchair.

I reached for the phone on my desk and punched in the number. Five minutes later, I had managed to talk Rigós into lending me his musician for that Tuesday afternoon. I made another quick call to a local college student, who I often hired as a server.

She was available for that Tuesday afternoon and promised to bring another friend to help. As I hung up, there was a knock on the library door. "Come in," I said.

Robert poked his head around the edge of the door. He was no longer wearing his Santa Claus costume -- he was back in his butler's uniform. "There's an Officer Skinner from the Clairmont Rangers to see you, Kate."

"Oh?" I hoped my voice didn't sound too interested. "Well, send him in, Robert."

I stopped breathing for the half-minute it took Robert to "go fetch him." When Matt the Knight appeared in the doorway, it took all my concentration to act my age. Unlike our earlier encounter that morning, this time I did a more thorough inspection of his appearance. The day had had its effect on him. His bright blue denim shirt had lost its freshly pressed look, his yellow and gray patterned tie was slightly askew. A lock of thick black hair had fallen down across his forehead, and a five o'clock shadow was beginning to creep across his jaw. I was shocked at the sudden rush of something primitive and hormonal that surged inside of me.

"Hello, Ms. Cavanaugh." Officer Skinner greeted me with a slight nod of his head. His voice was deep and tired sounding. "Sorry to intrude again, but this will only take a minute."

I was wishing he'd come because he wanted to see me, but I remembered inviting him to come and meet with Preston's lawyer. I was wrong on both counts.

Officer Skinner ran his hand over the late-day stubble on his cheek. "I understand that Terry Poole is here. I'd like to speak with him."

Why?

CHAPTER FIFTEEN ....

I knew I wouldn't get an answer from Officer Skinner if I directly asked why he wanted to speak to Terry. So, I tried a different tactic. "What's wrong? Has there been an accident, Ranger Skinner?"

"No, ma'am, everything's okay. I just need to speak to him. By the way, it's *Officer* Skinner."

Robert was still standing by the door, so I sent him off to find Terry. I glanced briefly at the lawyer, who now seemed to be struggling to get up out of his chair. I gestured toward him and looked back at the policeman. "This is Mr. William Sanoma, the attorney I told you about, who is handling Preston Schneider's affairs."

"Oh, yes," Officer Skinner reached out to shake the older man's hand, "we spoke earlier on the phone."

"Yes, yes. Yes, we did." The two men finished shaking hands. There was an awkward silence. They both turned and looked at me as if it were my job to keep the conversation going. Well, if they were leaving the choice of topic up to me, I figured I might as well fish for personal information. "Have you been with the Clairmont Rangers long, *Officer* Skinner?"

"One year -- but I was on the Cincinnati force for fifteen years."

"Oh. My impression is that Clairmont doesn't see a lot of violent crime. From what I understand, it's mostly speeding tickets and investigating when a security alarm goes off accidentally. What do you do with all your time?"

No sooner had those words left my mouth, than I realized I had put my big foot in it. Matt the Knight arched his brow slightly, and his lip twitched a little with what I took to be irritation -- at me. That was the typical pattern of my love life. Every time I was attracted to a man, his presence would make me so nervous I would blurt out dumb comments without thinking first. So I tried to smooth things over. "What I meant was, you must be sitting around waiting for something to happen. There can't possibly be enough crime to justify paying a full-time detective's salary."

"I am not a detective, Ma'am. I have other duties."

Oops. Officer Skinner's warm, chocolate pudding eyes seemed to turn cold and dark. I felt like a door had been slammed in my face.

Just then, Robert showed up, leading Terry Poole into the library. Terry had a quizzical look on his face. "Officer Skinner," he said, extending a hand. "What can I do for you?"

"It's concerning the statement you gave me this past Thursday evening."

"Yes?"

"I'd like you to come down to the station and go over it one more time, just in case you've remembered something else."

"Right now? Is it that urgent?"

"Frankly, yes. I need to reconfirm some of the details before I can go any further in my investigation."

An almost-forgotten rebellious attitude towards police

surfaced. I had many encounters during my traveling days. Some of the worst ones were in Arabic countries, but I had my horror stories about the London bobbies, too. Mind you, my traveling companions and I didn't look like very conservative, law-abiding citizens, but we didn't deserve the unfair treatment we received. Suddenly, I didn't trust Matt the Knight, whose shiny white armor was now beginning to turn black. I felt like I had to take the opposite side in order to protect someone I knew and trusted.

I turned to Mr. Sanoma. "Don't you think Mr. Poole here needs legal representation?"

Mr. Sanoma cleared his throat. "Umm. Officer Skinner, are you charging this man with anything?"

The policeman took a deep breath. "No. I just want him to review the statement he has already made."

We all looked at Terry.

"It's okay, Kate," Terry said, appearing his usual calm, unruffled self. "He's just doing his job." To Officer Skinner, "I don't remember anything other than what I've already told you, but sure, I'll come down and check my statement. Just give me a minute to tell my wife."

Terry was almost out the door when he stopped. "Oh." He turned and faced Officer Skinner. "Did you find out if the ring Preston had in his hand was his own?"

Mr. Sanoma and I exchanged surprised looks.

"No," replied Officer Skinner. "But we're working on it."

"Can I be of any help?" Mr. Sanoma stepped forward. "I'm quite familiar with Mr. Schneider's valuables."

Officer Skinner paused and seemed to be considering something for a moment. "Do you happen to know if Mr. Schneider owned a gold signet ring with the initials PS?"

Mr. Sanoma gave a slight shrug. "Well, yes. He wore it all the time. I doubt he ever took it off."

"Hmm. That information is consistent with the mark we found on his finger. But he was holding the ring in his other hand,

102

and we need to have it identified by someone who knows it was his."

"I'm quite sure I can do that for you."

Terry said, "I'll tell my wife I'm going with you -- meet you right here in a couple of minutes."

As I watched Terry leave the room, I had the overwhelming feeling that he was calmly walking right into the worst trouble of his life. I did not trust Officer Skinner. Too many people at the luncheon had expressed the opinion that Terry had a motive for killing Preston. I couldn't believe this Clairmont Ranger was unaware of the friction between those two.

I was sure that Matt Skinner, Ace Detective/Ranger -- or whatever he wanted to be called -- had a complete list of the people who were on the church grounds that Thursday evening, and I expected that Frank Meyer probably told him the same story he told me. I didn't believe Terry was being asked to "review the statement he has already made" just to make sure he hadn't forgotten anything -- I figured Skinner had other intentions.

And then a question popped into mind. "How," I asked Officer Skinner, "did you know Terry was here?"

"I spoke with --" He pulled out his little notebook, flipped through it, and found what he was looking for. "I spoke with a Reverend Donald Luebens over at Clairmont Community Church. When I couldn't reach Mr. Poole at home, I tried the church's office and spoke to the Reverend, who told me I would find Mr. Poole here."

Mentally, I began calling Reverend Luebens names -- "Judas", "Benedict Arnold", "Brutus". I knew I was overreacting, but to me it seemed Terry had this big, glowing neon arrow hovering over him, pointing straight at his head and flashing on and off the words PRIME SUSPECT.

I also knew I was being unfair to Officer Skinner. On one hand, a slip of my tongue revealed I didn't think there was enough violent crime to justify his employment. On the other hand, the man

103

was trying to do his job, which I was paying for through my rather high real estate taxes. I couldn't help myself. It was bad enough that a good friend had been murdered, but the idea that another good friend seemed to be under suspicion was too much for me to accept.

My insides were yinning and yanging like crazy. The conservative side was saying that I was being too hasty and jumping the gun in concluding that Officer Skinner was zeroing in on Terry. But my rebellious side had firsthand experience at being on the receiving end of an overzealous cop, who was convinced that a person was guilty until proven innocent.

CHAPTER SIXTEEN ....

I handed the menu back to the waiter and said, "I'll have the T-bone steak and stuffed lobster tail platter. That comes with a salad, doesn't it?"

"Yep." The waiter nodded and wrote down my order. "What kind of dressing?"

"Blue cheese. Could we have a basket of those great sour dough rolls you make? And bring some extra butter pats."

"Kate." Cherry shrieked at me from across the table. "We've been stuffing our faces all day."

"Well, maybe you were, but I haven't eaten a thing. Besides, I like the way JJ cooks his steaks."

"What do you mean you haven't eaten a thing?"

"I never eat when I'm on a catering job. I'm too wound up, and the sight of all that food makes me sick. But as soon as it's all over and the clean-up work's done, I'm ravenous."

It was about eight-thirty that Saturday night, and Cherry and I were at my favorite hangout -- JJ's, a local jazz club in a refurbished Colonial house in Old Montgomery. Besides offering good music, it was also a place where you could get simple, straight-forward food, cooked by an expert, and so it became the favorite place to unwind for all the chefs in the area.

Cherry decided to try the local brew and ordered a mug of Hassenbacher pilsner, while I requested a glass of Zinfandel. "Kate, the party was a blast. But your mother looked totally bummed out at the end...is everything okay?"

I wasn't going to tell Cherry she was a source of some of Mother's distress. Dancing around half-naked in her slinky black number, flirting with Uncle Cliff, and arm wrestling with Patrick Sloane was not considered appropriate lady-like behavior in Mother's book.

"My mother's always getting upset over something, but what really did her in, this time, was the policeman showing up to escort one of her guests to headquarters. It had something to do with the murder of my friend Preston."

"A cop was at the party, and I missed him?"

"Yeah. You would have fallen for him in an instant."

"So, they're already zeroing in on someone?"

"Officially, no. But my guts tell me they're going to try and pin it on Terry."

"Terry who? Did I meet him?"

"No, you probably didn't even notice him. He kind of blends into the background. He's very middle-class, family man, mild-mannered..."

"Boring." Cherry took a swig out of her beer bottle. "But you never know -- those quiet ones -- BOOM!" She flung her arms up over her head. "Bodies all over the place."

"Oh, Cherry. No, no, not him."

"Well, then who do *you* think did it?"

That question had been blaring in my brain for the past twenty-four hours. The sultry notes being played by the piano, bass, and sax trio made me feel like I was in a Mike Hammer episode.

I watched a dark figure climb the wide stone steps and enter the doors to the First Community Church of Clairmont. I ran as quickly and silently as I could to catch up, and pushed my way through the heavy doors. I stood in the front vestibule and peered across the dimly lit sanctuary, looking for the mysterious stranger. I couldn't see him, but I could see Preston, bathed in a spotlight, playing the organ.

Suddenly, out of the shadows, a silent figure lurched towards Preston. The stranger raised a brass candlestick that gleamed in the bright spotlight. A quick strike. Preston slumped down onto the keyboard. The killer turned. I could see a face. And then another face. And another. The faces kept changing -- one melting into another -- before I could identify any of them.

"Hello in there." Cherry waved her hand in front of my face. "Do you want me to repeat the question?"

"No." I shook my head. "I have no idea who killed Preston. But it's totally ludicrous to think that Terry did it."

Cherry looked at me and raised an eyebrow. "How come you're so sure about him?"

I filled Cherry in on my cancer story and explained how Terry and Marilyn helped me deal with it. In the meantime, the waiter brought my salad. "Terry is a very spiritual man," I said. "He has very strong religious beliefs and I just can't see him going against them."

"Humph!" Cherry said, seeming to bring that topic to a close. Her expression switched from boredom to concern, and she leaned across the table towards me. "So, life for Kate Cavanaugh hasn't been such a breeze."

"What are you talking about?" I shoved a forkful of salad greens with a heavy coating of thick blue cheese into my mouth.

"I mean," Cherry continued, watching me eat, "just look at you. People probably think you've got it all together -- no problems -- the attractive, successful Chili Heiress. 'What has *she* got to worry about?' But it must have been pretty scary to be told you had cancer, especially when you're single." Cherry quickly straightened up in her chair and frowned at me. "Why *are* you still single?"

I gave her my automatic flippant answer. "I haven't found the man who could put up with me."

"Don't give me that. If I could live with you for six months in a hut made out of cow dung on a beach in India, and not kill you, then it's safe to say you're easy to get along with."

I laughed at the memory, but Cherry was right. The truthful answer was much more complicated than that. "I guess I still haven't found a soul mate -- someone who would understand me. I get so focused on my business, I tend to shut people out. Who wants to live with that?"

"But why did you come back here to Cincinnati? Your chances of running into someone who understands you in this place are pretty slim. Don't you ever feel like hitting the road again?"

"No...well...maybe sometimes. But I like my comforts and I love running my own business. I have a big ego to feed, and the reputation I've built here seems to satisfy it. Besides, I'm an oddball. It doesn't matter whether I'm in Clairmont or India, I never feel like I fit in." I took a sip of wine. "After all those years of moving around, looking for someplace to feel at home, I finally realized I'd have to create my own world. That's what I've done on my farm. The Boones are my family ... still, it's lonely, waking up at three o'clock in the morning and there's no one in bed beside me."

Just when the conversation was beginning to get too uncomfortable, the cavalry arrived. The server set a huge heavy plate down in front of me, the steak and lobster still sizzling. The smells made my stomach growl. Cherry eyed my dinner and I could see in her expression that she was changing her mind about the amount of food she could consume.

Oh well, it *was* a fourteen-ounce steak, sided by three stuffed lobster tails...Cherry was soon digging into a hefty sampling of my dinner which I'd piled onto a bread and butter plate for her.

As we ate, we entertained each other, remembering the crazy things that happened to us on our travels together. Cherry reminded me of the time we sneaked across the Turkish border in the middle of the night in a truck loaded with Persian carpets. "Oh, yeah," I said, "remember that truck driver played his Neil Diamond tape over and over, all the way across Iran." We both broke into "She got the way to move me, Cherry. She got the way to move me. Dun ... dun ... dundundun...dun dun dun..." People at the next table gave us a cold stare. We waved to them.

Forgetting that we were disturbing our neighbors, we howled over how we failed to recognize the famous rock and roll star who serenaded us with his latest hit song in a hotel room in Bombay. Cherry said, "I guess we left a giant bruise on his ego."

I was just finishing my wine and wiping the tears from my eyes, when I caught sight of JJ at the bar across the room and waved to him. He picked up a bottle of wine and made his way over to our table. "Evening, Kate," he said in a gravelly voice and focused his attention on Cherry. "Looks like you two are having a good time."

I could see that Cherry's magnetic attraction was working again, so I introduced them.

JJ turned back to me. "Everyone around here's talking about what happened to Preston Schneider. I guess most of it is stuff you've already heard. But I thought you'd want to know what happened here Thursday night. Your pal Martin Wolfenden really went ballistic."

CHAPTER SEVENTEEN ....

JJ refilled my wine glass, ordered another beer for Cherry, pulled up a chair and sat down at our table. "I just thought that Wolfie was blowing off steam. I didn't take what he said seriously -- until I saw the TV news on Friday. You know how Wolfie is -- he's had such a tough year, and the guy's real emotional. I could understand he'd be angry, and maybe even make some threats, but..."

It had been a long day and I didn't have the patience for JJ's usual rambling prologues. "So, what happened?"

JJ stroked his graying walrus moustache and gazed at me with his tired, bloodshot blue eyes and smiled. "Okay, Kate. I'll get to the point." He grabbed an empty water glass and poured wine for himself. "It was around six-thirty and Wolfie was here, sitting quietly, having his dinner by himself, when this suit comes in and plunks his expensive leather briefcase down on the table, opens it up and hands Wolfie some papers.

"Wolfie stops his dinner in mid-bite while this guy reads to him whatever's in the papers. And whatever it was... Wolfie's face

110

turns purple. So he slams his fork down, grabs the papers, gives them a quick read, then throws them back in the guy's face. The suit never blinks an eye. He just turns around and walks out like nothing happened.

"Wolfie picks up the papers and stuffs them in his pocket. He gets up and stomps over to the bar and asks me for a double shot of Johnny Walker. That goes down pretty easy, and he points at his glass for a refill.

"So I ask him, 'What the hell's going on?' He doesn't even look at me, just shakes his head and keeps drinking. Then he pounds his fist on the bar and says, 'Damn, damn, damn.' Just that, nothing else."

I asked, "Did you know the guy who came in?"

"Nope. Never seen him before. But he sure looked like a lawyer."

"Wolfie's had enough trouble lately. What else could have happened?"

"I tried to find out, but he wouldn't tell me. He just sat there, drinking and muttering into his glass. Then I hear him say, 'I'm gonna get him. Some day, I'm gonna get that bastard.'

"Well, that opens a floodgate. Wolfie looks me straight in the eye and lets loose with some nasty remarks about Preston." JJ took a sip of wine. "I have to admit, Wolfie had reason to hate Preston. I mean, those restaurant reviews he wrote about Papillon were vicious. And if he hadn't written them, the restaurant would still be doing okay. But poor Wolfie's still out on the street, looking for a steady job. It's like Preston put a curse on him."

"But that happened a year ago," I said. "You have no idea what that man gave him?"

"No. When I asked him, he just started ranting, 'That overstuffed little butterball is a detriment to the culinary life of Cincinnati!' Then he says, 'I'm gonna cut off his tongue and serve it back to him on a roll with mustard!'

"And then he stormed out of here."

CHAPTER EIGHTEEN ....

Leaving the jazz club, I drove my Jeep Cherokee up Montgomery Road and turned right onto Kemper and continued east. The road wound through a quiet residential area, up over a hill, and plunged down into a dark wooded stretch. I was driving on automatic pilot, and Cherry seemed to be in the same reflective mood I was in. I turned on the radio. A deep bass voice announced, "This is The WAVE. Keep your dial set here -- we'll take the rough edges off your day." Smooth sax sounds filled the jeep, but the day's edges were more than a little rough -- they were like the teeth of a shark.

We sped along through the cold, moonless night, emerging from the dark, winding street onto the main thoroughfare going through Loveland. The garish lights of the car dealerships and fast food places made me squint.

"Well, this is an attractive place," Cherry remarked as we continued through the strip of mini-malls, gas stations, and lumber yards. We crossed the Little Miami River and traveled along the two blocks of brick storefronts the city officials liked to call Historic Loveland, then turned left and plunged once again into the blackness of a two-lane country highway leading into the northwest tip of Clairmont.

I was anxious to get home. The darkness that stretched before me became a backdrop to my imagination. The Stranger With Many Faces reappeared in my mind, only this time I could see the faces long enough to know who they were.

Each face seemed to jump out at me from behind the leafless trees that lined the road. First was Wolfie, then Frank Meyer, followed by Terry. I peered into the eyes of each one trying to figure out who had the look of a killer.

Suddenly, a string of greenish-white eyes, like big marbles, glowed through the darkness right in front of me.

"Katie! Watch out!" Cherry yelled just as I stomped on the brakes. "Wow, look at that. Aren't they beautiful?"

We sat and watched the family of deer cross the road, clamber up the other side, and disappear into the woods.

A few minutes later, I drove up the private lane leading to my farmhouse. Home. The tiny multicolored Christmas lights outlining its architecture made it glitter invitingly like a precious jeweled box. I parked around the side and we went in the back door leading into the family kitchen. The lights were on, but the Boones had already gone to bed. Boo-Kat greeted us with his favorite chew toy and tried to tempt us into a game of tug. Even though it was past midnight, he was wound up and starving for attention.

Cherry was just as wound up and the two of them chased each other around the house, while I pulled out a couple of mugs and made hot cocoa.

"So, Katie," Cherry said. We both sat at the kitchen table, sipping our cocoa and eating marshmallows from a bag. "Who's this Wolfie guy? Did I meet him?"

"No...oh, yeah. He was carving the roast goose today."

"Right. The one with the forks." Cherry's face scrunched

up in bewilderment. "I was wondering about that. How did you get that goose to swallow those forks?"

I threw a marshmallow at her. "Smart ass." Cherry threw one back at me. It bounced off my head, fell onto the floor, and rolled across the kitchen. Boo-Kat's four paws sounded more like a dozen, as he frantically scrambled out from under the table and tried to catch the dust-covered marshmallow, but it disappeared under the refrigerator. So I threw him another one.

"They're heat conductors," I said.

"What? The marshmallows?" Cherry asked.

"No. The forks. They're supposed to help the bird cook more evenly."

Cherry shrugged her shoulders. "Well...whatever. I just know the bird tasted great." She got a serious look on her face. "So, I take it this Wolfie guy had a restaurant, but Preston didn't like it. Was Preston right? Or was he just being malicious?"

"Well, Wolfie and Frank had their problems when they first opened. But most restaurants do. They usually get them straightened out over a short period of time. It was a nice place. It should've survived."

"Who's Frank?"

"Frank Meyer, an acquaintance of mine, who was in partnership with Wolfie."

"So Wolfie was the talented chef and this Frank was the money man?"

"You got the picture."

"Seems to me that Frankie boy also got burned by your pal Preston." Cherry popped a marshmallow into her mouth.

"Yeah." I nodded. "They both have a lot of work ahead of them to patch up their reputations. People lost confidence in Frank as an investment counselor with good sense, and Wolfie's talents as a chef have been called into question."

"Meaning they both had motives for getting even with Preston."

114

I poked at the marshmallows trying to drown them in my cocoa. "That's what I'm thinking."

"So, the police are going after the wrong guy?"

I sighed. "I have a problem thinking it could be Frank or Wolfie or anybody else I know."

"I'm sure the cops know what they're doing."

"Cherry, you're too kind. Remember that time in London, when the bobbies broke down the door of our apartment in the middle of the night thinking we were the former renters and they were going to find a big stash of coke or something?"

"Yeah? So? They made an honest mistake."

"Mistake? More like total incompetence." Just the memory of that night made my teeth clench. "They never listened to us -- just stormed in and began tearing the place to pieces and didn't stop until the apartment had been completely turned upside down. Even when they found out the people they were after hadn't lived there for more than a month, still, they treated us badly. Those cops wouldn't admit they were wrong -- figured 'Might as well look for drugs anyway.' Then the next day -- I couldn't believe it -- one of them came back to ask you out on a date. And you said yes." I reached over and lightly rapped Cherry on the top of her head. "You lose all sense when you're around policemen."

"You'll never let me forget that, will you?" Cherry laughed. "Besides... the date was a dud -- you know that."

"Anyway, back to my point. The cops *don't* always know what they're doing. I think this Officer Skinner is looking for the most convenient suspect. And as a suspect, Terry fits the bill. Here's the bad stuff." I started counting off the potentially incriminating facts on my fingers. "One, Terry was found standing over Preston's unconscious body and holding the weapon. Two, there were eyewitnesses to some kind of antagonism going on between those two just an hour before. Three, Frank Meyer told me Terry and Preston have been feuding for years. That Preston ruined any chances Terry had of having an operatic career in this city. On top of that, Pastor Luebens forced Terry to accept Preston as soloist for the Christmas concert over his objections."

"Boy," Cherry said, shaking her head, "if that's all it takes to get killed or be put in jail around here, then I don't want to stick around."

"That's what I mean -- it doesn't make sense."

"So, you think the cops have already made up their mind that Terry's guilty, and they're not going to look for anyone else?"

"I think Officer Skinner likes things neat and tidy. To him this could be an open and shut case. I just don't trust him. I felt this hostility coming out of him. Maybe I'm overreacting, but I'm afraid he's going to settle for an easy answer and not do a thorough investigation."

"Wouldn't that come out in court?"

"Only if Terry can afford a really good lawyer. You don't make much being a worship and music minister for a church -- even in Clairmont."

Cherry tapped her lower lip with a forefinger. "You don't think much of this Skinner guy, do you?"

"He's an attractive package, but I'm not sure where he's coming from. I just feel that Terry's being pulled into big trouble and he'll need every friend he can get. He's an innocent and thinks his God will protect him. Besides, I know Terry -- he's just not capable of killing anyone."

"Yeah, you've always been loyal and protective like that, Mother Lion. You saved my butt many times." Cherry sipped her cocoa, and then looked at her cup, lost in thought for a moment. "Clairmont may not be Casablanca -- I mean, there's certainly nothing exotic about living in the Cincinnati area -- but somehow you've managed to surround yourself with some pretty interesting characters."

Casablanca. Walking around that city you could never relax -- you were always on edge and wary of the people around you. That nervous energy was bubbling up inside of me once again.

116

Sunday, December 17th

CHAPTER NINETEEN ....

Boing! My eyes flew open. It was still dark, and I felt as alert as if it were nine o'clock in the morning, but my clock-radio said it was three-thirty. Boo-Kat whimpered, engrossed in some doggie dream. I looked down at him in his bed beside mine and saw his dark form posed in his flying Superdog position, on his back with legs stretched out high in the air.

I had all these lists in my mind -- lists of what to do for Preston's Creepy Gypsy Funeral Luncheon. I was wishing I could sleep in, but I knew that within half an hour I'd be up. People who could sleep for eight hours every night were truly gifted human beings. I sighed, rolled over and punched up my pillows and clamped my eyes shut, trying to will myself back to sleep. Cabbage rolls, schnitzel, and dumplings danced in my head and leaped over a fence -- replacing the usual sheep -- to the feverish violin strains of Hungarian Rhapsody.

Groaning, I reached across the bed, turned on the light, and grabbed the TV remote. I aimed and fired. "...and so the Midwest should be seeing the effects of this arctic front pushing down from Canada over the next three days. Back to you, Jennifer." The young, clean-cut, catalog boy meteorologist smiled at the camera past his comfort time, as it appeared that the director in the TV control room was a bit slow in calling for the switch to the news anchor. It was the graveyard shift on CNN, and a new group of trainees was obviously manning the station.

The camera cut to a perky, strawberry blond, with impossibly white teeth. "Fans of CRYPTOMANIA were saddened by the news that Preston Schneider -- also known as Cryptoman --" I popped up out of my semi-prone position in bed and turned up the volume. "-- died in a Cincinnati hospital this past Thursday night. He died as he lived, leaving a puzzle. Mystery surrounds his death -- he was found suffering from a blow to the head in the sanctuary of the church in which he was to star as guest soloist for a gala Christmas concert.

"Fans of his daily newspaper feature knew to expect unusual logic in the solution to his code puzzles. The police are investigating, but no arrests have been made."

Unusual logic. More like twisted thinking. Preston did have a strange way of communicating his ideas to people sometimes. Did he try to leave a clue? His lawyer, William Sanoma, said he had more communications from Preston. But had Preston left anything at the scene of the crime itself?

I remembered Terry and Officer Skinner talking about a ring. The next news story broke in on my thoughts. "...and so, the latest research study indicates that smoking males may have a link to breast cancer." Video tape ran of some poor woman trying to smile, while a technician squashed her breast in between two plates of plastic.

"Genetic mutations, possibly resulting in cancer, have been found in the children of fathers who smoked. It is believed that the mutation is passed on through the sperm of the father."

Oh, for crying out loud. The Paranoid Patrol was at it again.

I jammed my thumb on the power button and turned the stupid TV off. Dad never smoked. They're always throwing these theories around. First it's high fat diets, then the birth control pill. Radioactivity from power lines. What kind of booze you drink. Nitrites in your lunch meats. On and on and on. Why can't they just admit they don't have a clue?

I was so wound up, there was only one thing I could do. At times like this, I was glad I had my personal gym built. I quickly changed into my sweats and tied on my sneakers. Boo-Kat gave me a sleepy look and dragged himself out of bed. He stretched, yawned loudly, and followed me out of the room.

I moved silently through the dark hallway and passed Cherry's bedroom. The night-light that normally illuminated the landing was out, and it was an overcast and moonless night. I felt my way down the staircase, clutching the railing. I reached the bottom of the stairs, made a u-turn through the foyer, and then a left down the main corridor, past the commercial kitchen and pushed through the door into the gym.

I flicked on the overhead lights and winced, shutting my eyes for a moment until they could adjust to the fluorescent glare. Looking around for a basketball, I found one by my Soloflex machine. Boo-Kat's tail automatically began wagging and he got into his ready position. He liked this game. I bounced the ball a few times and he immediately ran to and stopped under the basket.

I slowly dribbled the ball to the top of the half-court key. Memories of being on the Clairmont High School Cougars grew stronger as the rhythmic sound of the bouncing basketball filled the gym. I picked up speed and cut behind the imaginary screen of teammate Jeannie Peters.

Jump shot. Yes!

Adrenaline shot through my body as I made my first basket. Immediately, I began to feel good. Boo-Kat tried to rebound the ball with his mouth, but I grabbed it away from him and dribbled it across the floor. He raced alongside me, trying to intimidate me with his growly trash talk. I countered with, "Oh, yeah? Your mother's a bitch." Back and forth we went. I shot. He jumped.

As Boo-Kat's yelps got louder, I began to worry that Cherry might hear him. I'd been having these predawn workouts for the past dozen years and knew that the Boones, sleeping on the other side of the house, weren't disturbed. But the two guest rooms were a lot closer to the gym.

On second thought, I remembered that once Cherry finally went to bed and her head hit the pillow, it was impossible to rouse her before ten o'clock in the morning. That was an absolute fact I learned back in Athens, when we were renting an apartment next to a Greek couple who were in a constant state of war.

It was always at four o'clock in the morning, and Cherry and I would have been in bed for only an hour or two after a long night of bar hostessing. The entire apartment building would shake as the front door slammed. The husband would come lumbering up the stairs, groaning and muttering to himself. As he opened the door to his apartment, his wife greeted him with the same bellowed accusation night after night. There'd be an hour of crying and curses yelled at the top of their lungs, punctuated by the sound of dishes smashing against the wall. The only thing I could decipher from the racket was that he drank too much ouzo and he was a lousy cardplayer.

Anyway, Cherry always slept through, and never heard a sound.

Boo-Kat lost interest in our game and curled up under the bench of the Soloflex machine as I dribbled the basketball to the foul line and began practicing my foul shooting. I bounced the ball three times. My fingers gripped the basketball along the seams, I shot, and rebounded. I got into a rhythm. Bounce, grip, shoot, rebound. Bounce, grip, shoot, rebound. My body clicked into the familiar routine and my mind began to wander.

Remembering our time in Greece made me think about Demetrius again. Many times, when we were talking in the bar, something would set him off, and I saw the same kind of passionate explosiveness within him as I heard coming out of that apartment next door.

What did that Athens newspaper reporter know that led to his murder and Demetrius' suicide? Demetrius was always quick to lash out at any insult to his reputation, imagined or otherwise. If just protecting his good name was the reason for violent action, then I could think of a number of people here in Clairmont who were just as worried about potential damage to theirs.

But once again, the two people who immediately came to mind, whose reputations and financial well-being were in fact severely damaged by Preston Schneider, were Martin Wolfenden and Frank Meyer. *They* certainly had reasons to lash out at Preston.

Preston knew he might be killed. According to his lawyer, Mr. Sanoma, my friend had been anticipating the possibility of his own murder for at least a year. But why? Maybe he had some information he was going to use against someone, and that person couldn't stand the truth coming out. Preston thought of himself as a guardian of society -- "I am a searchlight shining into dark corners."

I didn't understand why Preston gave his lawyer the instructions to wait until his wake to reveal the rest of his "communications". I couldn't recall exactly what Mr. Sanoma had said. Were these meant for me?

I stopped bouncing the ball and froze at the thought that Preston might be dumping on me the very information that got him killed. All of a sudden, this Gypsy Wake of his was looking even creepier. The thought of jumping on Cherry's motorcycle and heading for New Orleans sounded very appealing.

Who did I have to be worried about? I didn't know who was on Preston's guest list, because Mr. Sanoma would be personally contacting them. But I knew there were twenty-five -- two of them might be Martin Wolfenden and Frank Meyer.

I knew that Wolfie was really pissed off at Preston.

According to JJ, Wolfie had threatened to cut off his tongue the same night he was killed. JJ said that Wolfie was having dinner around six-thirty, when the stranger in the suit handed him the papers that instigated Wolfie's tantrum. Judging by the way JJ told the story, I assumed that Wolfie stormed out of the club no more than an hour later. That was plenty of time for him to get to the church, find a hiding place, and stalk Preston after the rehearsal, smashing him over the head with that brass candlestick. It was no secret that Preston was to be the soloist for the church concert. He had been bragging about it to everybody for weeks before hand.

I wondered what information was in the papers that upset Wolfie so much. Did it open up that old wound Preston inflicted on him a year ago when his negative reviews closed down Papillon? Or was this something new? Whatever it was, he sure acted strange at Mother's luncheon when I asked if he had heard of Preston's death.

Then, of course, there's Frank Meyer. It was his money that backed Papillon's start-up, so he, too, was hurt pretty badly -- not just financially, but reputation-wise. From the gossip I heard, it seemed that people were not so quick to follow his financial advice. Local conservative investors who made up his clientele no longer considered Frank the guru they had believed him to be.

For the past year, Frank had been trying to win back their confidence, but the death of that Mount Adams bistro was still haunting him. I could imagine Frank's vicious streak egging him on to revenge -- he was not the type to forgive and forget. This was a man who was used to being the one in power, bulldozing over everyone else. But when Preston squashed his restaurant, maybe Frank decided to squash fat little Preston the same way he, as a young boy, squashed those frogs he captured down by the Little Miami River.

So, *could* he have killed Preston? I knew he was on the church's finance committee, so there was a good chance he was at their meeting on Thursday night. According to James Wagner, the meeting broke up in plenty of time for the members to watch the end of the choir's dress rehearsal. Maybe Frank went back downstairs, where they had held their meeting, and hid there, waiting for his chance?

On top of that, Frank made a point of telling me about the quiet feud between Terry and Preston. I'm sure he passed that information on to Officer Skinner -- a pretty good way of diverting attention from himself.

Hmm. That made more sense than Terry being the killer...or Wolfie for that matter.

Now I was faced with a very difficult task. I looked up at the clock on the wall. It was almost five-thirty. I had plenty of time to get ready. I knew half of Clairmont was going to be shocked by my actions.

I was going to church.

CHAPTER TWENTY ....

All the detective mysteries I've read and all the trials I've seen on Court TV point to one basic fact: you have to visit the scene of the crime to get some idea of how a murder was actually committed. Church services started at nine-fifteen. By seven AM I had showered and was having breakfast.

Sunrise wasn't for another fifty minutes, so I could see my reflection against the cold darkness on the other side of my breakfast nook's bay window. I sat at the round oak table in my thick terry cloth bathrobe. My hair felt damp and heavy against my neck.

I had left the back door light on so I could see when Boo-Kat came back from his morning ritual. Snow flakes fell softly through the beam of light. Phoebe Jo would normally prepare and serve me a bowl of hot porridge with maple syrup poured over it on a morning like this. But I was here first, so huevos rancheros it was.

I wolfed down the eggs and, over a second cup of coffee, wrote Cherry a note telling her where I was going and when I'd be back. I gave her explicit instructions on how to put together her own huevos rancheros and made sure she knew where to find a couple of pieces of my homemade cornmeal bread. I left a little sauce pan of salsa on the stove to be heated up and poured over the eggs, and told her to sprinkle some shredded Mexican cheese blend on top.

"What did you eat?" Phoebe Jo had come into the kitchen and was peering down at my plate, her face screwed up as though there was a bad smell in the air.

"Eggs, Mexican style."

"Don't you want some porridge?"

"No thanks, I'm stuffed. Besides, I've got to get ready."

"This early on a Sunday morning?" Phoebe Jo put her hands on her hips. "Where're you going?"

"To church," I mumbled, starting to get up from the table.

"Where?" She cocked her head.

"First Community Church of Clairmont," I said a little louder.

Phoebe Jo's eyebrows arched and her eyes popped wide open. "Church?" She flung her arms heavenward, "Glory be," wrapped them around my waist, and danced me across the kitchen. "Praise God. Praise God."

"What's all the racket here?" Robert shuffled in, followed by Julie Ann.

"Miss Kate's seen the light. Praise the Lord."

I had to set them straight before they got too carried away. "No, no, Phoebe Jo. It's not what you think." My housekeeper stopped in mid-praise as I continued. "I'm just going to check out the murder scene. I have to see for myself where Preston was attacked. I'm driving myself crazy. My hyperactive imagination won't settle down and leave me alone until I do."

Phoebe Jo's face crumpled like a Yorkshire pudding after it's pulled out of the oven.

Robert poured himself a cup of coffee. "Well, at least it's a step."

125

Julie Ann was opening a box of Sugar Smacks. "Oh, you guys." Then she looked at me. "Just ignore them."

Phoebe Jo had regained her usual positive expression. "Well, it should be a good service. They'll be singing lots of Christmas carols." She gave me another hug. "We love you no matter what."

The last clang of the hundred year old bell sounded as I turned into the parking lot of the First Community Church of Clairmont, and pulled up into the only space I could find. Even though I thought I was a little early, the lot was full. My red Jeep Cherokee coated in a couple of weeks' worth of mud stood out from the rows of sparkling Mercedes, Lincolns, and BMWs. I really hadn't thought this out. As I walked across to the Gothic style church's main doors, all of a sudden it hit me that I was on unfamiliar ground. Old insecurities Mother had planted in me as a young girl began to surface. I looked down at my royal blue silk pants and tunic and wondered if it was an appropriate outfit for this conservative bunch. I looked up at the stone bell tower which represented to me a suffocating conformity that I had rebelled against as a young teenager. But that had nothing to do with why I was there, so I pushed it all back down.

A sharp, biting wind slapped my cheeks and made my long wool coat billow out. I had braided my hair, but it was still damp so it made the air feel even more frigid. I ran the rest of the way across the parking lot, up the front stone steps, yanked open the door, and entered the vestibule.

The first person I saw was a freshly scrubbed young man smiling and offering me a little pamphlet. "Good morning. Welcome to the First Community Church of Clairmont."

Well that was it. I was committed. No turning back now.

The young man -- I later found out he was one of the deacons -- said, "It's unusually crowded today. Can I help you find

126

a seat?"

"Umm. I'm just looking." I knew that didn't sound right, and the young man's smile didn't waver, but his eyes had a *she doesn't belong here* look. I stood at the bank of windows separating the vestibule from the sanctuary and tried to find a familiar face. There were mink coats and gray heads everywhere. No sign of Mother.

Everything was decorated for Christmas. There was a large wooden cross hanging on the wall behind the pulpit at the back of the choir loft. Underneath it were five pine trees covered in tiny white lights. A huge wreath with four unlit candles hung down low from the ceiling. Pots of red and white poinsettias covered the front of the altar. All down the sides of the sanctuary were wreathes and floral arrangements. It actually looked warm and inviting.

I realized this was the first Sunday I had attended in more than twenty-five years. I had been to Christmas concerts and weddings in this building, but not a regular service. I couldn't even remember what they did. But then I saw Terry Poole sit down at the piano and begin to play, so I figured I had better get a seat. The pews were full, except for the front row. And it was noisy in there, people talking and laughing like they were at a cocktail party. I saw Mabel Crank yakking away with Charles Hassenbacher on one side of the main aisle. Over on the other side, the large Yankovitch family were in the same seats I vaguely remembered them sitting in back when I was a little girl attending with Dad and Mother.

I cringed at the thought of making a late entrance in front of the entire congregation, but I saw Marilyn sitting right up by the piano and an empty seat beside her. So with great reluctance I reached to open the center door. Mister Smiling Deacon stopped me and pointed to the side aisle. Whew.

As I made my way up the side aisle, heads turned and I could hear whispered comments. "That's Kate Cavanaugh." "It's Tink's daughter."

I should have realized that a six-foot three-inch blond

woman was never going to go unnoticed. Still, I tried to unobtrusively slip into the seat next to Marilyn -- and in doing so, just about caused her a heart attack.

"Kate," Marilyn whispered, "what are you doing here?"

"Well, I --"

Marilyn quickly patted my arm. "I mean, I'm glad to see you. It's just such a surprise."

I didn't want to tell her that I was snooping around the scene of the crime. "It's Christmas ... and I didn't get to go to the Christmas concert this year ... so I'm here for my yearly dose of Christmas carols. I mean Christmas atmosphere."

Marilyn smiled at my awkwardness and patted my arm again. "I'm glad you're here."

Terry finished his preservice piano medley, and the organist took over with a crashing, all stops pulled out, entrance. The cocktail chatter throughout the sanctuary immediately ceased and all eyes were fixed on the back of the woman at the organ's keyboard.

She was playing a stirring piece of music, and Terry joined her in a piano-organ duet. Every now and then, the organist would look over her shoulder toward Terry, who would acknowledge her with some kind of head nod and facial expression. It seemed a very impractical arrangement for the organist not to have a clear view of what was going on around her. I whispered to Marilyn, "Isn't that irritating for the organist to have to keep turning and looking over her shoulder. Seems like a crazy way to have things arranged."

"There's usually a mirror in front of her so she could see what's happening behind her and watch for Terry's cues."

"What happened to it?"

"Terry found it on the floor, broken, the same time he found Preston Schneider."

Oh. No one ever mentioned Preston struggling with his killer.

Just then, the young deacon who greeted me at the door came up the center aisle carrying a long, thin, brass pole with a flame on the end. He used it to light the candles on the altar and three of the four candles on the low hanging wreath. A second young man pulled on a rope, raising the wreath towards the ceiling and securing it.

There was a commotion. I turned. It was Mother climbing over a few legs to get to the empty seat in the row behind me. There wasn't really enough room for both Mother and her enormous mink coat to squeeze through. But that didn't stop Mother. Her face was red and flustered. "Excuse me. Oh, dear. I'm sorry. What a dreadful morning." As she fell into the seat, she clutched at my shoulder and whispered loudly, "Kathleen, what's the matter? What are you doing here?"

Before I could answer, the music stopped and Pastor Luebens stepped up to the pulpit. "Good morning." Sixty years old, with white hair framing his bald head, and wearing a long black robe with a purple stole, he was the cliché minister. I was starting to yawn already, but swallowed it. I turned to Mother and mouthed the words, "I'll explain later."

A trumpet-like fanfare burst forth from the pipes of the organ. Terry had moved to the top of the dais next to Pastor Luebens and motioned for the congregation to rise. As we sang *Oh Come, All Ye Faithful*, the choir, dressed in burgundy and white robes, began to move up the center aisle from the rear. The first two people were carrying banners with gold letters -- one spelling out Peace, the other one Joy. When they got to the front they set up the banners, one on either side of the dais, and took their places in the choir loft.

It was a large choir, and a lot of its members were elderly looking. As half of them filed past me, I found myself looking down on a lot of little bald heads, but then I recognized Patrick Sloane and Holly-Berry Wagner, both of them giving me a startled look as they went by.

Their little parade ended and everyone sat down.

Pastor Luebens smiled out at us. "It's great to see you all

here in God's house." He made a few comments about how large the crowd was and how many new faces were in the pews. I thought that a lot of them probably came for the same reason I did -- to the see the scene of the crime. I guess it was the same mentality that slows everyone down on the freeway when there's been an accident. Even if there's nothing to see, we all have this need to look. He continued with a few announcements, and then Terry took over leading the choir in a rousing medley of Christmas hymns. I was beginning to feel quite festive. Then Pastor Luebens said a long prayer and began his sleep-inducing sermon.

Clairmont's favorite pastor was a very sincere man, but not a gifted speaker. I'm sure he worked long and hard on that sermon, but for me it had all the emotional power of a directory assistance computer rattling off telephone numbers. It was apparent he wanted to convey some important message -- however, it was a classic case of the message being mangled by the messenger.

I tuned him out and examined my surroundings, trying not to be too obvious about it. I looked at the organ and imagined Preston sitting there. Every now and then, a word from Pastor Luebens' sermon broke into my daydream. I'd listen to his next few sentences, then tune him right out.

Now that I was actually at the scene, I saw there weren't any hiding places close to the organ, from which a murderer could quickly lunge out and attack with a brass candlestick.

Maybe the murderer didn't need a hiding place.

CHAPTER TWENTY-ONE ....

"It was so embarrassing," Mother said as we made our way through the enclosed walkway to the church's Welcome Center. "I just didn't like doing it."

I clicked my tongue. "All you did was ask Loretta for a lift to church. What's so embarrassing about that?"

"I don't like asking favors of the help."

There was more to it than that. "Loretta is more like a member of the family than just your hired housekeeper."

"Well..." Mother shuddered and clutched the collar of her fur tight around her neck. It was more of an emotional reaction than a physical one -- the walkway was overheated. "It's that vehicle of hers."

"Now we're getting to the real reason. What's the matter with it?"

Mother snapped a look at me and pursed her lips. "It's a truck -- a *dirty* pickup truck."

"You're overreacting."

"No, I'm not. Look at this." She stopped her march, turned, and flared out her coat for me to inspect it.

"What?"

"I had to sit on a dusty old seat."

"It looks fine. There's nothing on your coat."

Mother huffed and rewrapped herself. "You're blind."

"At least you got here on time. It was nice of Loretta to bring you."

Mother's face softened a little. "Yes, it was."

"Have you made any arrangements to have your tire changed? Or do you want me to do it. I mean, change the tire?"

"Oh, for heaven's sake, dear. No. Loretta's called the Auto Club. They'll take care of it." She waited a beat and launched into playing her favorite game -- interrogating me. "What *are* you doing here?"

I decided to be honest, and took in a deep breath. "I wanted to see where Preston's murder took place."

"That's ghoulish curiosity."

Hmmph. I didn't want to get into an argument by pointing out the larger than usual Sunday morning crowd at church today. "No, no. I thought that I might be able to see something that would help Terry."

Mother's eyebrows lifted.

I answered, "I'm afraid that the police are going to take the easy route and pin the murder on him."

"Don't get involved."

How could I not? But I held my tongue, because it wasn't the time to get pulled into one of Mother's verbal tug-of-war games. I changed the subject. "Oh, look. There's James Wagner."

We had entered the Welcome Center, a large, newly built, one-story structure attached to the church. It housed Sunday School classrooms, an auditorium, and a commercial-sized kitchen. We headed towards the line of people slowly making their way into the kitchen.

"Kate, what a wonderful surprise," James said. The two people standing in line ahead of him turned. It was Nate, James' younger brother and Nate's wife, Holly. They smiled at me ... well, at least Holly and James did. Nate was his usual pallid and repressed self. He twitched his lip and nodded.

"Good morning," I said, sneaking a look around for Terry Poole.

Holly reached out and patted Mother's arm. "Tink, such an elegant luncheon, yesterday. Just when I think I've been to the best party ever, the next year is even more fun."

Hmm. I guess I was just the hired help. The little frozen tart could have at least thanked me for the use of a bedroom for her secret tryst with Patrick Sloane.

The line inched its way into the kitchen.

"Tink, did you sleep in this morning?" James asked.

Mother's bright Cavanaugh smile was pasted in place. "Car trouble, James."

"How did you find each other?" James said, turning from Mother to me. "It's so impossibly crowded today. Someone I'd never seen before was sitting in my seat."

"Yes, isn't it awful?" Mother replied.

I pondered that statement for a moment. I thought a crowded church was supposed to be a good thing.

Mother continued. "Thankfully, one of those nice, young deacons recognized Kate, and led me to where she was sitting."

"So," James said, directing his gaze at me, "what did you think of Pastor Luebens' sermon?"

Before I had the chance to finish forming a diplomatic answer, a "Good morning, folks," landed in the middle of our conversation. We all turned to greet the man, himself.

"I hope there are enough donuts to go around," Pastor Luebens said with a wink.

We entered the kitchen and looked over the selection of Krispy Kream donuts -- boxes and boxes of them. James Wagner

133

pounced on a vanilla cream, Day-Glo sprinkled monstrosity. Nate reached for the same thing, but Holly gave his hand a quick slap. "Not that kind." She pointed to a plain donut. "Get one of those."

Nate shook his head. "I know what I want."

"You know I'm on a diet. I just want a bite of yours."

"But I want *all* of mine. Get your own -- money's no object."

Holly pouted and held up the line while she studied a pile of plain donuts, seeming to mentally calculate the deadly calories lurking within the doughy rings.

Mother chose a sugared cruller, while Pastor Luebens balanced an éclair on top of a jelly-filled donut. I by-passed the lot and settled for a styrofoam cup of weak, black coffee. At the end of the line we each dropped an appropriate donation into a small wicker basket and exited the kitchen. Nate and Holly wandered off, and the rest of us found a corner to stand in.

Between mouthfuls, Mother asked Pastor Luebens, "Will we have our Christmas Concert this year, or have you canceled it outright?"

Pastor Luebens wiped his mouth unsuccessfully, a smudge of chocolate donut goop hung off the corner of his mouth and kept my attention as he answered. "Unfortunately, we -- the church elders and I -- have decided to cancel it this year."

Mother nodded. "I understand, but it's such a shame. The choir has worked so hard these past few months."

James swallowed the last of his ugly donut. "Terrible situation."

"I agree," Pastor Luebens said. "The choir's finale at dress rehearsal was inspired -- don't you think, James?"

"Oh, yes. Yes, indeed."

"Especially hearing it from up in the balcony."

James wiped some bright pink sprinkles off his chin. "Yes. It sounded positively angelic. I haven't been up there in years, ever since Terry had all that hi-tech sound equipment installed. I know it's necessary to have a loudspeaker system for the church, but it's like a recording studio. That soundboard is enormous -- takes up half the seating. Not a very worshipful atmosphere."

"Terry's done great things for the music ministry of this church," Pastor Luebens replied, "and I agree, change is difficult at times." He looked at me. "We even let him have his contemporary service one Sunday each month, in the hopes it would bring more people like you into the church, Kate."

Great. I was now the church's official token heathen. I wanted to get back into the sanctuary to look around while no one was there. "Well," I said to everyone, "it's been nice having brunch with you all, but I have to look for Terry." To Mother, "I'll give you a call later."

I quickly retraced my steps. In contrast to my first impression that morning, the sanctuary was now dark and quiet. The bright spotlights that had been directed at the choir during the service were turned off, as were the Christmas tree lights. The candles were all snuffed out. The only sound breaking the silence was the swishing together of my silk pant legs as I ascended the carpeted steps to the organ.

I sat down at the keyboard and began to feel anxious -- like I was trespassing. But I wanted to experience, as much as I could, what Preston must have seen just before he was struck. This new vantage point confirmed what I had observed from my seat in the pews during the service. There were no hiding places from which someone could attack. I looked at the space in front of my left shoulder where the mirror had been, and could appreciate how necessary it was to be able to see what was going on behind me. I felt very vulnerable having my back to the dark, empty sanctuary.

"Auditioning, Kate?"

I almost cracked the ceiling with my head as I jumped to my feet. I whipped around. "Patrick Sloane. Where did you beam down from?"

The chunky Texan laughed. "Never expected to see you in

this place, Kate. What brings you here?"

I gave him my stock "Christmas music fix" answer.

Patrick looked at me suspiciously. "But what does sitting here in an empty church, staring at the organ, do for you?"

I was tired of fabricating reasons. Besides, what did I care what anyone thought. "I'll tell you what it does. It gives me a chance to look over the murder scene."

"Ha! Kate Cavanaugh, Private Eye."

"What're *you* doing here? And while we're at it -- where were you on the night of the murder?"

Patrick feigned surprise, slapped the palm of his hand against his chest, and raised his bushy eyebrows. "What? Am I under suspicion?"

Why not? I didn't answer, just gave him a calm look as though I knew a secret of his -- which I thought I did. After all, I had seen him come out of one of my guest bedrooms with Holly Berry-Wagner. Patrick walked up to a seat in the choir loft, picked up a black folder and waved it at me. "My music -- I'm always forgetting stuff."

My prolonged silence made Patrick visibly edgy. I studied the optic effects his red and green plaid sport coat was producing. He sat down in a choir pew, and looked up at me. "Let me tell you what I saw that night," he said, scratching his chin. "Now, I told you at the party that Preston was making Terry very angry over some minor detail."

I stopped him right there. "That goes along with what Holly told me, but contradicts what James Wagner says. His opinion was that Holly had blown things way out of proportion. Said he didn't sense any antagonism between the two."

"Hfww! That old man's not very observant. I was a lot closer to the action than he was -- and so was Holly. I mean, we were both standing within a few feet of them. Where was James?"

"Up in the balcony, from what I understand."

"See? My point exactly. Anyway, as soon as the dress

rehearsal ended, I left as usual."

I remembered Eleanor telling me a different story. According to her, his usual routine was to hang around the church after choir practice, chewing the fat with some of the other guys. But I wasn't going to stop him from giving me his version of reality.

Patrick continued. "I was driving over to Montgomery to get some cheese cake at that bakery next to the cigar smokers' club. I was almost there when I realized I had picked up the wrong scarf on my way out of the rehearsal. It was the same color as mine, but it didn't have my monogram. Now, I knew that if I came home without my expensive cashmere birthday gift, Eleanor would kill me. So, I turned around and went all the way back to church."

I calculated the driving time back and forth to be about forty minutes. A long way to go.

"I entered the sanctuary," Patrick went on, "and headed for the coat rack, but before I got that far, I noticed Terry standing by the organ. He looked real scared and was holding on to one of the brass candlesticks from the communion table. As I walked over to him and got closer, I saw a body lying on the floor at his feet. It was Preston."

I sat back down on the organ bench.

"Preston was still breathing, but unconscious. There was a big red welt on the back of his head, but no blood. Terry said he'd just come up from his office down in the basement to lock up, and found him like that. I stayed with Preston while Terry ran back downstairs to call 911." Patrick leaned towards me. "It sure as hell looked like he did it, Kate."

"What're you two doing up there?" A voice sounded from the center aisle and startled both Patrick and me. Patrick waved. "Morning, folks."

As I turned to see who it was, the thought occurred to me again that it was damn easy to sneak up on someone in this church. "Marilyn. Terry. I was hoping to run into you."

"We were just coming in to lock up. Thought the place was

empty." Terry bounded up the steps, followed by Marilyn. "It's great to see you here. What did you think of the service?"

"I liked the music," I said, hoping he wouldn't ask what I thought of the sermon. Terry looked like he was holding his breath, waiting for me to say more. "It's very, um, Christmasy in here ... I really liked the music." Out of the corner of my eye, I saw Patrick nod to Marilyn and quietly leave.

"I must say, Kate, I was amazed to see you at services."

"Yeah," I replied, "a lot of people were. I could hear them buzzing my name as I walked up the aisle." I hesitated a moment. "But the real reason I showed up today was to get a look at the murder scene for myself."

Terry looked down at the floor and nodded, his mouth scrunched with disappointment. "I kind of figured it had something to do with that."

Marilyn bit her lip. "It's all everyone's talking about. Terry's having trouble doing his job. We don't know who's on our side."

I placed a hand on each of their shoulders. "Terry, I believe you're innocent." I turned to Marilyn. "Dumb as it sounds, I thought I might be able to help, so I'm gathering as much information as I can." Looking back at Terry, I asked, "Can we talk about that night?"

"Sure. Come on over to our place this afternoon around three o'clock." He smiled. "Don't worry, Kate. The truth always comes out in the end."

The end was nowhere in sight.

CHAPTER TWENTY-TWO ....

"I can't believe you've got me doing this," I told Cherry, as I drove south on Loveland-Madeira Road in my Cherokee. It was almost noon and, at Cherry's request, we were heading to the nearest Crown Chili Parlor for lunch.

"I'm starving," Cherry whined. "Besides, don't you like your own family's cooking? You should -- it's your inheritance."

"You're starving? After that nutritious breakfast?"

"It was too much work. And you assumed I knew how to fry an egg."

"But tortilla chips and salsa?"

"Chips are a grain, aren't they?" Cherry looked at me, her eyebrows lifted in mock innocence. She settled back into the front passenger seat. "I've had worse."

"Yes, you have -- and I was there with you. Remember the sheep brains in Cairo?" We both made gagging noises. "Well, I wanted to take you to a more upscale brunch place," I continued, "but you're my guest, so your wish is my command. I suppose everyone should try Cincinnati chili once in their lifetime."

I beat the yellow light, turned right into the strip mall, and pulled into a parking spot right in front of the free-standing red brick building with a giant gold crown on the rooftop.

Cherry jumped out and surveyed the chili parlor. "So, this is one of yours." She placed a hand on her hip. "Hmmm. How many of these little moneymakers are there?"

"Fifty-two," I said automatically.

Cherry looked straight at me. In a skeptical voice, she asked, "Your mother doesn't actually run the company day to day, does she?"

"No. Dad had a great staff of executives who have been able to carry on very well since he died fifteen years ago. Mother is the primary stockholder, with me and Uncle Cliff as minor stockholders. Mother's smart enough not to mess with something that's working smoothly. She may give the impression that business is all beyond her, but she's on top of every detail -- right down to how many jars of chopped garlic they're using each week."

"So she releases her need to meddle on you?"

I laughed. "You noticed." Linking my arm in hers, I said, "C'mon, let's have some lunch."

The chili parlor was pretty empty -- not surprising for that time on Sunday. The manager snapped to attention when she saw me. We were an unusual looking couple -- Cherry, a five foot tall red head in a black leather jacket, skin-tight black jeans, and red cowboy boots -- me, well over a foot taller, with my long blond braid, but wearing an unassuming green parka and blue jeans.

But that's not why the woman snapped to. She probably thought I was on an inspection tour, since I never came in as a customer.

Cherry stared at the menu board, creases gradually forming between her eyebrows. It was one of those rare times when I saw her helpless. "Katie, what's this one-way, two-way business? I didn't know chili could be so complicated."

I suppose it might be a little overwhelming to a non-Cincinnatian, but whether you wanted your chili plain, on spaghetti, with beans, cheese, or onions, it was all described in great detail on the board. The various combinations were coded: one-way, two-way, three-way, four-way, or five-way. Simple.

After I read the menu out to her, she still gave me a zombie stare, so I ordered a four-way for her -- everything but beans.

"And what can I get for you, Ms. Cavanaugh?" the manager asked.

I quickly said, "A two-way, please."

"What's that?" Cherry asked, even though I had just explained the code.

"Chili on spaghetti." We moved across to the register and I paid the bill. The manager was on her toes and had our orders ready before I received my change. "Over there," I said, indicating a booth in the corner. Cherry led the way.

"Hey," Cherry said as we sat down, "for a junk food place, it's pretty nice -- padded seats, real plants. And look at these place mats." She pulled one out from under her tray. "What is this? Some kind of game or something?"

"No. See? This is what you do." With my thumb, I punched out the paper crown along its perforations, curled the edges around, hooked the ends together, and placed it on Cherry's head.

"Dum da da daaaa! I feel like I'm in a margarine commercial." Cherry carefully took the crown off her head and studied it. "This is great. Betcha the kids love these."

I pointed at her plate. "You better start eating. It's best when it's hot." I twirled spaghetti around my fork. "Grandpa came up with the paper crown idea right from the start. It was such a big hit that he kept using it, until my dad took over in the sixties. Dad tried to cut costs and did away with it, but there was such an uproar of complaints that, within a month, the paper crowns were back."

Cherry had taken a huge mouthful of spaghetti, cheese, onions, and chili. She held it in her mouth for a second or two. Her eyes went a little funny. Oh no, I thought, she's going to spit up.

Cherry chewed a couple of times and then swallowed. "That's not like any chili I ever had. But it's damn good." She began shoveling it into her mouth. I could see the manager out of the corner of my eye watching Cherry's reaction, and giving a silent sigh of relief.

"So," Cherry said, "is this a new habit of yours -- going to church? I mean, that was kind of a shock, waking up to your note and an empty house. Well, except for Boo-Kat. Almost tripped over him when I opened my bedroom door. I thought the Boones would be around. Where are they? And how come you don't..."

"Wait, wait." I waved my hand at her. "Can I start answering some of these questions? First off, I know from past experience that your day is ruined if someone gets you up before ten, so I left you alone. And even though the Boones are at their church all day, I wasn't worried about leaving you alone, knowing you had a highly developed ability to entertain yourself." I shoved a forkful of chili into my mouth.

"And?" Cherry motioned for me to continue.

"What?"

"Church. You. Since when?"

"Since this morning," I answered. "I was looking over the scene of the crime."

Cherry slurped a strand of spaghetti. "Oooo...Have you cracked the case yet?"

"No, but I'm working on it."

Something caught Cherry's attention and she looked past me towards the front of the restaurant. Her eyes lit up in appreciation of what she saw. "Don't turn around," she whispered.

"What's the matter?" I whispered back.

"He's just your size and he's coming this way."

CHAPTER TWENTY-THREE ....

"Well, I take this to be a good sign," Officer Skinner said as he approached our table. "If the owner's daughter eats here, it must be okay. Especially if she's a famous caterer." He stopped at our table, carrying a tray full of food.

"Oh," Cherry said, "you know each other. Take a seat and join us." She quickly slid over, giving him room to sit beside her and across from me.

"Thanks, I'd like to." Officer Skinner smiled, took off his tan parka and stuffed it behind himself as he sat down.

I was not ready for this. Even though he looked a little less uptight in his burgundy and navy blue plaid flannel shirt and denim jeans, I felt my muscles tense as I wondered what we were going to talk about.

"Katie?" Cherry said. "Aren't you going to introduce us?"

I did, and Cherry immediately gave me an eye signal that told me she'd follow my lead. It occurred to me that if I handled this chance meeting right, I could get a line on how Skinner's investigation was going. "Do you eat here often?"

"Every Sunday," he replied.

"What is that?" Cherry pointed to the mounds of cheese on his tray.

"Cheese Coneys." He picked one up and took a bite.

It seemed Cherry couldn't take her eyes off him. "Mmm, looks good. What's in it?"

"Just a hot dog with chili and cheddar cheese," I said.

Skinner wiped some chili off his chin with a paper napkin. "*Just* a hot dog? Ms. Cavanaugh, you are too modest. These are the best. My doctor told me I could indulge myself once a week, food-wise. Crown Chili is my choice."

"Your doctor?" I asked.

"You look pretty fit," Cherry added.

"High cholesterol. And ..." He paused. "About a year ago, I came close to having a heart attack."

My opinion of Officer Matt Skinner softened a little. It sounded like he'd had a good scare just like me at an early age. "Didn't you say you've only been with the Clairmont Rangers for the past year?"

He swallowed a big mouthful and nodded his head. "Right. I was a homicide detective on the Cincinnati police force for fifteen years. But with this heart problem, my doctor strongly suggested that I get a less stressful job. And I hit the jackpot. Cops all over the country want to sign on with the Clairmont Rangers, but openings are few and far between."

"What makes it such an attractive job?" I said.

"Most policeman get tired of the 'Starsky and Hutch' routine in the inner cities. But I liked it, only my body didn't."

"So, you're not happy being a Clairmont Ranger?"

"Don't get me wrong, this is a first class outfit." Skinner leaned forward. "Your tax dollars are well spent, Ms. Cavanaugh."

I caught a whiff of the same warm woodsy scent that had

mesmerized me the previous morning. Again, it was a pleasant moment. Very pleasant.

"Call me 'Kate'," I said, regaining control. I smiled. "But you didn't answer my question, Officer Skinner. Are you happy with your job?" I avoided looking at Cherry, who was giving me a cross-eyed goofy look just outside Skinner's peripheral vision. She could tell that, despite my distrust of policemen in general, I was attracted to this particular cop, and she was trying to throw me off balance.

"You can call me Matt."

Cherry quickly licked her index finger, marked one point in the air, then pretended to scratch her nose just as Matt turned towards her to reach for a fresh paper napkin.

"The guys I work with are great," Matt said, wiping his fingers, "there's no real stress patrolling Clairmont, but..."

"But what?" I said, kicking Cherry's leg. She was flashing another goofy grin at me.

"It's going to take a while for me to adjust to the slower pace. I still get antsy even a year later. Sometimes I feel more like a security guard than a policeman. Our major job seems to be answering complaints when these spoiled rich kids decide to have a little three-hundred-guest party while Mom and Dad are out of town.

"Then, when Mom and Dad are *in* town, we spend a lot of time trying to explain why we can't just rip up the speeding ticket we gave their kid. Almost every resident of Clairmont is someone important in business or politics and they're used to having their own way." Matt paused. "Well, I shouldn't be complaining to you. It's a good job, and the lack of stress will probably lengthen my life."

"Well," I said, "isn't a murder investigation stressful no matter where you are?"

Matt smiled, and I found myself admiring his nice white even teeth. "You're right. It is stressful, but I wasn't expecting to have to deal with this in Clairmont. In fact, as you probably know, this is the city's first murder. Officially."

"What do you mean, 'officially'?" Cherry said, while twirling the last of her spaghetti around her fork. "Is there something under the carpet?"

Matt laughed. "There's one incident where the Captain thinks the coroner was wrong. Seems that a few years back, the Captain and the rest of the guys on the force were sure they had a murder case on their hands. But the coroner came along and ruled it 'Death by fright'."

We laughed. I know that's awful -- I mean a person died -- but I couldn't help myself. It was an instinctive reaction. "So," I said, "how's the investigation going? Or have you got it all figured out already?"

Matt was about to bite into his second Coney. He stopped, fixed his chocolate brown eyes on me and raised one eyebrow. Damn. I told myself that I'd better watch my mouth. I hadn't intended to sound cynical. I quickly added, "Preston Schneider was a good friend of mine and I'm anxious that you get his killer."

Matt stared into his soft drink and swished the ice around with a straw. "We're sifting through all the physical evidence, and considering all possible suspects." He looked up at me. "We've got to be real careful not to jump too quickly."

At times, I'm suddenly aware of the character traits that have been handed down to me genetically. It's a shock when I open my mouth and I hear one of my parents' voices come out. This time I heard Mother in my voice trying to make a helpful, but meddling, suggestion. "I was at church today and I found out about the broken mirror. Now, to me, that says there could have been a struggle that night between Preston and his assailant. What do you think?"

"Sorry, but the Captain would have my head if I said anything before we made an arrest." Matt the Knight paused. "But I promise you that every lead is being investigated."

I was somewhat reassured and relieved that he at least stated there was more than one possible suspect. It looked like this cop might not be such a bad guy after all.

CHAPTER TWENTY-FOUR ....

By two-thirty, I was cruising along the Ronald Reagan Cross County Highway, singing along with Vince Gill on B-105 Country. Several years ago, the officials of Hamilton County sprang on its citizens the fait accompli of adding the Teflon president's name to the Cross County. Even though I didn't vote for the man, no president deserved to have his name associated with this pothole ridden stretch of road.

I was heading for Finneytown and my three o'clock meeting with Terry Poole.

I hoped Cherry would be okay -- she seemed to understand it was best I go alone. She promised a very attentive Boo-Kat that she would take him for a walk around the farm and surrounding woods. Boo-Kat enjoys exploring on his own, but it's the highlight of his day when a human comes along. I, in turn, promised to be back as soon as possible, so that Cherry and I could do something together.

The sun was trying to burn away the gray clouds, and beams

of light were shooting out here and there -- the midwestern sky looked like a hokey painting you'd buy at a Starving Artists sale. I turned off at the Winton Road exit and headed south towards North Bend Road, driving past rows of small, brick bungalows, with small, neat yards.

It was interesting how Terry's present-day existence was so different from when we were elementary schoolmates in Clairmont. Back then, his life was full of so much unhappiness in the middle of wealth and privilege. Now, with his transplanted roots in middle-class Finneytown, he appeared happy and fulfilled. Even though his job was in Clairmont, he said he could never picture himself returning to live there.

I pulled into the driveway and was about to turn off my engine, when the radio announcer started his newscast with, "A Clairmont police spokesperson still has no comment on the murder of Preston Schneider, other than to say they're sifting through all the physical evidence, and considering all possible suspects." I had heard that very same quote from Matt Skinner just a few hours ago.

I turned off the engine, killing the radio. Damn. I still had to make up Preston's menu. I fished around in the depths of my leather purse, pulled out my handheld recorder, and dictated a quick reminder to settle on a menu that night. I left the recorder sitting on the front passenger seat to remind myself to listen to it. My memory was getting bad.

I zipped up my parka, pulled the hood over my head, and got out of the Jeep. Where shafts of light had, earlier, pierced through the clouds, the sky had filled in and was now a thick blanket of gray. It looked like the clouds were filling up with snow. My breath made smoke signals in the air with each exhale as I walked up to the front door.

Terry opened the door while the bell was still chiming. "Get in here, quick. It's freezing."

I stepped immediately into the living room of the small house. Marilyn was poking at a log in the fireplace. "Hi, Kate," she said. "It's been a long time since you've visited."

"I know. Things have been really crazy."

Terry took my parka. I sat down on the sofa, warmed my hands by the fire, and looked around the room. A Christmas tree with presents piled underneath dominated one corner of the cramped living room, and a Nativity scene was displayed prominently on a table in front of the bay window. Marilyn had disappeared into the kitchen and returned with a plate of Christmas cookies and a thermal carafe of coffee.

"Daniel and Joshua are over at a friend's house," Marilyn said, offering me a cookie. "We thought it'd be easier to talk without them."

Deciding there was no gentle way to begin our conversation, I launched right into it. "Terry, I've been hearing some gossip about a feud between you and Preston. I've known you almost all my life, and this is the first I've heard of this. What's the story?"

Terry took a deep breath before answering. "Preston and I have had our differences -- I suppose some people might call that a feud -- but it wasn't something I've discussed with other people." Marilyn handed me a cup of coffee and poured one for Terry. He reached for it and continued speaking. "I've always wanted to sing with the Cincinnati Opera, even in the most minor role -- it didn't matter. Preston was on the opera board and somehow he had influence over the director. I'd audition for parts over and over again, but was never chosen. I heard through the grapevine that Preston had something to do with that."

Marilyn glared at Terry. "Why don't you tell Kate what that was really about?" She quickly turned to me. "This is politics, pure and simple."

"Calm down, Marilyn," Terry said. Then he put down his coffee cup. "Preston hated ... um ... I was too ..." I waited while Terry seemed to be searching for words. He finally said, "Essentially, Preston could never stomach my conservative values. He was pro-abortion. I'm not. Somehow he couldn't accept the fact that I had as much right to my personal convictions as he had to his. I've stated publicly, time and time again, that I am not in favor of using intimidation or violence as a means of change and that no human being is in a position to condemn another. In the end, we will all have to answer to God for what we do on this earth.

"When I told Preston I suspected he was the reason I never passed any auditions, he said, 'The Cincinnati art scene doesn't need your kind.' Preston considered the arts and entertainment scene to be his territory. So then, when Preston wanted to sing in the Christmas concert, I stooped to the same narrow way of thinking and reacted as if he was invading *my* territory. I tried to retaliate. I admit it was an immature response -- I couldn't help it. But it wasn't worth killing him for. Nothing is."

Boy, I had no idea that there was so much negative stuff going on between the people I knew. "What do you mean by 'retaliate?' What did you do?"

"I tried to talk Pastor Luebens out of letting Preston take part in the Christmas concert."

"I thought you were in charge of the music for the church. Didn't you have the final say?"

"Not in this instance, I didn't." Terry took a sip of his coffee. I looked at Marilyn. She had a hard expression on her face that seemed out of character. Terry continued. "And the thing that riles me is that it all comes down to money."

"Money?"

"As head pastor of the First Community Church of Clairmont, Pastor Luebens overruled me with regard to Preston. It seems that Preston was making a big year-end donation, and Pastor Luebens didn't want to offend him."

That coincided with what Frank Meyer told me the previous day.

"And," Marilyn slammed her coffee cup down on the table, "he doesn't come to church all year -- just Christmas and Easter -- throws money around and expects everybody to kiss his feet."

151

Terry turned to Marilyn, "Honey, he was Kate's friend."

Marilyn burst into tears. "It's all too much."

I reached across the table, took her hand in mine, and tried to console her. "I know Preston made a lot of enemies because of his actions and attitudes. A person would have to be made of stone not to feel anger at some of the things he did."

Terry stood up, stuffed his hands in his pockets, and walked to the window. "No matter what Preston did, there is no justification for murder."

I handed Marilyn a tissue and she composed herself, wiping her tears. "Terry," I said, "what happened Thursday night?"

Terry looked out the window. "I started out that day in a bad mood and was not looking forward to that dress rehearsal. I'd been trying for weeks to change Pastor Luebens' mind about Preston, especially after the way Preston treated me in the couple of brief rehearsals we had during that time.

"In the dress rehearsal, with all its added tensions -- the orchestra trying to get their entrances straight, and the sound people running around setting up microphones -- Preston was even more intolerable. He kept interrupting the rehearsal with his complaints and 'helpful suggestions'. I had a hard time keeping my cool while he was trying to tell me how to do my job. I wasn't too successful at hiding my anger -- the whole choir could see it. That put them on edge, because they weren't used to seeing me that way."

"So," I said, "how did Preston wind up playing the organ?"

"I didn't want him around one minute longer, but he was standing next to Pastor Luebens when he told me he wanted to hang around and play the organ for a little while. In fact, Pastor Luebens was nodding 'yes', before I had a chance to answer.

"So, I left them in the sanctuary and went downstairs to my office to finish off some paper work."

I swallowed my mouthful of brown sugar shortbread cookie. "Was anyone else up there with them when you left?"

"The musicians were packing up their instruments and the choir members were putting on coats and leaving."

"I've never heard Preston play. Was he any good?"

Terry rolled his eyes up to the ceiling. "He had the ability to make that organ, which is the finest in this area, sound like a cheap circus calliope."

I laughed. "And I had imagined Preston playing Bach's *Toccata and Fugue in D Minor*."

Terry looked at me, his face all screwed up in a "Huh?"

I shrugged. "It's the only organ piece I know. It was my favorite part in the movie *Fantasia*. You know -- where it gets all psychedelic."

"Oh, yeah? Well, all I heard him play was a mangled version of *Oh, Holy Night*. I blocked the rest out. Only in his dreams could Preston play a Bach toccata."

And in the fantasies of my hyperactive imagination. "So, how long were you in your office, and what happened when you came back to the sanctuary?"

Terry sat down next to Marilyn and poured himself a cup of coffee. "Let's see ... the dress rehearsal ended around nine-thirty, and I immediately went downstairs. I sat at my desk and worked until I started feeling tired. I looked at my watch and it was ten-thirty. All was quiet, but I couldn't tell you when Preston stopped playing the organ, because I had blocked it out. I decided it was time to lock up and go home." Terry took a sip of coffee. "I remember thinking it was strange that Preston didn't stop by to tell me he was leaving.

"The first thing I saw when I entered the sanctuary was a brass candlestick lying on the steps leading to the choir loft. I thought someone had unknowingly knocked it off the communion table, so I picked it up. When I turned to go up the steps, that's when I saw Preston lying on his side on the floor by the organ."

I felt my eyebrows instinctively pull together in a frown. "That's not what the news reports said."

"I know. The media likes to play up the drama. Preston was *not* slumped over the organ, his blood dripping off the keys."

Hmmm. That was even more gruesome than *I* had imagined. "*Was* there any blood? Or sign of struggle?"

"The organ mirror was on the floor and shattered. He had a gash across the palm of his left hand."

"Wasn't he holding a ring in his hand?"

"When I picked up his cut hand to feel for a pulse, I noticed he was holding a ring in his other hand. It crossed my mind that this could have been an attempted robbery that went bad. The sanctuary doors were all open -- anybody could have come in.

"Anyway...Preston had a huge welt on the back of his head, but he was still alive. I was just deciding to call 911 when Patrick Sloane showed up. He stayed with Preston while I went downstairs and made the call."

My mind was sorting through all the stories I'd heard over the past few days, trying to make them fit. Patrick Sloane told me that he left the church that night, immediately after the dress rehearsal, to go and buy some cheesecake, then came back to look for his scarf. I had calculated that his trip took about forty minutes. Terry said that an hour had elapsed between the end of rehearsal and when he found Preston. That left Patrick Sloane with twenty unaccounted-for minutes.

"Was Patrick acting normal when you saw him?"

Terry rubbed his forehead. "I guess so .... maybe ... I don't know .... the whole evening was abnormal." He stopped rubbing and looked at me. "That was pretty much it. Then the ambulance and the police came. Preston was taken to the hospital and I answered all the Rangers' questions. They let me go home, but one of the officers followed me so he could collect the clothing I had been wearing."

"What?" I asked.

"They wanted to check for blood or hair or whatever the forensic guys look for in these cases."

Damn. I'd been right all along -- they were really going after him from the start. But then I thought, they won't find any concrete evidence. The police would be forced to admit they've been going after the wrong person.

The doorbell chimed. Marilyn got up and opened the door. Our jaws dropped. It was Matt Skinner looking very official behind his policeman's shield, and backed up by a pair of tall uniformed Clairmont Rangers. He looked past Marilyn, into the room and directly at Terry. He ignored me.

I knew what was coming.

"Terry Poole?" Skinner announced in a deep, authoritative voice. "You are under arrest for the murder of Preston Schneider."

"NO!" Marilyn shouted.

CHAPTER TWENTY-FIVE ....

"Good Lord!" Phoebe Jo said. "So, what did you do?"

"Well," I replied, "there wasn't much we could do. Officer Skinner read Terry his rights, while the two Rangers handcuffed him. Then they took him away."

It was seven o'clock, and I was sitting around the kitchen table with the Boones and Cherry. Phoebe Jo had prepared one of her comfort meals -- her timing was always impeccable.

As I filled them in on the afternoon's events, we passed around a platter of country ham, bowls piled high with mashed potatoes, collard greens with bacon, and corn pudding. We helped ourselves to a basket of freshly baked biscuits sitting in the center of the table.

"That poor Terry," Phoebe Jo said, "he's had such a tough life. The devil's been following him around, messing up his life, just like he did to Job."

"Who's Job?" Cherry said to me, as she reached for a biscuit. "Is he another one of your friends who's in trouble?"

The Boones and I laughed. Phoebe Jo answered. "It's from the Bible. Job was a God-fearing man, who never deserved any of the bad things that happened to him."

"That sure describes Terry's life," I said to Cherry. "Terry grew up in Clairmont, the only child in a wealthy family. His father was an alcoholic, who went into rages. One day, when Terry came home from school -- we were both thirteen -- he found his mother in her bedroom, shot to death. He found his father sitting in the den, holding a gun. According to Terry, his father looked at him, calmly raised his gun and shot at Terry, who turned and ran out of the house. Then his father committed suicide."

"That poor boy," Phoebe Jo said. "He was left all alone -- no relatives. But God always provides, and a minister and his wife living out in Finneytown adopted him."

Cherry asked, "But what about the family's money? Didn't Terry inherit it?"

I said, "Turns out it was all gone -- bad investments. The police figured that's what sent his father over the edge."

Robert got up and went to the kitchen counter and sliced some more ham. "So, Kate, the Rangers took Terry away in handcuffs -- what happens now?"

"I immediately called Uncle Cliff and explained the situation, and he's agreed to defend Terry. That's all I know."

* * * * * * *

"Cherry," I said, "this is not what I had in mind when I promised we'd do something together this evening."

"I'm just glad to see you sitting still for a few minutes."

After pigging out on Phoebe Jo's delicious dinner, Cherry and I had gone upstairs to my bedroom to just lounge around and gab the night away. "It does feel good to stay home," I said to Cherry, who was sprawled on my loveseat, with her legs hanging over one of the arms. I was sitting cross-legged on the floor beside

157

her, with Boo-Kat's head on my lap, his hind legs stretched out in ecstasy as I brushed his fur.

We had a lot of catching up to do. Twenty years was a long time -- Cherry had fallen in and out of love hundreds of times and it sounded like she had been around the world at least twice since our trek. She also had updates on many of the people we had encountered on the road. Some were dead. Some had settled down. And others were still wandering.

"Expect some of them to show up on your doorstep one of these days, Katie. I'm spreading the word -- Cincinnati's not to be missed." Cherry reached over and yanked on my braid. "I'm having a great time, and nobody's even asked me to go to bed with them, yet."

"Cherry." I punched her arm. "You haven't changed a bit."

There was a timid knock on the bedroom door. We turned to look. Julie Ann peered around the edge of the door and in a shy voice asked, "Kate -- um -- can you brush my hair?"

"Sure," I said, "Boo's done. You're next." I pushed my terrier off and got up. Boo-Kat gave me a grumbly growl, went over to his bed, circled around a couple of times, then flopped down with a grunt.

I took the brush from Julie Ann's hand and sat down in the wing chair across from Cherry. Julie Ann brought a footstool over to the chair, sat down with her back towards me, and took off her eyeglasses. I pulled the brush through her straight brown hair and said, "It's really growing fast, soon you'll have a braid as long as mine."

Out of the corner of my eye, I noticed Cherry cock her head and study me. "Katie, I've never seen you without that braid. Didn't you lose your hair when you had chemo?"

Julie Ann laughed. "Kate looked like a fuzzy-headed duckling. She had this little tuft on top of her head, and that was it."

"Talk about bad hair days. You must've just died," Cherry

said, "all that beautiful, long, blond hair gone."

"Well," I said, "first, I had it all chopped off -- as short as yours, Cherry. I didn't want all that 'beautiful, long, blond hair' clogging up the shower drain."

Cherry shook her head. "You're always so practical."

"You know, even with all the trauma I went through -- the diagnosis, the chemo, and the surgery -- losing my hair *was* the most difficult part of the experience. But hair grows back. Too bad tits don't."

Julie Ann turned red and Cherry squealed. "I love it!"

I said, "Remember how Demetrius used to call me his 'amazon'? Do you know what that really means, Cherry?"

"Yeah -- someone tall and gorgeous like you."

"No, get this ... I looked it up in the dictionary. In ancient Greek mythology, the Amazons were a race of strong, tall, female warriors, who used bows and arrows in battle. They all had one of their breasts cut off so that it wouldn't get in the way when they drew back their bows. The word amazon comes from the Greek 'a (without) mazos (breast)'."

"Wow." Cherry sat up straight. "Kate Cavanaugh, Amazon Warrior."

* * * * * * * * * * * * * * * * * * * *

I yawned, rubbed my eyes, and looked at the clock on my bedside table. Eleven-thirty-five. I thought, if I looked at another recipe for tokány, or any other Hungarian stew, I'd go mad. Well, at least I had the menu finished for Preston's Gypsy Funeral Lunch. I slammed the cookbook shut and added it to the piles around me on the bed.

I was tired, but I needed to process the day's events before I would be able to sleep, so I reached over and pulled a green notebook off the nightstand shelf. I usually needed just one page to record what kind of day I had, but it was five pages later when I finally put my pen down. Before closing my journal and putting it away, I reread the last few lines.

> I am absolutely convinced that Terry is innocent. Why isn't that obvious to everyone else? My view of the world is always so different from others'.
>
> Someday I hope to find someone who thinks like me. Ha! Fat chance! It certainly isn't going to be Matt Skinner! Now there's another page to write, but I don't want to waste the paper!
>
> I need to get to sleep now, but I can't get out of my head something Cherry said this evening. "The newspapers are full of stories about God-fearing killers."

Monday, December 18th

CHAPTER TWENTY-SIX ....

"'Morning, boss." Tony-Z bopped in through the side door of the commercial kitchen.

"Good, morning," I called back. "The game plan's on the board."

I flipped the sheet pan over and banged out the chocolate cake for the Hungarian dessert onto a waxed paper-lined towel. I rolled it up and left it sitting on the counter to cool.

"Transylvanian?" Tony-Z said, in a Bela Lugosi-ish voice. As I turned towards him, he brought his apron up in front of his face with a flourish. "Ha! Ha! Ha! Haaa! I assume we're not using garlic in these dishes?"

"Very funny," I replied in a monotone. "That's vampire joke number one. How many of these am I going to have to listen to, today?"

Tony quickly made a cross with his index fingers. "Back away, Woman in a Bad Mood."

I curled a lip and snarled.

"Okay, okay." Tony waved his hands. "No more. What should I start on?"

"We can't do anything until we go shopping. I've already called in the meat order. Carl promised to deliver at noon, but we have to make a trip to Trolley's for the produce. Let me just give you a quick run-through of the menu."

I went over to the bulletin board and pulled down a couple of pages I'd printed off my computer. One was the menu plan, and the other was a shopping list. I laid them out on the counter top, and Tony looked over my shoulder as I read. "Okay. We're going to have a buffet lunch. Preston requested a sit-down meal. But with the menu he's given me and the time constraints, I decided to change it to a buffet. If we did it the way he wanted, there wouldn't be enough time for the guests to eat and get to the cemetery on time for the burial service.

"First, as an appetizer, we'll have Breaded Fried Cauliflower. Then, there will be a kind of salad bar layout with Green Bean Salad, Cucumber Salad, and Pickled Beets."

"Yuck." Tony made a face.

"Wait, it gets better. Then we'll have some warming pans. One will have Stuffed Cabbage, and another will have Braised Red Cabbage with Apples. Then, Transylvanian Beef Stew, and Wiener Schnitzel. Finally, for dessert, I've started making a Chocolate Log."

"Sounds awful, Kate. Did you come up with this menu after one of your funky food dreams?"

I pinned the menu back on the board. "These are Preston's personal choices -- his comfort food. He once told me about his Hungarian grandmother's huge Sunday family dinners. One day before you started working for me, Tony, Preston came over and cooked a couple of his favorite dishes for us. There was certainly nothing trendy about them, but it was food for the soul."

I waved the shopping list in front of Tony's face. "C'mon, we gotta get going, because after this, I have to go over to Preston's house to check on the setup."

I could hear Phoebe Jo vacuuming the hallway. I poked my head out the kitchen door to tell her we were leaving. "And would you please help Cherry find something decent to eat for breakfast when she finally gets up?"

"Don't you worry, Miss Kate. I'll fix her up a nice bowl of oatmeal."

I waved. "Whatever. See you later, we should be back in an hour."

Tony and I took the white 'Round the World catering van down Loveland-Madeira Road and across Kemper, past JJ's on Montgomery, then took Cooper Road into the city of Blue Ash. All the small suburban cities on the eastern side of Cincinnati blend into one another, so the trip only took twenty minutes.

I made a left into the little parking lot in front of a yellow brick building. Mike and Pete Trolley had the best produce around, and I could count on them to supply me with whatever I needed at the last minute.

The parking lot was empty, except for an old, beat-up, green Jaguar. There was only one like it. "Wolfie's here."

Tony cursed under his breath.

"Here." I handed the shopping list to him. "You start on this ... I want to talk to Wolfie."

"Have fun."

As we walked the short distance to the store, I clutched at the collar of my unzipped parka, pulling it tight around my neck. It was a sunny morning, but colder than I expected it to be.

I pulled open the door and, immediately, my mood was elevated. The bright oranges and yellows of the citrus fruit, and the sweet, earthy smells of the produce were a tonic for the depressive reality I had been dealing with. I saw Wolfie poking around in the lettuce bin, but I decided to delay that meeting, and go sniff some mangoes.

More than any other sense, smell can completely transport me back to a favorite time and place. I held the smooth-skinned, red and yellow mango up to my nose, and breathed deeply.

I was sitting on a white, sandy beach on the western coast of India. The warmth of the sun soaked into my coconut-oiled skin. I could hear the fishermen chattering excitedly, as they pulled their boatloads of fish up onto the beach. A young Hindu woman wrapped in a flowing, purple sari, and wearing silver, jingly bracelets around her ankles, walked towards me, balancing a large basket on top of her head. She stopped in front of me and smiled.

"Hey, Kate -- must be another emergency." Pete Trolley's cheerful voice pulled me back to Cincinnati. I looked down into his red-cheeked face. His full, thick beard almost hid his easy-going smile.

"Yeah," I answered, "another one of those crazy last minute jobs. Tony's got the list."

"I know. He's in the back looking over some half-crates with Mike." He jerked his head towards the opposite side of the store. "Your pal Martin Wolfenden's here."

"I saw him. I was just about to go talk to him."

Pete gave me a nod and started unloading tomatoes from a crate, arranging them in neat rows. He gave each one a little turn until the most perfect side was facing up. "These are the best tomatoes you're gonna get in December. Flown in this morning, straight from the field in Florida."

I didn't need any, but I picked out half a dozen anyway and dropped them into a plastic bag. I figured Phoebe Jo would probably find a use for them.

This was one of those times when I wished tact was one of my more dominant qualities. I had to ask Wolfie about his outburst against Preston that Thursday night at JJ's. But I had no idea how I was going to introduce the topic without it being taken as an accusation.

Ever since last Saturday, when I saw Wolfie's weird reaction to Preston's death, I'd wanted to talk to him. It was unlike Wolfie to be so distant -- to me at least. Add to that JJ's story, and I had too many questions that needed answers. Now with Terry under arrest, it seemed the police were satisfied he was guilty and had stopped looking for anyone else. I was determined to keep the investigation open, but I dreaded the thought of *another* friend being a suspect. I hoped Wolfie had an alibi for where he was at the time Preston was attacked.

I braced myself and walked towards Wolfie. Help. I shot a silent prayer to the heavens, but I wasn't sure anyone was listening.

I came alongside Wolfie. He appeared to be very focused on the inner core of a head of leaf lettuce. "Hi, there. Find any bugs, yet?"

Wolfie's whole body jumped, and the head of lettuce dropped back into the bin. He quickly regained his composure. "Oh. Hi, there, Kate."

"How are you?"

"Fine." Wolfie resumed his lettuce inspection.

"I've been concerned about you, ever since my Mother's luncheon on Saturday."

"Oh?"

"Well, you didn't seem to be yourself. And then I was at JJ's place the other night, and heard from him that on Thursday you'd met with someone who made you very upset. Just wondered if you were okay."

Wolfie placed a head of lettuce into his shopping cart. I could see a muscle on the side of his cheek tense up as he clenched his jaw. But then he turned to me and said, "I'm fine," and gave me a stiff smile.

Oh stop it. Don't do this, I thought. Cooperate. I'd passed the ball over to Wolfie, and it was in his court. But he wasn't even picking it up. Now I had to think of something else to say.

"Uh. Oh. Hmm." I sputtered.

Wolfie looked up at me. His eyes narrowed. "You think I'm stupid, Kate? I know what you're getting at." He started pushing his shopping cart away from me.

I followed him. "Wait a minute. Wolfie, I just..."

"You want to know if I have an alibi." He stopped, spun around, aimed a stubby little index finger at me and used it to accent each word. "Why can't you just come straight out and ask? Don't pretend to make polite conversation -- that's an insult."

So much for being tactful.

"You want to know what I did that night? I'll tell you what I did!" Wolfie wheeled his way down an aisle, picking up vegetables and throwing them into his cart without looking at them. I kept following him.

He said, "I received a phone call close to five o'clock that afternoon from an attorney who said he represented someone I had just gone into partnership with."

"A new partnership? Who is it?"

"No one you know. Just a suit new to Cincinnati and looking for something trendy to invest in. I had plans for a new restaurant. Anyway ... this lawyer said he had some papers that he needed to hand-deliver to me. I told the guy he'd find me at JJ's -- I was going there for a quiet dinner by myself."

We rounded a corner and started up the garlic and onion aisle. I let Wolfie continue. "I'd had two or three bites of my filet mignon when he entered the restaurant and walked up to my table. He's got this look on his face that says, *Don't shoot me, I'm only the messenger.*

"I took one look at the papers he handed me and knew it was all over. The investor was pulling out at the last minute because of what Preston had written about my first restaurant." Wolfie looked at me. His eyes had a flat, spiritless quality, and I could see dark rings under them. "Months of planning -- down the tubes. I will never do that to myself again -- getting my hopes up when someone else is controlling the purse strings.

"I lost my cool and I guess I created a bit of a scene -- but at least I didn't punch out the lawyer, even though I felt like it. He left and I got good and drunk."

"How long did you stay there?"

"Until about seven-thirty or so. Then, I remembered that Preston was at that stupid Christmas Concert rehearsal of his. The church had plastered all the stores in the area with posters listing him as the prima donna soloist. Well, I decided I was going over there and give him hell for screwing me over a second time. I wanted to bite his head off."

Or, I thought, according to JJ, cut off his tongue and serve it back to him on a roll with mustard.

We were hitting the dried fruit aisle and heading towards the garbanzo bean dip display. Wolfie kept talking. "I waited in that church parking lot for half an hour thinking I'd catch Preston, but only succeeded in freezing my buns off -- the old Jag's heater needs an overhaul. My anger turned into depression and I decided to go home and crash.

"The next morning, Frank Meyer called me up and told me what happened to Preston. We got together for a celebratory lunch on Mount Adams and gave a toast to whoever it was who did us all such a favor."

We passed by the popcorn balls and jujubes, and arrived at the checkout. Wolfie started unloading the contents of his shopping cart onto the counter. "Oh, by the way," he said, "I just got an invitation to the social event of the year."

"Oh? What's that?"

"Preston Schneider's wake."

That statement ka-chunked in my brain. Wait a minute, wakes are for friends -- especially if they're by invitation only. What was I thinking? You don't get invited to a wake -- you just show up -- normally. However, Preston Schneider wasn't a normal person, so I had to allow him his eccentricity. On the other hand, Wolfie was an enemy, so why did he get an invitation?

167

In my imagination I could hear Preston chuckling. That old windbag was up to something.

CHAPTER TWENTY-SEVEN ....

"Okay, Tony," I said. "So you know what you're doing with the filling for the stuffed cabbage?"

"Yeah, Boss," Tony called back, as he unloaded the last crate from the rear of the van.

"I'm going over to Preston's place to check on his kitchen supplies. We probably won't have to bring anything over, but I better make sure. I won't be gone any longer than an hour."

"What do you want me to do when I finish the filling?"

"Start cutting up the vegetables, and cook up the green beans for the salad," I told him, as I started up the Jeep and pulled out onto the gravel road.

I drove south on Loveland-Madeira Road, heading towards Preston's house. The mid-morning traffic was light, but I was right behind one of the dark green Clairmont Ranger patrol cars, so I had to stay within the speed limit. I wondered if it was Matt Skinner. After two miles of an excruciatingly slow and painful 35 mile per hour crawl, the patrol car moved into a left turn lane. As I passed, I took a quick look, but it wasn't him.

Then I wondered, why am I thinking about Officer Skinner, anyway? What do I care?

I stamped on the gas pedal and sped up to a more comfortable 50 miles per hour.

Five minutes later, I was driving along the quiet sidewalk-lined streets in the part of Clairmont where Preston had lived. It was considered the poor section of Clairmont, where the homes are on one acre lots and in the low $500,000 range.

I was still a couple of blocks away from my destination, when I came upon a heavy-set man in unflattering, baggy, gray sweats. He was jogging in place, waiting for me to go past so he could cross the street. He waved, and I stared at his puffy, red-cheeked face trying to figure out if I knew him. The man was breathing hard, and big clouds of carbon dioxide exploded out of his mouth into the crisp air.

It was Patrick Sloane. I waved back and continued on my way. In my rearview mirror, I could see him cross the street, then, instead of going straight, turn and follow me.

Two short blocks later, I pulled into Preston's driveway. Even though I hadn't been there in the last couple of years, I had no problem figuring out which house was Preston's. Nobody else on the street had a mailbox with a laughing gargoyle on the top of its post.

I stepped out of the Jeep and looked down the street in time to see Patrick Sloane a block away, lumbering along the sidewalk. He turned a corner and disappeared from sight.

I redirected my gaze to the front of Preston's house, a two-story, red brick colonial with green shutters, set back a good seventy feet from the sidewalk. Like all the other houses on the street, the front yard had a mix of large evergreen and shade trees. I walked up to the front door, past a thick planting of evergreen shrubs and dry clumps of dead chrysanthemums. There wasn't anything extraordinary about the outside of the house. But boy, the inside was another story.

I fished around in the bottom of my purse and pulled out the gold chain with Preston's keys attached, and the piece of paper with the home security code, supplied by Mr. Sanoma, Preston's lawyer. As soon as I unlocked the door and stepped into the vestibule, I quickly punched in the code on the security panel and shut the door.

I'd forgotten how claustrophobic Preston's home was. Everything seemed dark and heavy. The vestibule walls were covered with a rich burgundy, fuzzy paper. Starting to feel hot, I took off my parka and dropped it on an ornately carved, dark wood chair, that looked more like a medieval throne.

I flicked on a light switch and looked up. Hanging over my head was the scariest-looking chandelier I'd ever seen. It must have been one of Preston's more recent acquisitions. I certainly would have remembered it, had I seen it before. It had two tiers of candle-shaped bulbs, each candle being held up by, what looked like, a real deer antler. I turned the light back off and went into the spacious living room.

Instead of trying another light switch, I went over to the front windows and opened the heavy, bronze-colored, velvet drapes. The winter sun poured in through the windows, and I imagined the figures in the large oil paintings, hung around the room, squinting in the harsh, unfamiliar light.

At the sight of Preston's shiny, black grand piano, with the bust of Beethoven perched on a green marble pedestal beside it, I burst into tears.

Surprised at myself, I plunked down onto the brocade sofa in front of the cold fireplace. "I miss him," I said out loud. There were times when that man could irritate me to no end with his criticisms, and there were times I hated him for the way he treated other people. But I was going to miss his friendly interest in my career, his periodic challenges to my culinary talents.

More than that, Preston and I had recognized in each other

the same loneliness and feeling of being disconnected from the people around us. But we never spoke about it.

I pulled out a tissue and blew my nose. There was a lot to do and I couldn't spend the morning sobbing on Preston's couch. I dug out my mini-cassette recorder, left the living room, and found my way to the back of the house where the kitchen was.

Preston had a well-equipped kitchen with gleaming, stainless steel, commercial quality appliances -- plus all the latest gadgets, grinders, mixers and processors that any chef would ever want. But, like the rest of the house, it also felt dark and closed up. The cabinets were dark walnut and the countertops looked like a richly grained, green marble. I longed to open the curtains and let some light in, but realized there weren't any curtains. Huge evergreen trees in the back yard were cutting off the sunlight.

I did a quick inventory. Maybe too quick. As I tried to yank out a sheet pan from the top shelf of a cabinet, Preston's extensive collection of baking pans came crashing down on top of me. I spent the next ten minutes trying to put them back the way they were.

"Don't bother making the pickled beets," I said into my recorder, after I opened up another cabinet and found eight jars of them. They looked homemade. I wondered if Preston had preserved them himself.

I decided to check out the refrigerator. I was going to need a lot of fridge space, so I figured I might as well clean out the food that was probably going bad in there. I confess that my intentions weren't totally professional. In the same way other people read the titles on your bookshelves to try and figure out what kind of person you are, I found the contents of someone's refrigerator just as interesting and probably more revealing.

The first thing I noticed when I opened the door was a half-empty bottle of champagne. That wasn't surprising. There were neat stacks of plastic boxes with white labels stuck on the sides describing their contents. I read: Mango Chutney, Fried Rice, Szechuan Slaw, Apricot Pork Roast. There was one entire shelf on the door filled with bottles of different oriental sauces. I opened the vegetable drawers, and found a collection of slimy lettuces and what looked like bundles of rotting herbs. All that went into a plastic garbage bag I'd found under the sink. Then I took out the cartons of milk and orange juice and dumped them down the drain.

I decided to take a quick peek into the freezer. What I saw both shocked and pleased me at the same time -- a stack of red and gold cardboard boxes.

"Crown Chili Frozen Dinners -- I don't believe it." I stood there for a moment, just staring at them. Preston had never admitted to me that this was part of his regular diet. He always said that my grandfather's secret recipe was good value for the ordinary person, but intimated it would be a rude assault on his own highly developed taste buds.

I chuckled to myself and said out loud, "You are what you eat. What does this make you, Preston?"

Nobody answered, so I left the kitchen and went into the dining room to see how much space I had to work with. Not much. It was too small to handle twenty-five guests.

"Set up the bar in the living room," I said into my recorder, "and we'll need three round tables and twenty-five folding chairs for the family room. Get Tony and Robert to move some of the bigger pieces of furniture out of the family room into the living room to make way for the buffet table."

I went to the china cabinet, opened it up, and counted the plates and silverware. "Bring enough settings for ten, and four tablecloths."

There wasn't anything else for me to check out, but before I left, I felt compelled to look at the rest of the house. I went back to the vestibule and climbed the staircase.

I had never been upstairs, and my curiosity was killing me. In the back of my mind was the childish hope that I would miraculously find some information that would point to Preston's real killer.

I reached the upper landing and walked along the corridor, opening doors -- a bathroom, the linen closet, a couple of guest bedrooms, a second bathroom -- nothing very interesting. At the end of the hallway was Preston's master bedroom -- another dark and gloomy room.

Beside his imposing four-poster bed, on a round marble table with a heavy stone pedestal, was what I guessed to be his bedtime reading. I picked up the thick, bound volume and leafed through it. A musty, acrid smell stung my nostrils and made me sneeze. It wasn't really a book, but rather a bound collection of pulp magazines from the 1930s.

"Well, Preston, this isn't what I'd call great literature." I put the book back down on the table and left the room.

At the other end of the hallway, over the three-car garage, was the one remaining room left for me to explore. I opened the door. "Jackpot."

I had discovered Preston's Inner Sanctum.

Floor-to-ceiling bookcases lined three walls. To my right, in a corner, was an overstuffed easy chair. Beside it, on a small table, was a large blue and white ceramic vase in the shape of an elephant. On the fourth wall, there were a pair of dormer windows with a view of the front lawn and street. A large mahogany desk sat in the center of the room. On it was a computer terminal, a cordless telephone, a couple of file trays, and a letter holder -- not a loose sheet of paper or stray paper clip in sight.

But what caught my eye was the crystal ball.

I walked over to the desk, set down the mini-cassette recorder I'd been carrying, and plucked the glass orb out of the clutches of a carved wooden gargoyle squatting beside the PC. I rolled the baseball-sized, solid crystal ball around in my hands. It had a nice, smooth, sensuous feel to it.

I placed it back into the outstretched claws of the waiting gargoyle and leafed through the letters and contents of the file trays -- just some bills, newsletters from a wine tasters club, and articles ripped out of food magazines. I moved around to the other side of the desk and sat in the high-backed executive chair. I sank back into the soft leather, swiveled from side to side, and glanced down at the computer keyboard. Stuck on the top edge of it was a piece of masking tape with a series of letters and numbers written on it that read: SSEIVNESN-1-2.

Something about sitting in Preston's chair made me feel guilty. "Oh, for God's sake." He'd given me the keys to his house, so I knew he considered me his trusted friend. But sitting in a dead man's chair gave me the creeps. It was too intimate -- like crawling into his bed.

I jumped up and moved away from the desk.

I noticed a CD player on one of the bookshelves, and went over to it. "So, Preston, what kind of music soothed your soul, as you sat here and gazed into your crystal ball?" I pressed the play button. "THERE'S NO BUSINESS LIKE SHOW BUSINESS," sang Ethel Merman, her lungs blasting out the words at an ear-splitting volume. I turned it down.

Curious about the contents of the bookshelves, I began browsing. Preston's collection of CDs consisted mainly of Broadway musicals and opera. There were cookbooks, recent best sellers, glossy art books, and a number of old, worn volumes dealing with codes and cryptography.

Built into one of the large bookcases was a glass enclosed display cabinet. Inside was a collection of childhood memorabilia: toy soldiers, comic books, Shadow pulp magazines, and old photos of Over-the-Rhine -- the neighborhood Preston grew up in. There was also a yellowing photograph of his parents in front of the family grocery store.

I saw a plaque, but couldn't read the inscription on it, so I opened the glass doors, and pulled it out. The inscription read: "To Helmut Schneider, 1965 Cincinnati Small Business Man of the Year." I replaced the plaque and took a closer look at the framed photograph beside it. It was easy to see it was a picture of Preston's father receiving the plaque. He looked a lot like Preston, only with a pencil-thin mustache. The overweight man with the crewcut making the presentation also looked familiar, but I couldn't place him.

"What's this?" The colors red and gold attracted my attention. I reached into the cabinet and pulled out a couple of sheets of clear plastic. "Wow, I remember these." Encased in the clear plastic sheets were a couple of old Crown Chili paper place mats with the punch-out crowns still intact. I could tell by the design that these were the original versions from the 1950s. They were in mint condition. I put them back.

I never realized Preston was so sentimental. The memorial to his childhood gave me some insights. I had to assume the items in the cabinet were things that made him happy. That helped explain why his freezer was full of my family's Crown Chili -- it was comfort food. It also helped explain why he treated me so much better than he did others. I had reaped the benefit of all that good feeling he had towards what my family produced.

My watch beeped, reminding me that the half-hour I'd allotted for my inspection tour was up. I turned off Ethel Merman and was about to leave the room, but something stopped me. It was a gut feeling.

I turned and looked at the computer. Preston had been prepared for the possibility that he might be murdered -- and sure enough, it had happened. He must have had suspicions of potential killers -- maybe even had a list. I couldn't leave until I checked out what was in the computer. My hope was that if there was such a list, Terry's name wouldn't be on it.

The computer went through the usual crackles and whirring sounds when I turned it on. I looked over the menu and began pointing, clicking, and opening files. There were expense accounts, Preston's latest food column, his Cryptoman puzzles, tax material, and then a roadblock. I couldn't get into what he had named the T-File. The instructions "Please enter password" appeared on the screen. What password? I looked down at the keyboard, saw the piece of masking tape, and typed SSEIVNESN-1-2. The computer beeped at me and the instructions disappeared for a couple of seconds, then reappeared with the same request. I retyped. Same reply. I was stuck. Instead of getting lost in one of those computer hells where I've spent hours trying to untangle myself from the mess caused by haphazardly punching keys, I took a breath and did the prudent thing -- I shut down the computer.

Maybe there were hard copies of his so-called T-File somewhere. I yanked on the file drawer in the desk, but it was locked. "Well, I have a key for that, but it's downstairs in my purse." I looked at my watch and shook my head. "I'll come back later, tonight. There's too much to do right now."

I rushed downstairs, grabbed my purse and parka, reset the alarm, and locked up.

As I drove home, I started planning my afternoon activities. At a stop light, I reached into my purse for my recorder. "Damn." I'd left it somewhere in Preston's house. I made an illegal U-turn and sped back. The whole reason for having the recorder was to compensate for the fact that I had a sieve-head. But it wasn't going to help, if I couldn't remember to keep it with me.

I left the Jeep running in the driveway and quickly let myself into the house, almost forgetting to punch in the alarm code. "Where'd I leave that stupid thing?" I hurried through the rooms on the bottom floor, scanning the tables and counter tops. Nothing. I took the stairs two at a time, looked in the master bedroom, and then headed for Preston's office.

From the doorway, I could see it on his desk. "There it is." Right beside the gargoyle. I entered the room and marched across to the desk and grabbed my recorder.

Something was wrong. The desk's file drawer was open and there were papers scattered on the floor. I hadn't done that.

I sensed a presence behind me. A sharp pain started at the back of my head and tried to burst through my eyeballs. White pinpoints of light danced in front of me. Click. All went dark.

CHAPTER TWENTY-EIGHT ....

A giant gargoyle stared at me and laughed. It jumped straight up and landed on the antler chandelier, joining several other gargoyles, who were holding onto the horns and swinging back and forth. The chandelier exploded and the hideous creatures came tumbling down towards me, screeching and howling. I had the sensation of rising up through the darkness, while they fell past me. Soon, there was only one gargoyle left, looking down at me from the black void above. He was holding a glass orb. The creature's body began to undulate as though it was made of water. My vision blurred. I blinked. The gargoyle was solid again, this time looking down at me from a ledge -- a wooden ledge.

I thought, where am I? The gargoyle didn't move -- it couldn't, it was made of wood. I became aware that I was lying on the floor, looking up at Preston's desk. The back of my head throbbed. Pain shot down one leg and I realized it was bent underneath me in an awkward position. I straightened it out and kicked something that made a grating sound as it skidded across the hardwood floor. Rolling my head to one side, I could see pieces of blue and white pottery around me. They used to be Preston's ceramic elephant vase.

The lump on the back of my head complained when I touched it. I looked at my fingers -- no blood.

What the hell happened? The last thing I remembered was reaching across the desk for my recorder. The desk file drawer -- who opened it? Who hit me on the head? I pulled myself up to my feet and leaned against the desk. I took a deep breath and punched 911 on Preston's telephone.

"I've been attacked," I said, when the operator asked how she could help me.

"Where are you?"

I gave her Preston's address.

"When did this happen?"

I looked at my watch. I couldn't believe what it said, it must have stopped. I felt like I'd been unconscious for hours. "What time is it?"

"Eleven-thirty, Ma'am. Do you know who your attacker was? Is he still there?"

"No, I think I'm alone in the house. I was hit from behind about five minutes ago."

"I'm sending the paramedics and the Rangers over right now. Do you have any injuries?"

"My head aches and I feel kind of woozy."

The operator told me to stay where I was until help arrived, and then hung up.

I punched in my telephone number.

"'Round the World Catering," Tony-Z answered in a flat voice. "Can I help you?"

"Get over here, Tony. Bring Cherry, so she can drive the Jeep back."

"Kate? You sound funny."

"And I haven't even told you a joke yet. Come and get

me."

"Did you have an accident? Where are you?"

"At Preston's. Someone just tried to use my head for batting practice."

"Holy shit. Be right there, Boss." Tony hung up.

I punched the "off" button on the cordless phone and held onto it while I staggered over to the easy chair in the corner. My head wasn't pounding quite as much as it had been just a few minutes before. As I waited for the Clairmont Rangers to rescue me, I sorted through the confusing chain of events.

Someone -- Preston's killer? -- had somehow broken into the house in the few short minutes I was away? Without tripping the alarm? I was sure I hadn't forgotten to set it. Or -- another possibility occurred to me that made me even more uncomfortable -- he, or she, had slipped into the house while I was making my inspection tour and taking notes.

The pounding in my head had stopped, but I could hear a rumbling noise. It was coming from outside the house. "The Jeep." I jumped up and tried to hurry out of the room, stumbling, and bouncing against the walls as I went down the hall. I'd left the engine running when I came back to look for my recorder.

I made it as far as the top step of the staircase, but had to sit down and lean my head against the bannister.

The front door opened and a squad of uniforms rushed into the vestibule. My heroes had arrived -- followed by Ranger Skinner. "Hello," Skinner shouted into the living room, while the other three men scattered, searching for me.

I peered through the stair railings. "Up here," I shouted as they were about to disappear into different rooms.

Ten minutes later, the medics had pronounced me fit as a slightly dented fiddle, though they had wanted me to go to the hospital for some scans. I refused -- I had too much to do -- but I promised them I'd go if I experienced any of the symptoms listed on the sheet of paper they left with me.

"Well, Officer Skinner," I said, giving him a half-hearted smile, "this is getting to be a daily habit, you and I running into each other." I was back in Preston's office accompanied by Skinner and a second Clairmont Ranger, who had done me the favor of turning off my Jeep.

"What exactly are you doing here, Ms. Cavanaugh? From all appearances, it would seem we are both investigating Preston's homicide."

Yeah, but I'm the only one trying to find the truth. "I've been retained by Preston's estate to cater his last party." And you can't come.

Skinner pulled out his note pad and gave me a stony *just the facts, ma'am* look. "What were you doing when you were attacked?"

I related my story about forgetting the cassette recorder and having to come back. Meanwhile, the second Ranger was busy collecting the broken pieces of the blue and white pottery elephant, and placing them into a plastic evidence bag.

I wrapped up my account with, "The attacker either had his own key to the place and knew the alarm code, or he sneaked in while I was making my inspection tour of the house."

Skinner looked up from taking notes. "And you didn't hear anything?"

"I made a lot of noise banging pots and pans and listening to Ethel."

"Who?"

I was standing by the CD player and punched the play button. Ms. Merman belted out *Doing What Comes Naturally.*

"Okay, okay." Skinner covered his ears. "You made your point." Ethel was deafening even at normal volume.

I pointed to the open desk drawer and the papers scattered on the floor. "I'll bet it was Preston's killer who broke in and stole something from there."

Skinner didn't look too impressed with my deduction. In

fact, the only response he made was to look up to the ceiling for a second and then back at me with a skeptical lift of his eyebrows. That just made me want to push my point even further.

"Why," I said, "would anyone other than Preston's killer be looking into his files? A thief had plenty of things to steal downstairs in the lower part of the house. The killer was probably looking for some information Preston had linking him -- or her-- to some crime. And it couldn't be Terry Poole, because you've got him locked up."

"Interesting theory, but we've already gone through Mr. Schneider's personal effects. We obtained a search warrant a couple of days ago, and didn't find anything unusual in those files -- just ordinary correspondence and some fan mail."

I pointed to the computer. "What about that?"

Skinner followed my finger. "Went through that too."

"And what did you do when you got to the T-File?"

"Nothing. Couldn't get in." Skinner breathed deeply and then rubbed his temple. "I don't have to discuss this with you, Ms. Cavanaugh, but I will tell you this -- we have all the physical evidence we need."

"But maybe..."

Skinner held up his hand. "You can only go so far without finding any solid leads. We have to follow the physical evidence at the scene of the crime. That evidence points to Terry Poole. I can't go on a wild goose chase, in God knows how many possible directions, without a physical connection. You can say 'But maybe, but maybe' all you want. I have nobody to connect with Schneider's death but Terry Poole."

"But someone searched through those files and then attacked me. That's evidence -- isn't it?"

"You probably surprised a thief, who heard you coming, hid, then whacked you over the head in order to escape."

"Why didn't he just run away?"

Skinner sighed. I could see he wasn't going to indulge me

much longer. He said, "Maybe he was shorter than you and thought you'd catch him, so he attacked, then ran. I don't know. We'll dust and see if we come up with some short cat burglar's prints."

What a jerk.

Skinner pocketed his note book. "Preston Schneider's career was based on making people angry at him, and just because he may have offended someone, that's not enough grounds for suspecting that person of murder. I need a physical connection. Talk to Terry Poole's lawyer." He tilted his head and squinted at me. "Is he a relative of yours?" Skinner didn't wait for my answer. "Well, check with him. The prosecutor's convinced the judge that there is enough evidence to warrant this case going to trial."

"Kate!"

"Katie!"

I heard Tony and Cherry shouting downstairs, followed by the sound of feet pounding up the staircase. I poked my head out into the hallway. "Hey, guys. In here."

I felt Officer Skinner come up behind me and touch my hair. I spun around. "What're you...?" He smiled and indicated with his forefinger for me to turn back around. I found myself succumbing to his smile and followed his instructions. I felt my hair being moved. I looked back. Skinner was holding a small piece of the blue and white ceramic elephant. "The medics didn't get all of it," he said.

I mumbled a thank you.

"Katie, are you okay?" Cherry rushed up to me. Tony was right behind her. They hit me with a pile of questions, which I tried to answer in order. In the meantime, I could see Officer Skinner looking at the computer. I wondered if I had made him reconsider his decision to ignore the T-File. Nope. I saw him shake his head.

"Let's go home," I said, "I need to lie down." But first I asked Skinner if it was okay to take one of Preston's books. I mean, I didn't want to be accused of stealing evidence.

He shrugged. "No problem."

I grabbed a book titled Codes and Cryptography. I was planning to spend the entire night trying to crack Preston's code which I copied from the masking tape.

We all went downstairs to the vestibule, where Skinner said, "I'm sure we'll be running into each other again, Ms. Cavanaugh." He saluted me a goodbye and left with the other Ranger.

Tony stood outside on the front steps, waiting, while I put on my parka.

"This place is like some kind of weird museum," Cherry said, peering into the living room. "You sure have strange friends, Katie."

I laughed. "No kidding."

I was about to punch in the alarm code, when my memory started to work. "My recorder." I stomped up the staircase.

CHAPTER TWENTY-NINE ....

I was sitting across from Cherry at the kitchen table, my head hanging over the steaming bowl of beef-barley soup that Phoebe Jo had made that morning. Boo-Kat was sitting at attention right beside my chair, waiting to pounce on anything that fell onto the floor. I groaned and breathed in the comforting warmth and aroma of the soup, hoping that somehow it would reach into the back of my head and soothe the aching lump that throbbed at the base of my skull.

Phoebe Jo placed a wicker basket in front of me. "What's the matter, Miss Kate? You usually love my soup."

It was one of my favorites, and I wondered if dunking my head into the bowl would make my boo-boo feel better.

Underneath the cloth napkin in the basket I found a couple of my home baked whole wheat rolls, which Phoebe Jo had heated up in the oven. I tore off a piece of roll and dipped it into the broth, pushing aside big chunks of carrots and parsnips. I popped it into my mouth. It was rich and flavorful, with just the right amount of salt. While I had spent thousands of dollars going to one of the best culinary schools in the country, Phoebe Jo was an instinctive cook. My appetite was jump-started, and I picked up my spoon and began to eat. Maybe it was a purely emotional reaction, but the soup made me feel better.

"How ya feeling, Boss?" Tony swaggered into the kitchen. "I've been looking over the menu and I know I can handle it myself. So, you just take the rest of the day off."

"I'll do no such thing," I said, choking on some barley.

"Now, Miss Kate," Phoebe Jo wagged her finger at me, "you've had quite a bang on the head. You're lucky to be alive. Take it easy. I'll help Tony."

Cherry slapped her hand on the table. "I'll bring samples up to your bedroom for you to taste. You can shout down on the intercom and tell them what they're doing wrong."

I could live with that.

"*And,*" Cherry announced, getting up onto her feet, "I'm not letting you out of my sight -- consider me your bodyguard."

"Ha." Tony let out a laugh.

Cherry shot him an irritated look. "Did someone say something funny?"

"Well," Tony gestured at her, his hands extended, "look at you. You've got a nice body -- I mean you're in really good shape, but you're not exactly Wonder Woman."

Cherry plucked a wooden spoon from my kitchen utensil jar and sauntered across the floor towards Tony. "Take this dangerous weapon. You're the mugger and I'm the poor, defenseless female walking through the big, bad neighborhood."

Tony held up his hands. "Now, wait a minute. I can really hurt you."

Cherry tapped him lightly on the butt with the spoon. "That's what you think." She grabbed one of his hands, placed the wooden utensil in it, turned and slowly walked away from him.

Tony looked at me and Phoebe Jo, shrugged his shoulders

186

and quickly followed after Cherry. He clutched her shoulder. In one fluid motion, Cherry turned, grabbed Tony's arm, shifted her weight, and flipped him over her hip, but kept him from landing hard on the kitchen floor. The demonstration ended with Cherry standing over Tony, her foot on the back of his neck, playfully spanking him with the wooden spoon.

"Okay, okay, I give up," Tony said. "You're right. I'm wrong."

"You're hired," I said. "Just one problem."

"What's that?" Cherry asked, helping a humbled Tony to his feet.

"You've got to start your day the same time I do."

"Yeah, I've been meaning to ask you about that." Cherry put a hand on her hip. "You seem to need even less sleep than you did twenty years ago. You always got up early, but now it doesn't seem like you even go to bed."

"It's my body clock." I shrugged. "Must be old age." I moved my chair away from the table in order to stand up, causing Boo-Kat to scramble out of the way. "Cherry, I'm honored that you would make such a sacrifice, but visiting me is supposed to be fun -- not a job."

"I haven't had this much fun since I took that job modeling the latest leather fashions for Motorcycle Mamas at the Harley-Davidson convention. In fact, you might have trouble getting rid of me."

Out of the corner of my eye, I saw Tony smile. I said, "Thank's for the offer, but there's no reason for you to disrupt your sleep pattern." I picked up my soup bowl and -- still slightly dizzy -- shuffled over to the dishwasher. "Don't worry, I can take care of myself -- I'm a big girl."

"Yes, you are," Cherry replied. "Just the same, I'll be up at the crack of dawn tomorrow with you and the birds and your little dog, too."

* * * * * * *

It was mid-afternoon. I was lying in bed, listening to some soft jazz on the radio. The combination of soup and Motrin made my head feel a lot better, and I found myself wanting to do something -- but without getting out of bed. I'm a Boomer and I want it all.

I looked at my bedside telephone and decided Uncle Cliff should know what happened to me that morning. We could exchange information, with him telling me what happened at Terry's court hearing. I had the phone in hand, when a soft knock sounded at the bedroom door.

"Yes?" I craned my neck, trying to look around the partly opened door.

"Kate?" Julie Ann peeked into the room and pushed her glasses up against the bridge of her nose.

"Hey, there." I waved her in and patted the spot beside me on the bed, indicating for her to sit down.

"Are you feeling better?" Julie Ann said. "Mom told me what happened."

"Sure. What's up?" I saw the code book I'd borrowed from Preston's office in her hand, and pointed at it. "Good reading?"

"Oh, yeah." Julie Ann placed the book on her lap as she sat down. "I was hoping you'd let me borrow it. This stuff is real interesting to me."

"That's right, I'd forgotten you liked that sort of thing." I sat up in bed. "Maybe you can help me break the code."

Julie Ann's eyes widened. "Cool." She frowned. "What code?"

I dug a scrap of paper out of my pocket. "This was what was written on Preston's computer keyboard. It could be an access code."

"SSEIVNESN-1-2?" Julie Ann scratched her head. "Did you try it?"

"Didn't work."

"Hmm. I betcha I can figure it out. I've learned a lot about how to peek into someone else's PC from some of the guys in the computer club at school. Oh." She put her hand up to her mouth and looked as though she just realized she had let a secret slip. "But I would never break into one, myself." With that, she hopped off the bed. "I'll get started on this right after I finish my homework."

"That'd be a great help, Julie Ann. We'll solve this mystery together."

"You bet." She left the room.

I reached for the telephone again and pressed the automatic speed dial for Uncle Cliff's cellular phone.

"Clifford T. Vasherhann speaking."

"Uncle Cliff. Kate." I filled him in on my morning adventure in Prestonland and reassured him I was recuperating quickly. "Now it's your turn. What happened in court, today?"

"The prosecutor's got a lot of evidence -- circumstantial at best -- but enough for the judge to send it over to the grand jury."

"Like what? So Terry was holding the brass candlestick -- what does that prove?"

"I'm afraid it's a bit more complicated than that, K.C. The police found traces of blood on Terry's pant leg."

Blood? "I spoke with Terry yesterday and he didn't mention anything about getting blood on himself."

"The prosecutor's theory is that Terry and Preston broke the church organ's mirror during their struggle, cutting Preston's hand. Blood got on Terry's pants when Preston reached out as he fell 'stricken by the candlestick blow.' "

"The prosecutor sounds kind of melodramatic."

Uncle Cliff laughed. "You got that right, he was a member of the drama club in college. The courtroom's his stage now. Anyway, Terry's explanation is that he was holding Preston's wrist, checking his pulse, and when he let go of it, the cut hand must have brushed against his pant leg, leaving some blood."

I processed that. "Sounds like a reasonable explanation."

"Wait, there's more. The only fingerprints found on the candlestick were Terry's and one mystery print. The other candlestick found at the scene was on the communion table, and that one had church deacons' fingerprints all over it, but not one that matches the 'mystery' print."

"How do the police know they were deacons' prints?"

"Everyone at the church was fingerprinted."

"Everyone?"

"Well ... some of the members on the finance committee and in the choir didn't go along with the Rangers' request. They all refused on the same general principles of protecting their privacy."

"You can do that?"

"Yep. They weren't obligated and the police didn't think they had strong enough suspicions to pursue it." Uncle Cliff paused briefly, then added, "I guess I'll see you tomorrow at Preston's funeral service?"

"If I survive his wake. See you there." I clicked off the phone, sank back into my pillows, and stared up at the ceiling. I was tired and overwhelmed. Never before had I so willingly handed over all the preparation for an event to Tony. Not that he wasn't capable, it's just that I was such a control freak. "Hmm. Just like Mother." That was someone I should call, but first I wanted to talk to Marilyn about who, other than the deacons, would have any reason for handling those candlesticks. Finding the owner of that mystery print was going to be a process of elimination, which the police -- having charged Terry -- were obviously not going to pursue.

But I really didn't feel like talking to anyone. The phone rang a couple of times and stopped. Seconds later, my bedroom door opened slowly. Phoebe Jo stuck her head in and stared at me, not saying anything. "I'm awake," I called out.

"Oh. Do you want to talk to Marilyn Poole?"

It must have been one of those flukey ESP connections.

Marilyn thanked me for getting Uncle Cliff to represent Terry. I asked her my fingerprints-on-the-candlestick question. She paused a few seconds before answering, "No. Nobody else handles the candlesticks -- just the deacons. I sure wish there was some way to find out who owned that lone fingerprint."

"Sit tight, Marilyn, we haven't heard the last from Preston. Tomorrow's wake might stir up a lot of interesting possibilities."

"Hhmmm ... Just as I was leaving the house to go to court this morning, an invitation to the wake was hand-delivered to us. Sounds pretty weird -- I'm certainly not going without Terry."

First Wolfie, now Terry. Preston's guest list was beginning to look like a collection of non-mourners. What did Preston have in mind when he made his selections?

Marilyn and I said our goodbyes.

I lay back down and pondered the scroll work on the wallpaper border edging the ceiling. A cold, late afternoon light filtered in through the window. I pulled the comforter up over my legs. I wondered if Cherry was going to bring me something to sample -- I was getting hungry. But stronger than my desire to eat was my need for a little sleep. My eyelids drooped and I didn't try to keep them open.

Preston, wrapped in a bronze-colored velvet curtain, sat on his carved wooden throne, shoving food into his mouth with both hands. "More. More," he kept shouting, as I brought plate after plate of his favorite Hungarian dishes and set them down on the large wooden table in front of him.

I watched until he ate the last morsel of food and wiped the plate clean with a piece of bread. Preston patted his mouth with the tassels on the edge of the curtain, and then removed the ring from his finger and, stretching forward, held it right in front of my eyes. It was his signet ring with the initials PS. He said, "Here. You'll know what it means."

I awoke with a start. PS -- obviously it meant Preston Schneider. But it also could stand for Patrick Sloane. I didn't know anyone else with those initials. But wouldn't it be too much of a coincidence -- the killer having the same initials as his victim? I remembered Patrick jogging close by Preston's house that morning. He was also the one who just happened to be right there in the church's sanctuary when Terry Poole found Preston's body. It was all fitting together too easily.

Questions: Did Patrick allow the police to fingerprint him? And if PS *did* stand for Patrick Sloane, what pushed him to murder?

Tuesday, December 19th

CHAPTER THIRTY ....

"Uuuhh," Cherry groaned.

I stopped beating my raspberry buttercream and looked over at her. She sat at one corner of the same stainless steel table I was working at, with one hand propping her head up and the other clinging to a large commuter mug of coffee. I said, "You're doing great, kiddo. Just another fourteen hours and you can go back to bed." She looked pretty good, too, in a short, straight, black skirt, black tights, and a black sweater.

Cherry yawned, opened one eye halfway, and looked around the commercial kitchen. "Where's the clock? What god-awful time is it, anyway?" Her search stopped. She fixed her squinting eyes on the far wall and groaned again. "Eight o'clock? How do you get up so early, Katie? Not just you, but everyone in this place -- and you're all so chirpy and energetic." Cherry took a swig of coffee. "I can't believe it, we've been awake for two hours and the sun's just now showing up."

Tony came out of the walk-in storage closet, with an

armload of table linens, singing, "Ka-tie Cavanaugh had a farm, Ee-yi, Ee-yi-o. And on this farm she had a guest, Ee-yi, Ee-yi-o. With a bitch-bitch, here. And a bitch-bitch, there ...."

I said, "Okay, okay, Tony. That's enough."

Cherry glared at him and muttered, "I used to think he was cute."

I dipped a spoon into the buttercream and handed it to Cherry. "Taste this -- tell me what you think." While she was occupied, I rubbed the back of my neck, massaging the lump. It was big, but, surprisingly, I felt pretty normal.

Cherry handed the cleaned spoon back to me. "It's too early. My taste buds won't be awake for another two hours."

"That's what I thought -- needs more kirsch." I picked up the bottle, splashed a bit more into the bowl, and stirred.

I unrolled the chocolate cake I'd made the day before, spread the raspberry buttercream over the cake, and rolled it back up. I piped a line of buttercream rosettes along the top and finished it with a sprinkle of shaved chocolate.

Phoebe Jo came rushing into the kitchen, tying an apron around her waist. "I'm here, Miss Kate. I'll get right onto breading the cauliflower and the veal. Julie Ann's caught the school bus, and I let Boo-Kat out to roam." She stopped and looked a little worried. "Oh, dear. I hope he doesn't come back dragging another snake."

I sighed. "We'll get Robert to deal with it this time." I turned to Tony, "Speaking of which, how's the loading coming along? Is Robert still out there?"

"Yeah, he's got all the chairs in the van, and I'm gonna help him with the tables next."

I went over to the bulletin board, checked the job list, and scratched off the ones I'd completed. Salads were next. For the next twenty minutes, under Cherry's sleepy surveillance, I chopped dill, parsley and scallions, and sliced cucumbers. I said a silent thank you to Tony for having already made the two salad dressings. I put the cucumbers and dill into one container, and the green beans Tony had cooked earlier, scallions, and parsley into another, poured the dressings over them, and stored them in the walk-in refrigerator to marinate.

On another shelf in the walk-in were three foil-covered pans. I peeked in each one. "Cabbage rolls ... beef stew ... red cabbage. Excellent." It was amazing to me that there we were, about three hours before serving time, and I was just then getting around to checking up on Tony's work. Once again, I had to come to the realization that I couldn't keep all those plates spinning by myself. Thank God for Tony.

If you don't mind the cold, a walk-in refrigerator is the perfect place to escape to when the world gets too stressful. And I was definitely starting to feel stressed out. I leaned against the shelving. It was absolutely quiet, and I felt like I'd stepped into another dimension where no one could get to me. "I really don't want to do this lunch." It wasn't just the events of the past few days that were overwhelming -- it was what they meant that had me depressed.

I was being exposed to the dark side of a person I thought I had known for years -- Preston. I knew he had used his power to abuse people, but I never realized to what extent. Someone repaid his actions with the ultimate evil act. I've always heard that everyone is capable of murder, but never really believed it. Now I found myself suspecting everybody. God, there was so much hatred and bitterness.

I focused on the people who might show up that afternoon. They'd probably be from the same group who were at Mother's luncheon. They would all be wearing their masks, pretending to be in control of their lives, just as I would as soon as I stepped back out into the kitchen. Even with Cherry ... I felt we weren't making a real connection. It made me sad. Maybe it had always been that way -- only now I expected more from people. I wondered if it was possible to live your life without a mask.

The feeling of loneliness I usually managed to ignore by

keeping myself busy suddenly seemed to pull and tear at every bone and ligament inside of me. My whole being ached, and the only party I wanted to throw was a pity party for myself. "Snap out of it, girl. Things could be a lot worse."

Rattle, rattle, rattle. Someone was having trouble trying to open the door from the outside. "Kathleen? KATHLEEN?" It was Mother. I opened the door.

"For heaven's sake, dear," Mother said, "what are you doing in there? You've had a concussion -- you should be in bed."

"It was just a little bump on the back of my head. This is my version of an ice pack treatment."

Mother stood there, in her black Vittadini dress and matching jacket, frowning.

I continued. "The medics told me to put ice on any sore spots, and right now, my whole body feels sore."

Mother kept frowning. "What? Sometimes I don't understand you." She waved me forward. "Don't hold the refrigerator door open."

I obeyed. "Would you like a cup?" I said, as I walked over to the coffee maker and set out a couple of mugs.

"None for me. My teeth are clenched already, Kathleen -- I'm angry at you."

"What did I do?"

"It's what you didn't do. I had to learn about the brutal attack on my only daughter from my brother, your Uncle Cliff."

"Well, I know it's love and concern that's motivated you to come over and yell at me."

Mother blinked, and I could see her eyes register a thought. She walked over to me and gave me a stiff hug -- she was out of practice, but I'll accept any little crumb.

"Now that I'm here," Mother said, looking around the kitchen, "I'll help supervise."

I followed her as she made her way over to Phoebe Jo's work station. As usual, Mother was showing, in her obvious way, that she didn't think I could handle things without her. I suddenly realized how important I was to Mother. I mean, who would she have to boss around, if she didn't have me? Ever since Dad died, she's needed me to lean on -- to step on -- to compete against.

Mother wrinkled her nose at what she saw. "What are you doing with that cauliflower?"

"I'm breading it, Ma'am," Phoebe Jo replied, dipping a piece of cauliflower in some egg and rolling it in bread crumbs.

Mother turned to me with a sour look on her face. "And then what happens to it?"

"It's gonna fry."

"That's thoroughly disgusting, Kathleen. Aren't you worried about your reputation?"

"You know, I've never eaten this dish, but it sounds good. Preston's grandmother used to make it for him."

Mother let out a deep breath. "Oh, dear." She walked over to the menu board. "What else do we have to look forward to?"

"Did you get an invitation, too?"

"Nooo." Mother looked over her shoulder at me. "And I intend to speak to him about ... Oh ... that's right ... he's dead." She blinked and touched her lips with a perfectly manicured finger. A second later, she waved off her thought. "Well, I was sure you'd need help after being mugged, so here I am."

From my vantage point of being able to see over the top of Mother's head, I noticed Tony and Robert come in the kitchen's back door. "Hey, guys. Back already?"

"Yep," Robert said. "The tables and chairs are all set up at Preston's.

"It's kinda weird in that house," added Tony.

I checked my job list -- everything was done. "We're in good shape." I glanced over at Cherry, who had almost found a way to be prone while sitting on her stool. "Well, most of us are."

"I'm awake," Cherry answered. She slid off her stool and showed she could stand up on her own two legs. "See? I'm ready to go."

I wasn't. There was usually a surge of adrenaline through my body just before a special event -- a feeling of excitement. This time there was a feeling of dread.

CHAPTER THIRTY-ONE ....

The laughing gargoyle sitting on top of Preston's mailbox greeted our caravan -- first was the 'Round the World Catering van with Tony and the food, then Mother in her white Mercedes. I brought up the rear with Cherry in my Jeep. We pulled into the driveway and parked behind a shiny black hearse and a dark blue Lincoln Continental.

Two young women got out of a small, beat-up car parked on the street and came towards us. Oh, good, the servers were right on time. I waved. Mother, Cherry, and I walked to the front door, leaving Tony and the servers to unload the van. As I turned the doorknob and entered into the vestibule, butterflies took flight in my stomach.

Immediately, I felt suffocated by the fuzzy wallpaper and the dark heavy furniture. There was a recording of a string quartet playing some monotonous sounding piece, and not only was the heat turned up too high, but a fire blazed in the living room's fireplace. The thick velvet drapes blocked out any light that would have come through the front windows. A couple of table lamps had been turned on, casting the room in a soft light.

As we were hanging up our coats, the cadaverous-looking Mr. Sanoma greeted us with his skull and crossbones smile. "Ah, good to see you, Ms. Cavanaugh. You look very elegant." Just before leaving home, I had changed into a long, straight, black, wool knit dress. As usual, I had my hair in a single braid. I felt Mother preening me from behind, brushing some microscopic speck of lint off my shoulder.

Preston's lawyer motioned to the big, hulking man standing by the gleaming silver metal casket positioned at the front end of the living room. "Mr. Peeks? I would like to introduce you to the caterer, Ms. Kate Cavanaugh."

As far as appearance went, Mr. Peeks was everything Mr. Sanoma wasn't. The funeral director had pudgy round cheeks and looked like the type of guy who could break into a raucous laugh at any moment. My hand disappeared into his big paw as we looked eye-to-eye, shook, and exchanged a pleasant "Hello."

I introduced them to Mother and Cherry.

I walked up to the casket. The grand piano and the bust of Beethoven perched on the green marble pedestal had been moved into a corner to make room for Preston. There were three floral arrangements on the floor in front of the casket. I stooped to read the cards. The most lavish arrangement came from *Cincy Life* magazine; a smaller, but tasteful, display was sent by the opera board. The embarrassingly ordinary-looking one came from Preston's newspaper syndicate. There were no personal tributes at all. I straightened up and stepped back away from the flowers -- their scent was overpowering. The combination of fluttery, anxious feelings in my stomach, excess heat, and the suffocating atmosphere was making me feel nauseous.

"I thought it would be opened," I said, pointing to the casket.

Mr. Peeks replied, "The autopsy. Even with all the cosmetic

200

tricks I know, I couldn't make him look good."

I turned my gaze back to the coffin and tried to imagine what Preston looked liked. I half-expected to hear him banging away on the inside and the muffled shouts of "Let me out. I've had enough of this joke." I squeezed my eyes shut and switched channels in my head. There was a job to do.

I looked around. For the big bear he was, Mr. Peeks had disappeared very quickly and quietly. Speaking of disappearing -- where was Mother? I could see Cherry studying the strange portrait of an ugly woman, hanging in the vestibule. I walked the other way, through the living room, past the self-serve bar Robert had set up, and into the large family room area. There she was, fussing over the way Tony and Robert had arranged the tables.

"Having fun, Mother?"

"These tables are too close together. We need to leave enough room for people to walk around with their plates of food, otherwise, there's bound to be a messy accident."

"You're right. And we need room for the roving gypsy violinist, too."

Mother's brows shot up. "What?"

"By order of our deceased host."

"What kind of a wake is this?"

I told her to lodge any complaints with Mr. Sanoma, and headed for the kitchen. Just outside the kitchen door, the two servers were setting up the buffet table, and I stopped for a quick look to make sure they were doing it right. They were managing well without me. I expected Tony was, too.

I pushed through the swinging door into the kitchen and found Tony with his headphones on, bopping in front of the stove. He was obviously listening to something with a more radical beat than the deadly string quartet music that was being piped throughout the house. The ventilating fan over the range was going full blast, sounding as loud as a jet engine as it sucked up the greasy smell of the frying food. I waited until Tony had finished dumping a load of cauliflower into the deep fryer and had stepped away from the stove, before I cautiously announced my presence -- I had visions of cauliflower florets flying through the air.

Even so, he jumped a couple of inches straight up off the floor and landed, clutching his chest. "Kate," he shouted, "you're gonna give me a heart attack."

I pulled the headset away from his right ear. "No need to yell, I'm right here."

"Sorry." Tony pulled his headphones off and let them dangle around his neck. I could hear the tinny sound of a mind-numbing beat escaping from the earpieces.

"Are you ready to take care of the veal, yet?"

"Just a couple more batches of cauliflower, then I'll start it."

I opened the oven door and peeked inside. There were two hotel pans, one with the Transylvanian beef stew, and the other with stuffed cabbage. The braised red cabbage was being heated on the stove top. Great. I went over to the supply box Tony had brought from the farm, and grabbed an apron. "I'll do the puliszka."

I mixed up a paste of cornmeal and water in a bowl. Tony already had water boiling in a large sauce pot. I poured the cornmeal paste gradually into the boiling water, stirred it for a couple of minutes, and left it to simmer.

Tony leaned over, looked into the pot, and made a loud snuffing noise. "Looks like something you'd feed pigs."

"It'll thicken up. With a lot of salt and butter it'll taste great." I gave the cornmeal mush a stir. "Preston insisted that the beef stew be served with puliszka. Apparently, that's what his grandmother did. The stew smells great, Tony."

"Yeah. Guess the Dracula Special's turning out okay."

"Well, you've done a fantastic job -- just want you to know how much I appreciate your hard work."

"Thanks, Boss."

I heard the sharp *click, click, click* of Mother's heels on the tile floor. "Something smells good," she said. "The guests are beginning to arrive -- and I think your gypsy's here."

"I'll be out in a few minutes -- got to finish this." After ten minutes of watching and occasionally stirring, I added more salt and beat in a stick of butter. I scraped the mush out into a warming pan, covered it, took off my apron and went out to greet the "mourners".

"Hi, Kate," Charles Hassenbacher said, as I entered the living room. Papa Hassenbacher was already at the bar, surrounded by the usual entourage of his four notorious sons: Thomas, Carl, John, and Henry. I shook hands with each of them, and we all spent the next few minutes conversing in clichés about how shocking it was to hear of Preston's death. Over Charles' shoulder, I saw a small, bald-headed man in a frilly shirt and a bright red embroidered vest, with a purple satin cummerbund around his ample waist. He had a look on his face as though he had just been beamed down from some alien spaceship and was wondering where the hell he had landed. A violin case was cradled in the gypsy's arms. I went over and told him to get himself a drink from the bar and pointed the way to the kitchen, where he could hang out. We wouldn't need his musical contribution until the guests were all seated and eating.

I could see that Mr. Peeks was greeting people at the front door and showing them into the living room. Mabel Crank appeared to be giving him an earful of her crabbing. I couldn't actually hear her monologue, but she was emphatically waving her arms around, ashes dropping from her ever-present cigarillo.

Siegfreid Doppler waved at me as he entered the living room.

"What's this all about?" I asked, pointing to the array of expensive camera equipment hanging around his neck and over one shoulder.

"According to Mr. Sanoma," Siegfried answered, "Preston wanted me to document the event. The estate's paying me quite handsomely, so I didn't question it."

Cherry suddenly appeared next to me. "There you are, Katie. I've already screwed up and let you out of my sight. That won't happen again." She stayed a discreet two steps behind me as I made my way towards Mr. Sanoma, who was standing by Preston's casket. I wanted to find out from him when I was going to receive the rest of Preston's mysterious communications. But before I was able to get to him, Frank Meyer set up a road block.

"Can I get a beautiful woman a drink?" Frank displayed his best come-on smile.

The only thing I wanted from him was information. I grabbed his arm. "Let's go to the dining room -- I've got to talk to you." I led Frank through the vestibule, turning my head to see him swaggering triumphantly, as though he was entering my bedroom. Cherry followed, her eyes expressing a readiness to pop him one if he tried anything.

"And what do you want to do in here?" Frank said, his eyes searching for a suitable surface.

"The last time we spoke -- just a few days ago -- you told me quite a good story about why you thought Terry was guilty of Preston's murder. I wasn't convinced. You then asked me, 'Who else could have done it?' Well, I've learned a lot since then."

Frank's eyes lost some of their burning desire. "Like what?"

"Like you and Wolfie getting together and celebrating Preston's murder."

That doused his flames. "So? There are a lot of people in this city who feel the same way."

"True, but not everyone was at the church that evening. You were." I could see anger flash in Frank's eyes. Cherry the bodyguard tensed up and took a step forward. "And you had a reason," I added.

A major vein in Frank's neck began pulsing. "I'm shocked, Kate. After all these years of friendship, you think I'm capable of murder?"

204

"It's no secret," I replied, "that ever since Preston helped kill the restaurant you and Wolfie opened together, people in this city have lost confidence in your business sense. You haven't been able to get another project off the ground."

Frank jabbed his thick forefinger at me. "I don't deserve this kind of treatment and I don't know where you get off playing detective. No. Wait a minute. I know -- it's that tall policeman -- what was his name? ...Skinner. It's hard to find guys bigger than you, isn't it." He smirked. "This is some weird way you have of flirting with him, feeding him information so that he could solve the first murder in Clairmont and be a hero."

For a guy, Frank was being real catty and I wanted to hit him. But more than that, I wanted to hear his alibi.

Frank started pacing back and forth and cracking his knuckles. "You want to know what I did Thursday night? I'll tell you. At seven o'clock I entered the side door that leads directly into the church's basement meeting room. I sat in the finance committee meeting for two hours. At nine o'clock, we adjourned and I went upstairs with Pastor Luebens and James Wagner, to listen to the choir rehearsal for a few minutes. They were still practicing when Pastor Luebens and I went to his office in the Welcome Center to discuss some of his personal finance matters. We wrapped things up at about nine forty-five. I got in my car and drove home. But I wasn't the last one to leave the church. Holly Berry-Wagner's and James Wagner's cars were still in the parking lot."

Frank stopped pacing, and looked directly at me. "You know, I got an invitation to this wake and I didn't really want to come. Everything connected with Preston always turned out rotten, and this is really starting to stink, too. But I've come to find out why he invited me -- his lawyer said there'll be a full explanation ... and I'm going to the burial service afterwards to make sure that bastard Preston is actually put into the ground."

CHAPTER THIRTY-TWO ....

"...and bless this food we are about to eat. Amen." Pastor Luebens had strategically placed himself in front of the buffet table just before saying grace. He turned, picked up a plate, smiled at the servers, and accepted with enthusiasm a helping of each dish.

I watched the other guests as they, too, picked up plates and started moving alongside the buffet table. Every one of them wore the same quizzical expression when they got their first look at the food. One of the servers plopped a scoopful of puliszka onto Mabel Crank's plate. Mabel's apple doll face scrunched up even more than usual. "What's this? Looks like corn mush."

James Wagner spoke up. "Kate? What is the theme of this repast?"

"Hungarian," I said.

"And why did you choose that?" James asked.

"It was Preston's choice. Seems that he wanted to share the culinary joys of his Hungarian roots."

Mother came up beside me, reached across the buffet table,

and delicately touched James' arm with her fingertips. "I thought it sounded awfully common, myself -- but then I sneaked a taste in the kitchen. It's wonderful. Reminds me of the meals my mother's cook used to make for us when I was a little girl."

I almost choked on the lump that suddenly formed in my throat. I wished I could replay Mother's statement, just to make sure that I had heard it correctly. It was the first time she had voiced anything positive about one of my events, in my presence. I felt a little tear trickle out the corner of my eye.

Mother looked at me. "Are you all right, dear? You sure you're up to this?"

I swallowed the lump and nodded. "I'm fine."

I surveyed the guests, who were now all seated and appeared to be enjoying their food tremendously. Mabel Crank seemed especially entranced by the gypsy violinist's flamboyantly romantic playing. Maybe there *was* something that could soothe her crotchety soul. Frank Meyer was doing all he could to avoid looking at me.

The tables weren't full, but, aside from Terry and Marilyn, I couldn't tell who was missing -- even at that point I hadn't seen the guest list.

"Ms. Cavanaugh."

I turned and saw Mr. Sanoma coming toward me. "I'm not expecting any more arrivals after this point," he said. "Seems we have nine no-shows."

"Well, there's plenty of food," I said, "help yourself to whatever you want, and ask Mr. Peeks to come and join us."

"Thank you." Mr. Sanoma gave me a little bow with his head. "That's most gracious of you."

I left my post behind the buffet table, and went over to greet the people I hadn't had a chance to speak with. As Yogi Berra would put it: "It was déjà vu all over again." James Wagner, Walter

"King" Yankovitch, Mabel Crank, Charles Hassenbacher, and Mother gathered at one table. Judging from their conversation, they all considered themselves good friends of Preston's -- though Mabel Crank did manage to get in her obsessive complaint about Preston not liking the brand of hot dogs she sold at her hockey games.

I moved over to the second table and greeted Nate Wagner and his wife Holly, Patrick and Eleanor Sloane, and Pastor Luebens. You'd think they'd all feel comfortable together, having the choir and church in common. But, strangely, the chit chat was tense.

It didn't look any better over at table three. Wolfie and Frank Meyer sat on one side of the round table and the four Hassenbacher brothers huddled together on the other side. There was no conversation whatsoever -- just six forks shoving food into six mouths.

This is a strange party you're throwing, I silently commented to Preston, just in case he was listening.

It was getting onto one o'clock and I was starving. I grabbed a plate and helped myself to everything on the buffet table. *Click!* Siegfried Doppler's camera caught me stuffing a gigantic piece of cauliflower into my mouth. I mumbled a protest between chews and retreated to the kitchen.

Cherry's raucous laugh sounded through the swinging door just before I pushed it open. Both she and Tony looked up in surprise when I entered. It appeared that Cherry was demonstrating some more of her self-defense tactics -- but I didn't ask.

Tony climbed up from his kneeling position on the floor. "Are they stuffing themselves out there?"

"Yeah. They're having a good ol' time." I set my plate down on the small kitchen table and sat between Mr. Sanoma and Mr. Peeks.

"This is great food," Mr. Peeks said.

"Yes," Mr. Sanoma added. "Quite delicious."

I nodded towards Tony. "Thank the chef over there -- he's done all the work." I swallowed a mouthful of stew, and said, "By the way, Tony, have you and Cherry eaten anything?"

"Picked at it while I was cooking," Tony replied.

"I didn't understand the cornmeal mush," Cherry said, "but I pigged out on everything else."

Mr. Sanoma looked at his watch, patted the corners of his lips with a napkin, and stood up. "It's time, Mr. Peeks."

Time? "Time for what?"

"We're all to gather in the living room," the lawyer announced. "Mr. Peeks, will you help move some of the folding chairs?"

I started following the two out the door.

Tony pointed to Cherry and himself. "Are we supposed to come?"

"Don't know," I said, shrugging my shoulders. "But you might as well -- it's bound to be interesting."

Mr. Sanoma was already herding the guests into the living room. "What's this?" "What are we doing now?" rippled through the gathering. Mr. Peeks grabbed two armloads of folding chairs, took them into the living room and set them up in front of the casket.

"Take a seat wherever you can," Mr. Sanoma instructed the guests. "Just make sure you're facing the casket."

I stood in the back of the living room with Cherry and Tony, and listened to the hubbub of grumbling and complaining as everyone else tried to sort out who got to sit where. It was like some crazy, confused game of musical chairs. When Mr. Sanoma rolled in a VCR stand and a large TV monitor, it was as if the music had stopped -- they each plopped into the nearest seat and gave him their full attention.

I guessed the equipment must have been stored in the dining room, but I hadn't noticed it when I was in there -- my conversation with Frank Meyer had required my total focus.

The way Mr. Sanoma positioned the VCR stand behind the casket, the TV monitor looked as though it was sitting on top of the casket itself. Noting that all eyes were on him, the lawyer loaded a video cassette into the VCR and, without any preamble, pressed the play button.

A closeup of Preston Schneider, looking smug and pleased with himself, appeared on the TV monitor. I quickly moved up as close as I could, without blocking anyone's line of vision. As the camera pulled back, we could see that Preston was dressed in a tuxedo and sitting in the easy chair in his office. Showing himself to be calm and in control, he reached over to the table beside him, picked up a bottle of champagne, and poured out a glass. We all watched in tense silence as he slowly took a sip, closed his eyes, and savored it. Preston had always enjoyed playing with people's minds.

Finally, he looked out at his audience and spoke. "At this very moment, my publisher's probably going crazy, pulling together a quick ad campaign to take advantage of my murder. I'm assuming I did not die of natural causes.

"Well, I don't think it'll mess up their plans if I reveal to you, my good friends, a little secret identity I've kept hidden for a number of years." Preston raised his glass of champagne in a toast. "To that indefatigable defender of truth, that bestselling author: me -- otherwise known as Wagging Tongue."

Preston tilted his head back and proceeded to drain the contents of his glass.

Charles Hassenbacher jumped to his feet. "That goddam sonofabitch." Obscenities were hurled at the TV screen by the rest of the Hassenbacher clan.

Walter Yankovitch yelled, "We've been inviting this bastard into our homes, calling him a friend, and all he did in return is betray us. Those mudslinging books of his are an abomination."

Mabel Crank rasped, "What the hell does 'indefatigable' mean?"

I don't know why I never suspected Preston of being Wagging Tongue before, but it certainly didn't surprise me. I looked at Mother, who was sitting on the brocade sofa. Her face was white with shock. She stared at the TV, frozen in place, her hand clutching at her throat. Preston had started speaking again, but I couldn't hear him above the shouts of indignation and profanity. I turned to Tony and Cherry, who appeared to be thoroughly enjoying themselves watching the commotion caused by Preston's nose-thumbing from beyond the grave.

Mr. Sanoma rushed to the front of the room and waved his arms in an attempt to quiet the outraged guests. He paused the tape. "Ladies and gentlemen, please control yourselves. Our time is limited and Mr. Schneider has a very important statement to make."

"He's dead -- who cares?" Wolfie shouted.

"Quiet. Please." Mr. Sanoma continued waving his arms. Finally, the angry mob settled back into their seats, and Mr. Sanoma rewound the tape to where Preston swallowed the last of his champagne and was getting ready to speak again.

Preston said, "Undoubtedly, you're all wondering as to my reasons for inviting you to this wake. I hope you enjoyed your lunch -- I've no doubt you did. Thank you, Kate, for your usual excellence."

I turned to Tony and gave him a Thank You wink.

Preston cleared his throat and continued. "Most of you have a motive for killing me. One of you probably has committed the act -- or maybe you've all pooled your resentment and resources and hired a thug to actually pull the trigger, or throw me in the Ohio River with cement shoes on my feet, or do me in with whatever other cliché method there is for committing cold-blooded murder.

"I'm sure each of you would like to be thought of as a highly moral, selfless leader of our community. But as I see it, most of you are being ruled by your love of money and motivated by greed, and I suspect you will stop at nothing to protect your reputations. You all want to look so proper and upstanding, but I have seen what's underneath your expensive facades.

"Let me begin with Mr. Patrick Sloane." Preston paused. I and everyone else in the room turned to look at his first suspect.

Patrick sat, rigid in his chair, eyes fixed on the TV screen. Eleanor Sloane stared at her husband, a silent "What?" on her face.

We all looked back at Preston as he continued. "This good old boy from Dallas comes riding into town with his sights set on being the next president of Rodger's, America's friendly grocery megastore conglomerate. Now you'd think Patrick would be a pretty smart guy -- what with him not only getting this far up the corporate food chain, but also having the good sense to marry a woman whose family is soaking in old oil money. Guess again. Like most cowboys reaching his age, Patrick needs to prove he hasn't lost any of his stud appeal. Unfortunately for him, my little spy network discovered his secret trysts -- including the latest one with Holly Berry-Wagner."

Eleanor screeched and swung her fleshy, dimpled elbow, smashing Patrick under his chin. Holly jumped up and screamed, "You're evil!" at the TV monitor.

Preston's video kept playing. "Sloane found out I wouldn't take a bribe -- I wanted the power to rub a rich person's nose in the truth."

James Wagner's face was flushed red as he shook his fist at Preston's image. "Liar. Must we stand for all this outrageous mud-slinging gossip?"

What happened next was so weird and unbelievable. Preston's wake had felt pretty creepy, but then I watched it degenerate into a Wrestlemania Main Event.

Suddenly, Nate Wagner, screaming a blood-thirsty yell, rushed across the living room and leaped onto the back of Patrick Sloane. Shy, wimpy Nate Wagner was like a person possessed, his slender fists pummeling the much bigger man.

They fell to the floor. First Nate was on top of Patrick, then Patrick was on top of Nate as they rolled towards the coffin. They slammed into the floral displays, knocking them over, and, at one point, the casket shook violently from the force of their bodies hitting its stand.

I yelled, "Someone stop them."

Mr. Peeks grabbed Patrick, pinning his arms behind him. Nate scurried away, towards the grand piano. He picked up the heavy bust of Beethoven and hurled it. I assumed he was aiming for Patrick, but Nate, not being the athletic type, didn't have control of his curve ball. In a sense, Preston died a second time when Beethoven hit his TV image -- right between the eyes. Thousands of tiny shards of glass showered down onto the top of the casket.

Nate flung himself again at Patrick, who was still in the clutches of Mr. Peeks. The three went down, with Nate on top swinging away at Sloane's face, bloodying his nose. Everybody was crowding around, like a bunch of kids watching a schoolyard fight. I went off to the kitchen to get some ice and a wet cloth. On re-entering the living room, I saw that two of the Hassenbacher brothers had managed to pry Nate off of Patrick, and Pastor Luebens was standing between the two fighters.

"Let's be reasonable," Pastor Luebens said. "Preston Schneider said some very disturbing things. But," he turned to Nate, "we don't know that it's true -- at this point, it's only gossip. Even so --"

"No it isn't," yelled Nate, "I've seen the way Patrick looks at Holly. I've suspected it for a long time."

I caught a faint whiff of what smelled like hot plastic, and figured it must have been coming from the blown-out TV monitor. Mother was comforting Holly, who was crying into a fistful of tissues. I passed by them and went up to Nate, gave him some ice wrapped in a towel for his swelling eye, and handed Patrick the wet cloth to wipe up his bloody nose. The two men glared at each other, but Pastor Luebens addressed all of us. "Even so, we should stay calm and hear Preston out -- apparently he had something to say to the rest of us."

Mr. Sanoma nodded in agreement. "That is my understanding." The lawyer walked around to the far side of the casket to the VCR stand. "There is another setup we can watch this

213

tape on. If you will all kindly adjourn to the game room downstairs, I will ... Oh, my!" Mr. Sanoma's finger hit the eject button on the video player several times. "It won't come out." He poked his finger into the cassette slot. His eyes widened. "It's gone!"

A connection was made in my brain -- that strange smell. I rushed to the fireplace. Globs of black plastic sizzled and dripped off of the logs. What had been the tape was now shriveling into tiny bits of ash. The others crowded around the fireplace. I pointed to the sticky mess. "There go Preston's final words."

"Good," said Charles Hassenbacher with a satisfied nod. "Just a pack of lies, anyway."

I said, "Did anyone see who did this?"

"If I did," Charles answered, "I'd say 'Thank you. You've done us all a great favor.'"

Mother slowly shook her head. "But now we'll never know what he had to say."

"And the world will be a much happier place." Charles smiled and indicated to his sons it was time for them to leave. As they headed for the vestibule and their coats, everyone else started moving around and making noises as if they, too, were going to leave.

Pastor Luebens held up his hand. "Wait. Don't just leave like this. A burial service is scheduled in half an hour at the Gate of Heaven cemetery, and I was hoping to see some of you there."

"I'll be there," Wolfie said, as he pulled on his overcoat. Then he walked up to me and added, "Just want to make sure that SOB gets planted six feet under."

I wasn't even sure I wanted to go to the burial service. I felt disgusted, angry, sad, and downright shitty. There've been times when I questioned what I was doing in Clairmont -- and this was definitely one of those times. I just wanted to get the hell out. Cherry was leaning on the piano, watching. I felt compelled to go over to her and whisper, "Let's get on your bike and go to New Orleans." But that wasn't going to resolve anything. Instead, I said,

"Preston's killer must be getting desperate."

"Why do you say that?" Cherry asked.

"The killer is trying to destroy any information that might point to him -- or her."

"Yeah," said Cherry, "and that sweet, lovable Preston seems to have left incriminating information all over the place."

"I've got to get into those locked computer files. The same person who knocked me out in Preston's office must be the same person who just threw the video tape into the fireplace."

"And that has to be the killer," we both said at the same time.

I just hoped Julie Ann's code-breaking abilities were better than the Clairmont Police Department's.

CHAPTER THIRTY-THREE ....

"Ashes to ashes, dust to dust..." *Rumble! Screech!* "...our stay on this earth is so short..." *Bang! Bang! Bang!*

Pastor Luebens' words of comfort were lost in the cacophony of construction noises. We were standing in a cold drizzle that was half rain, half ice. On top of that, we were surrounded by earth movers, cranes, and dump trucks. Everything was awash with slimy red mud as a crew worked on the new Meditation Garden addition to the All Saints cemetery. They had already dumped enough loads of dirt to create three new small hills, and were carving out one large, kidney-shaped pond.

I couldn't hear half of what Pastor Luebens was saying, but I could read Mother's lips as she mouthed "This is dreadful" to me. I nodded in agreement, but thought that at least she was standing next to King Yankovitch, under his bright red and yellow striped golf umbrella. The rest of us: Frank Meyer, Wolfie, Mr. Sanoma, Mr. Peeks, Cherry, and I were wet and miserable.

Thankfully, Pastor Luebens' message was short and, I think, sweet. We didn't actually see Preston buried -- that was to be done later. Everyone seemed anxious to get back to their cars, and barely said goodbye to one another before driving off in different directions.

216

"That's the weirdest funeral I've ever been to," Cherry said, as we buckled ourselves into the Jeep. "I don't understand how you could have been friends with that Schneider guy. I mean, like what I saw on that tape was totally obnoxious."

I nodded. "You're right. He was. I never realized until the last few days how mean he was to people. I'd like to wash my hands of the whole thing, but I've got to get into that computer."

We swung out onto Montgomery Road and headed south to Clairmont. I looked at Cherry out of the corner of my eye. "If you don't mind, I'd like to stop at Preston's for a few minutes. I have to check that everything's been cleaned up. Besides, I've just had a hunch on how to get into that T-File."

Ten minutes later, I pulled into Preston's empty driveway. My catering van and the servers' car were gone, and I found that Tony had locked the front door by pushing in the button on the doorknob. Mr. Sanoma and I were the only ones who had keys.

We did a quick tour around the downstairs. Tony and the two servers had been very efficient in cleaning up. The kitchen was spotless, the glass from the broken TV monitor in the living room had been swept off the floor, and the fire in the fireplace was out.

Cherry held up the bust of Beethoven. "Look, Ludwig's nose is busted. The poor guy couldn't hear, and now he can't smell." She placed him back up onto his pedestal next to the grand piano.

I made a face at her. "C'mon. Let's go upstairs and try out my bright idea."

My stomach pulled into a nervous little cramp, just before we entered the office. I hesitated at the door.

"What's the matter?" Cherry asked.

"Ghosts." I said, and forced myself into the room, sat down at the computer and switched it on. "Okay." I rubbed my hands together. "Here we go."

Cherry hung over my shoulder and watched as I typed in the words "Wagging Tongue."

CHAPTER THIRTY-FOUR ....

I flipped the last banana pancake over on the griddle, and put the warmed maple syrup on the kitchen table in front of Cherry, who did nothing to stifle a huge, slow yawn. Boo-Kat was lying, curled up, at her feet. He lifted his head and opened his mouth in a yawn just as wide, but much noisier and ending in a little squeak.

I, too, was suddenly overcome by a yawn, which was not surprising since I had been up half the night playing basketball, trying to work off my frustration.

Cherry propped her head on one fist. "Did you come up with any other ideas?"

"No," I said, and dished out the pancakes onto two plates. Wagging Tongue was not the key to unlocking the T-File. I watched Cherry take her first mouthful of pancake.

"What do you think?" I asked.

"Well, it's good, but it doesn't taste the same as the ones we had in India."

"Maybe I need to squat down on a dirt floor and cook them

218

over a little fire." I reached for the maple syrup. "We can't get jaggery here -- that would probably make a big difference."

"Oh, yeah ... what *was* that stuff? We poured it on everything."

"It's kind of like maple syrup, but it has a different taste 'cause it's made from palm tree sap."

We each wolfed down six pancakes, and Boo-Kat made out okay, too, with both Cherry and I slipping him little nibbles.

Cherry gulped a mouthful of coffee. "So, what's on today's agenda?"

"We're going to be detectives for real. After what happened yesterday, the only surviving solid lead Preston has left us is the affair between Holly Berry-Wagner and Patrick Sloane."

"Well, I think Patrick is the killer."

"Oh? Based on what evidence, Ms. Holmes?"

"Wasn't Preston holding onto a ring with the initials PS? There you go -- Patrick Sloane. Case closed."

I started clearing dishes from the table. "That's not the type of evidence that'll hold up in court. Not in comparison with what the Rangers have against Terry Poole. So go put on something presentable, we're going visiting."

My conscience had a brief struggle with itself, as I steered the Jeep down Drake Road, past the soccer fields and the Village Municipal Building that was located in the heart of Clairmont. I was about to commit a major no-no: paying a social visit without first calling ahead. But this really wasn't a social visit -- it was an inquiry in disguise. I couldn't let on that I was suspecting Holly might have something to do with Preston's murder. There might have been a confrontation between the two of them after rehearsal over her affair with Patrick Sloane. I was going there under the pretense of seeing if she and Nate were all right after yesterday's outrageous happenings. I had to be cool about it. What I might find out could help clear Terry.

We sped down the long driveway between monstrous pine

trees, coming to a halt in front of a newly built mini-mansion. Two-story Palladian windows sparkled in the sunlight and I wondered how much it cost to keep them clean.

"Wow." Cherry looked down at her black leather pants and jacket, and then at me. "Am I presentable enough?"

"Yeah, you're fine." I hadn't exactly dressed up, myself. My idea of presentable consisted of clean blue jeans, a maroon chenille tunic sweater, and my green parka.

The doorbell bonged once when I pressed it. Hmm, classy sound. Someone peered out one of the two long, narrow windows that flanked the polished oak door. A second later, the door was opened. Holly greeted us with a vibrant smile that was totally out of character. I almost didn't recognize her. She was wearing some sort of floaty, filmy, mint green bedroom attire.

"Oh," I said, "I'm sorry. I should have called first."

Holly opened the door wider. "No. Don't apologize. What a wonderful surprise. Come in, come in." And as we did, she called back over her shoulder, "Nate, darling, we have visitors."

This show of warm hospitality was not what I expected. And what was this "Nate, darling?" I looked over at Cherry and raised my eyebrows. Cherry shrugged. We followed Holly as she fluttered into the family room. Nate stood up from the long leather sofa in front of the roaring fireplace. He was also dressed somewhat exotically in silk paisley pajamas and a royal blue silk dressing gown. Still, he held out his hand and shook mine, as if he were greeting me in his best blue and white pinstripe suit.

"Please ... join us for coffee," Nate said, indicating where we should sit.

Cherry and I plopped down onto a flowered chintz love seat. "Thanks," I said, "but we've just had breakfast." I cleared my throat. "We came calling just to make sure everything was okay. You know ... after yesterday ... it was a strange, upsetting thing that happened at Preston's wake."

But as I said that, I realized that these two people snuggling

220

together on the sofa were far from upset.

"Oh, we've gotten over that," Holly said in a buoyant tone of voice. "But it was kind of awful, wasn't it? I've never seen my husband act in such a surprising manner." She smiled at Nate and gave his arm a squeeze.

Cherry's body hiccuped beside me, as she stifled a laugh. Just as I was wondering how to direct the conversation, Holly took off in a monologue that answered almost all of my questions.

"That whole affair with Patrick Sloane was a terrible mistake -- I was being very foolish. It started out innocently enough. It was a hot summer night after choir practice -- just this past summer -- you know that little place near the church where you can get frozen yogurt cones?"

I nodded.

"Well Patrick was going on and on about how good the raspberry yogurt was, and did I want to come with him and get some. Patrick can make anything sound irresistible. He kind of gets gushy for a man -- you know what I mean, Kate."

This time I just smiled.

"Well, anyway. The raspberry yogurt was good, and we started going there every week after choir practice. I think I made Patrick feel young -- we kind of clicked and laughed a lot when we were together. One thing led to another and we started going to this ---"

"Holly," I held my hand up, "you don't need to tell me any of this."

Her face flushed a little. She pulled her long, thick, brown hair into a ponytail over her shoulder and twisted it, while she spoke. "It's funny how things turn out. It's never what you expect. I pictured Nate and me raising a family, going on trips together. I was going to get involved in the PTA -- I had it all worked out. But then we didn't have any children -- and Nate's business became more and more demanding, and it seemed he could never get away."

Holly let go of her hair, laid her hands on her lap and

221

looked at me. "You seemed to have accomplished what you wanted to, Kate. You must be very happy."

I hoped she wouldn't make me respond to that.

Holly's face brightened and she pulled herself up straight. "Well, things are going to be different from now on." She glanced sideways at Nate and smiled. "We've made a new beginning -- and I've already told Patrick it's over."

I needed some hard information and figured this was my opportunity. "How did Preston find out about your affair?"

"I don't know. And it wasn't until your mother's luncheon that Patrick told me Preston had found out what we were doing."

So that's what they were up to in my guest's bedroom. I still felt it was safe to ask one more question. "Were you and Patrick together last Thursday night after choir practice when Preston was killed?"

Holly's forehead creased into a slight frown. I wondered if I'd blown it. But then she answered, "We didn't do anything -- just drove around in his car for about an hour and talked. Then Patrick dropped me off at my car in the church's parking lot and I drove home. As I pulled out of the lot, I noticed he was walking back towards the sanctuary. When I got home, Nate was sitting up, waiting for me as usual."

Nate, in his characteristic silence, had been watching Holly the whole time she related her story. But then -- *surprise* -- he spoke. "Darling, there was nothing usual about that night." Nate turned to me. "My sweet little wife is hearing this for the first time."

Holly's smile clicked off and a puzzled expression took its place, but Nate's arm around her shoulder seemed to reassure her. "For months, I'd been torn between being suspicious of Holly and wanting to trust her. That night, I was in a particularly distrustful frame of mind." He looked at Holly. "So I followed you to church and waited in the parking lot. I was surprised that you even went there -- I figured going to choir practice was just an excuse to get out of the house and you'd be heading somewhere else."

Holly stared at her husband, her eyes wide.

"After sitting in the parking lot and freezing my buns off for half an hour, I decided I was just being paranoid. Besides, I was beginning to feel pretty stupid about the whole thing. So I went home. When you showed up an hour later than usual, I actually believed your story about the dress rehearsal taking an extra hour."

Holly didn't say anything, but instead seemed to fix her eyes on her embroidered slippers. We all sat in silence and I found myself studying my own footwear, waiting for the awkward moment to pass. She raised her head, chewed on her lower lip, and said, "It was shocking to find out about Preston's death the next morning. And then to hear a couple of days later that Terry was arrested ..." Holly leaned forward towards me. "But I did see those two argue and I could just feel the antagonistic energy zapping back and forth between them throughout the evening. I know Terry's a dear friend of yours, Kate, but the Rangers wouldn't have arrested him, if they didn't have enough evidence."

Another awkward moment passed as I swallowed my outrage at the thought that someone who had dealt with Terry on a regular basis could say that he was capable of killing. It was my turn to redirect the conversation. "I guess you might say that Preston did you two a great service by spilling the beans yesterday."

Holly laughed. "It's a funny way to find out that your husband really does care about you after all. I've listened to women talk about this sort of thing on those awful talk shows on TV, but I thought they were all staged."

So that's how she spends her time.

"I feel so free knowing that it's all over and I don't have to slink around and lie about what I'm doing. But there's still one problem we have to deal with -- James."

"James?" I asked. "What does he have to do with any of this?"

"Well ..." Holly sighed and looked to her husband.

Nate accepted the verbal baton. "James is quite proud of the

Wagner family's spotless reputation." He took a breath and was about to continue, but Holly jumped in.

"I'm the bad guy now -- the first one to bring scandal into this family. James is so concerned about what everyone in Clairmont is going to think. For crying out loud, every family has its problems -- it's not the end of the world. But I know he's going to make things miserable for me." Holly put her hands to her face.

Nate hugged her close. "Don't worry, Hol -- I'll talk to him."

CHAPTER THIRTY-FIVE ....

Cherry and I left the two love birds in their nest and headed down Drake Road towards the "poorer" section of Clairmont.

"So," asked Cherry, "is Holly still on your suspect list?"

I groaned. "I ... No ... Guess not. She seemed pretty honest about the situation -- I didn't get the feeling that she was covering up anything."

Cherry slapped her hand on the dashboard. "I'm telling ya, Katie, it's Patrick Sloane."

I turned right on Shawnee Run. "Well, he could have had the opportunity to attack Preston."

"Holly saw him going back into the church as she drove out of the parking lot and headed for home."

"Hmmm, then he might have been leaving the sanctuary, heard Terry, then decided to come right back inside and pretend to 'discover' Terry standing over Preston."

I made another right.

"Hey," Cherry shouted, "isn't this the street that Preston's house is on?"

"Yeah, the Sloanes are a couple of blocks down." And Patrick was jogging in the neighborhood, just an hour before my head got bashed in. I had to admit that the pieces of the puzzle were beginning to fit together and it was looking more and more like him.

"Oooh." Cherry shook my arm and almost made me lose control of the wheel.

"What?"

"It's your sexy Ranger."

There he was, Matt Skinner, in his snappy green Clairmont Ranger uniform, coming out of the front door of the Sloane's brick colonial home. As he descended the steps, he put on his wide-brimmed Smokey Bear hat and headed towards a green Clairmont Ranger patrol car in the driveway. Despite my anger at him, my hormones surged. I couldn't put the brakes on that, but I brought the Jeep to a halt in front of the house, and sat, waiting for Skinner to pull out.

"See? I told ya." Cherry pointed at the patrol car. "Your Ranger's come to arrest Patrick Sloane."

There wasn't anyone in the patrol car, and Skinner was standing by the driver's door. I said, "He's leaving ... I think ... What's he doing?"

"He's waiting for us. C'mon, Katie."

This wasn't on my agenda for today. But then, what was he doing here if he had an open and shut case against Terry? I jumped out of the car and walked briskly towards him. I heard Cherry slam the passenger door and the heavy, clunky sound of her cowboy boots on the pavement behind me.

"Ms. Cavanaugh, I knew we'd meet again." Skinner's eyes were warm and friendly -- there was something sort of teddy bearish about them.

I felt the corners of my lips lifting into a smile, but I managed to keep from breaking into an embarrassing schoolgirl grin. "I'm visiting a friend. What're you doing? Here on business?"

"In light of some new information, I'm conducting more interviews."

"Oh." This time I didn't put the breaks on my smile. "I thought you already had your man."

Skinner arched an eyebrow. "Can't leave any loose ends dangling. Preston Schneider's lawyer told me what happened at the wake yesterday. Sure wish I knew what else was on that tape. Maybe I should be interviewing *you*, Ms. Cavanaugh. After all, weren't you a close friend of the victim -- good chance he told you what he was going to say."

I was speechless for a moment. That moment quickly passed. "Believe me, Ranger Skinner, if I knew what dirt Preston had on his potential killers, I'd have been pounding on your door the moment I heard that he'd been murdered, and I'd be pointing to all sorts of people other than Terry Poole."

I'd had enough of this conversation, said a curt "Now, if you'll excuse me," and marched up the pathway to the front door.

Cherry tugged on the back of my parka and asked, "Why do you always get so pissed off at him?"

I slammed the door knocker three times. Immediately, the door opened and Patrick was grinning at us. "I saw you out the window, Kate. Hi there, Cherry." He stepped back and motioned for us to "C'mon in." As I closed the door behind us, I saw Skinner's patrol car pull out of the driveway.

Patrick led us into the living room, his orange and black nylon jogging suit making a swishing noise as he walked. "So, what did I do to deserve a visit from two beautiful women? Sorry about the mess. Take a seat wherever you can find one."

There were a couple of duffel bags on the sofa with a pile of clothing in between them. A newspaper lay open on an easy chair, its pages sliding down onto the floor, and a second sofa had been taken over by two enormous white Persian cats. Patrick gathered up the newspaper and swatted the cats with it. Cherry and I took their places. White fur floated down onto our laps.

I said, "I just wanted to see if everything was okay between you and Eleanor after yesterday."

"Ha. Well, it's not." Patrick filled the easy chair with his bulk. He gestured towards the duffel bags on the sofa with a lift of his chin. "I've been sent packing -- for now, anyway. Eleanor says she can't stand the sight of me."

"I'm sorry to hear that." I paused a beat. "We ran into Ranger Skinner out in your driveway ..."

"Yeah." Patrick waved his hand in disgust. "As if I didn't have enough problems. He's busy snooping around some more -- turns out Preston's lawyer went blabbing to the police about the video. I don't see what bearing that has on anything."

Whoever threw the tape into the fireplace sure did.

Patrick slammed a fist into his palm. "That Skinner questioned me all over again about Thursday night. This time I added a few details I didn't think he needed to know the first time he questioned me."

"Like driving around with Holly after the rehearsal, instead of going for cheese cake?"

Patrick eyed me a little sheepishly. "You been talking with Hol?"

I nodded.

"Well, it still doesn't change anything. I told the rest of the story the same way I told it the first time. I still say I was going into the church to look for my scarf when I saw Terry standing over Preston." Patrick paused for a moment and looked past me and at something over my right shoulder. "Come to think of it, if Terry hadn't been arrested, and after Preston's blabbing yesterday, by now I'd probably be the next logical suspect."

He already was in my books. I bit on my lip. "By the way.... remember a couple of days ago when we saw each other? You were jogging, and I was on my way to Preston's?"

"Yeah?"

"Did you see anyone else around his house -- someone who wouldn't normally be there? Any unusual activity or strange-looking people in the neighborhood?"

Patrick shook his head and frowned. "Nah. I was on my way home when you saw me. I didn't notice anything when I went past earlier."

This was a waste of time. The only thing I got out of him was an admission that he'd lied to me earlier. It was time to wrap this up gracefully and get out.

I heard the sound of someone coming in the front door and slamming it shut.

"Are you still here?" It was Eleanor. "I thought I told you I didn't want to see you when I came home." She stomped into the room, her face red, and she pulled up short when she saw us. "Oh. Hi, Kate. Hello, Cherry."

As though on cue, Cherry and I immediately got to our feet. "Well," I said, as we quickly made our way to the door, "it's been nice talking with you, Patrick. Take care, Eleanor."

No sooner were we out the door, than I could hear the Battling Sloanes having a discussion at the top of their lungs, with Patrick wishing that "I *had* killed Preston *before* he had recorded that goddam video."

As we drove away, some new thoughts flashed through my head. Holly was fearful of James Wagner and what he might do to her in reaction to her affair. Patrick had to contend with Eleanor and the possibility of losing her family's financial resources. Both felt they had something to lose if their affair was exposed.

Maybe Patrick and Holly had conspired to commit murder last Thursday night and were covering up for each other?

CHAPTER THIRTY-SIX ....

Phoebe Jo ladled steaming porridge into thick, white, stoneware bowls. "Will Cherry be joining us for breakfast?"

"I don't think so," I said. "The last couple of days getting up early to be on the job as my bodyguard have left her suffering from sleep deprivation. I'm just going to leave her alone."

"You two sure are opposites, aren't you?" Robert had poured himself a cup of coffee and was sitting down at the breakfast table. "Must've been kinda difficult living together and traveling through all those weird places."

"Yeah, that's what made it so much fun," I said, pouring a thick covering of maple syrup over the top of my porridge. "We sure had a lot of laughs. I'm gonna miss her when she goes."

"Cherry's leaving? Oh, no." Julie Ann had rushed into the kitchen and grabbed her box of Sugar Smacks out of the cupboard, letting the door slam. "When's that happening?"

"Tomorrow morning," I replied, and began eating my porridge.

"Julie Ann," Phoebe Jo chided, "what in Heaven's name's got you so excitable?"

I turned to see Julie Ann mopping up a puddle of milk that was dribbling off the counter. "Oh, this stupid thing's too full," she said, twisting the cap back on the milk bottle and shoving it back into the refrigerator.

As Julie Ann picked up her bowl of cereal, she accidentally flicked the spoon out of the bowl and onto the floor. Sugar Smacks and milk splattered across the tiles, and Boo-Kat scrambled out from some corner and licked it up as if he hadn't seen food in days.

Julie Ann rushed over to the table and plunked herself down beside me. "Oh, Kate, I'm so excited."

"How come?"

"I've been working on Preston Schneider's computer code. And you won't *believe* this --" Julie Ann shook her head so hard, her glasses slid down her nose. "I've cracked it."

"You have? That's fantastic." I grabbed her skinny little face and planted a big smacking kiss on her forehead. "So, what is it?"

Julie Ann shoved a spoonful of cereal into her mouth and started chewing. My heart was pounding so hard I could hear it in my ears. Finally, she swallowed and said, "It was really tough figuring it out. That book about codes was really hard to understand sometimes. I had to figure out if there was any pattern to the letters you gave me, so I tried to think like my computer -- you know -- super logical. It looked like it was all one word, because there weren't any spaces. And the numbers 1 and 2 had me stumped for a long time."

"Yeah, Julie Ann -- Ranger Skinner and I were stumped, too." She was driving me nuts with this rambling preamble to her solution, but I knew it was important for her to let me know how hard she worked and the young mathematician in her needed to explain in a step-by-step process how she came to her conclusion.

Phoebe Jo pointed to the wall clock. "Don't take too long,

Julie Ann -- the school bus will be here in ten minutes."

Julie Ann pulled out a notepad from her backpack and wrote down SSEIVNESN-1-2. She continued. "From what I read in the book, I figured the '-1-2' had some relationship with the letters before them. There were so many possibilities, and I filled pages and pages before I finally decided it probably wasn't that complicated after all.

"Here, I'll show you." She wrote as she spoke. "-1 means you start with the first letter. And then the -2 means you write down every second letter. That's what I did, and look what I got."

I stared at what Julie Ann had written.

She said, "S-E-V-E-N -- leaving me with the letters S-I-N-S."

"SEVEN SINS." I turned to Phoebe Jo. "What *are* the seven sins, anyway?"

Phoebe Jo's forehead wrinkled as she thought for a moment. "I'm probably not remembering this exactly right, but they're things like ..." She began counting off on her fingers. "Pride, Deceit, Murder, Gluttony, Envy, Lust, and Hatred."

That was just like Preston -- he never missed an opportunity to point a finger and express his opinion.

The phone rang and Robert answered it with a "G'morning -- Cavanaugh residence." Someone on the other end said something that made him frown. "Just a moment." He covered the receiver's mouthpiece and, as he walked towards me, announced, "It's the Wagner woman and she sounds awful upset."

The Wagner woman? Who's ...? Oh, right -- Holly. But she hardly ever called. "I'll take it in the other room."

Julie Ann jumped up. "I'm gonna miss my bus. Bye, Kate."

I gave her a big hug. "Thanks, you're a genius. See ya later."

Walking down the hall to my study, I brought the phone to my ear. "Holly? Kate here. What's up?"

"Oh, Kate ..." Holly's voice was high and trembly. "He's dead."

"Who's dead?"

"Nate. He's been killed."

I was stunned.

"Kate? Are you still there? You've got to help me." Holly began to sob.

My brain clicked back on-line again. "Yes. I will. Tell me what happened."

I heard her blow her nose and take a deep breath before answering. "Late yesterday afternoon, Nate said he'd run a few errands for me -- going to the grocery store, picking up the dry cleaning -- things like that. He never came back. I waited until seven o'clock before calling the police. They didn't have any accident reports that sounded like him. I wanted to file a missing person report, but they said they couldn't do that until Nate had been gone for forty-eight hours. So all I could do was wait, it was the worst night of my life. And then at six o'clock this morning, two Rangers showed up at my front door, telling me that Nate's body was found an hour earlier on the Little Miami Bike Trail."

Holly broke into loud, wrenching sobs. "We were making a new beginning. You saw us, Kate ... it's not fair."

I asked, "Was it robbery?"

"That's what they thought. But then one of the Rangers told me Nate was found clutching a scarf with the initials PS on it. I knew it wasn't a simple robbery."

PS? Monogram. "Patrick's scarf?"

"I think so. I haven't seen it yet, but that's what it could be. I told them about my affair, and they asked me to come down to the station to talk some more and identify the scarf." Holly paused. "Um ... Kate ... would you come with me? I don't have anyone else to ask."

I immediately said, "Yes. But I've got to go to Preston's house first. I've just got my hands on the access code to the locked files in his computer and I know that the Rangers will find that information very interesting. I'll meet you at the station in an hour."

"Well, I know that whatever you find in those files can't hurt me any more than what I've already endured --- all my secrets have been told." Holly paused, and I could hear a sniffle. "Kate, I really appreciate this. I'm exhausted and I don't think I can handle this on my own."

"Did you tell James, yet?"

There was a moment of silence. "No. But I'll call him as soon as I get off the phone with you."

CHAPTER THIRTY-SEVEN ....

I sped south on Loveland-Madeira towards Preston's, having left instructions with Phoebe Jo to tell Cherry what had happened that morning and where I was going.

So much was happening that I felt like I was in a pressure cooker and the lid was about to blow. I hadn't had time to process the latest rush of events and didn't really feel like I had a good grasp on anything.

There were two murders in the last week, and each of the dead bodies was holding something with the initials PS. I couldn't remember if Patrick had told me whether or not he had found his scarf that night when he returned to the church.

I could understand someone having a motive for killing Preston, but not Nate. It was too coincidental that both the ring and the scarf would be pointing to Patrick Sloane. Maybe someone was planting evidence to implicate Patrick? No. The ring was definitely Preston's. What connected these two murders? It was too much to try and think about all at once. I decided to take the small step approach. First, I needed to focus on getting to Preston's and seeing what was in the computer. What I found would either clarify things or -- I thought with horror -- confuse them even more.

The Smiling Gargoyle greeted me from his perch atop the mailbox as I pulled into Preston's driveway. His smile was the type that said, "I know something you don't." I imagined him beckoning me over to the mailbox with a long gnarly claw, and whispering the secrets that he alone possessed now that Preston was dead.

No such luck. I turned off the engine and ran up the front steps, unlocked the door, turned off the alarm system, and took the stairs to the second floor two at a time.

I sat down in front of the computer in Preston's office and turned it on. My breath came in short, hard gasps as I waited for the menu to come up on the screen.

"Come on. Hurry up."

Finally. I rolled the cursor to the T-File. Clicked. A dialogue box with the instructions "Please enter password" appeared over the menu. Nervousness made my fingers feel thick and clumsy as I tried to type in "Seven Sins". Instead, I pounded out "Sven Sins". The computer beeped at me.

"Oh, shut up. I know, I know." I retyped.

The dialogue box disappeared, and the computer began making electronic chewing noises. My chest tightened, reminding me to take a breath. The screen blinked and I was in the T-File, which I discovered was officially titled the Truth File. "Oh, Preston ... how pompous."

There were dozens of documents, each labeled with a name. Some I knew, others were unfamiliar. I went to the first name I recognized -- Charles Hassenbacher -- and double clicked it open.

A few bars of the tune "Roll Out the Barrel" sounded from the computer's speaker as Charles' document opened up, revealing a record of his wheelings and dealings to get his philandering sons into the political arena. I exited. It was of no interest to me. Besides,

I didn't have the time to look under all those rocks.

I went back to the file's contents page and checked through the list of names. The next one I opened was Frank Meyer's. His file opened with a very familiar commercial jingle. Immediately, the rest of the words popped into my mind:

"...'cause if I was an Oscar Mayer Weiner,
everyone would be in love with me."

I laughed -- couldn't help myself -- it was so appropriate. Frank had always been an approval seeker. I clicked out and moved on.

Back at the contents page, I did a quick read through of the remaining names, passing by Terry Poole, Patrick Sloane, Martin "Wolfie" Wolfenden, and Walter "King" Yankovitch. When I got to end I was startled to see Richard James Wagner. What was clean, upright James Wagner doing on this list? It was like a question on an aptitude test where you're given a list of items and asked, "What doesn't belong?"

I opened James' document and listened to the few bars of music Preston had chosen for him. It was a classic orchestral piece -- something I knew and had heard many times, though I couldn't remember what it was. But the information I saw on the screen in front of me was far more compelling.

Apparently, James was not as wealthy as the impression he gave. Back in the 1980s, he made a lot of horribly bad personal real estate investments and experienced devastating financial losses. To keep up the rich facade and the status as a player in Clairmont's business and social communities, he began embezzling money from the family business, Wagner Savings and Loan. He called on his brother Nate's expert accounting skills to cook the books.

As I paged through the contents of the file, I noticed various communications from Harblock Investigative Services. They had conducted several interviews with a disgruntled Wagner Savings and Loan employee, who had secretly kept records of the illegal transactions. Reading between the lines, it seemed that Preston had targeted James and just wanted any dirt that could be dug up on him.

Why would he go after James? I wasn't aware of any relationship between the two of them other than they were serving together on the opera board. But so what?

Opera? *That's* where James' theme music was from. But I knew it best from Francis Ford Coppola's movie *Apocalypse Now*. I could picture the helicopters rising up into the sky, and hear the ominous *thmpf, thmpf, thmpf* of the blades slicing through the air to the beat of that music.

It was *The Flight of the Valkyrias* from Richard Wagner's opera *The Ring of the Nibelung*.

Wagner's Ring.

Preston's ring.

Both rings encircled James Wagner.

The PS on Preston's signet ring had nothing to do with his clue. It was the piece of jewelry itself that he had pulled off his finger, before slipping into unconsciousness, that was important. I guessed it was all he could do -- but it sure was convoluted. Quite possibly Cryptoman's most obscure puzzle.

A flash of movement in my peripheral vision caused me to glance up from the computer screen.

"Oh." I jumped to my feet. "James, you startled me."

James Wagner stood in the doorway, aiming his standard paternalistic smile at me. Even so, his pale blue eyes locked onto mine with a cold intensity that sent chills right through me. "Holly told me you'd be here. Do you need any help?"

I scanned the room, trying not to be obvious about it. I was looking for a weapon to defend myself with. My instincts told me that James had already attacked me once in that room with a ceramic elephant. I saw the gargoyle with the crystal ball on the desk next to the computer.

"No, I don't need any help," I replied. "What are you doing here?" I sidled around to the front of the desk and leaned

238

back against the edge of it. The squatting gargoyle offered me his baseball-sized crystal ball, which he held in his outstretched claws. I palmed the solid glass orb.

James stepped into the room. "Well," he said, patting the back of his perfectly groomed thick, white hair, "I'm interested in what you're doing."

I slapped on my Cavanaugh smile.

"What's the matter, Kate? You seem so nervous."

I guessed no matter how wide I tried to spread it, my grin wouldn't cover the fear I was feeling.

"Oh, I see." James reached into his coat pocket and pulled out a small gun. "You've already found my file."

"There are lots of files here. Preston had information on all sorts of people."

James squinted at me. "I can see in your eyes that you've come to a conclusion. I'm just curious, how did you figure out I killed him?"

"Preston told me."

James' face flushed. He yelled, "What do you mean Preston told you?"

"The ring in his hand. The theme music in your computer file."

James frowned.

"Would you like to hear it?" I asked and, without waiting for an answer, moved back around to the keyboard, reopened James' file, and watched him as the music played again.

His frown deepened. "Wagner's Ring." James spoke through clenched teeth. "That fat, insignificant, little man always had to have the last word. I thought I silenced him when I burned his video tape in the fireplace."

"How could you have done it, James, and think that no one would ever find out?"

"I killed Preston because he was a self-righteous bastard. When I found out that he knew about my financial misfortune and how I was saving face with some creative bookkeeping, I tried to pay him off -- several times. But he refused. The last time was in the sanctuary after the choir's dress rehearsal. I'd attended the church's finance committee meeting that evening, and stopped in at the sanctuary afterwards to hear the music. I waited in the balcony until everyone else had left the sanctuary, before I approached Preston. He was playing the organ.

"Preston bragged to me that he was Wagging Tongue and intended to expose me in his next book. He said, 'The public has a right to know what kind of crooks hide behind respectable facades.' Why couldn't he have just played the game?" James' eyes bored right through me as if I wasn't there. His gun hand began to tremble, and he continued with a crack in his voice. "I pleaded with him, but he ignored me and continued playing that órgan as though I were some insignificant homeless beggar with my hand out. The gall of that evil man. His arrogance was more than I could stand. I grabbed the nearest weapon and swung, then wiped the fingerprints off the candlestick with my handkerchief. I ran out of the church, not knowing if I'd killed him or just knocked him out. When I heard the next day that Preston had died in the hospital and that it was Terry Poole who'd found him unconscious, I knew who to frame.

"*I* told the police about the antagonistic relationship between Terry and Preston -- how Preston blocked Terry's attempts at an operatic career."

James' knuckles turned white as he tightened his grip on the gun. "Preston had hated me for years -- blamed me for his father's bankruptcy. It wasn't my fault Helmut Schneider couldn't pay off the loans he'd taken out on his family's little grocery store. Helmut didn't know what he was doing. One year he's voted Small Business Man of the Year, the next he's overextended himself to the point where I had to call in his loan. It was business, nothing personal. So then he committed suicide and Preston blamed me for that, too."

I looked across the room at the bookshelf where the photo

of Preston's father and the plaque he received were displayed. Now I realized it was a much younger and heavier James Wagner who was in that photo, presenting him with the plaque.

James saw me look and, still holding me under the point of his gun, stole a quick glance to see what I was looking at. He trained his eyes back on me. "Ah, yes. His family shrine. Preston was so proud of his father." He slammed a fist on the desk. "But what about *my* family? For over a century, the Wagner name has been synonymous with being solid and trustworthy. I couldn't let Preston destroy it. So I did what I had to do."

I saw in James' eyes the same expression of outrage and anger that I'd seen in Demetrius' all those many years ago in Greece. Demetrius got so despondent over the loss of his good name and status that he didn't care about life any more and killed himself. But not before taking down the person who knew of his illegal activities. If James was planning to commit suicide, he'd have no problem shooting me first.

I had been standing all this time. Suddenly, my knees felt weak. I wanted to sit down to stop my legs from shaking, but then I would be at a disadvantage if there was an opportunity for quick action on my part. I squeezed the solid crystal ball that I was holding close to my side. I knew that James could shoot faster than I could throw, so I prayed the trembling in my legs would stop, steeled myself, and waited for my chance to use it somehow.

I said, "You're the one who cracked the elephant over my head."

James nodded.

"You were there when Mr. Sanoma gave me the keys."

James took a deep breath. "I started staking out this house, knowing that at some point you'd come here. I planned to sneak in and hide somewhere until you left. I had to find Preston's files, but I was just starting my search in this room when I heard you return, so I hid behind the door and knocked you out when you entered.

"I thought getting rid of that fat little bastard would be the end of it. But no -- he had to have the last word." The intensity I had felt coming from James' eyes seemed to suddenly shift. The energy that had been focused on me was now turned inward. It was as if a veil had been pulled across his eyes and he was no longer aware I was in the room. He spoke as though to himself. "He made me kill my brother."

I was horrified at that revelation. My whole body tensed, ready to attack. Was this my chance? But he blinked and his cold eyes were once again locked onto mine. I had to keep him talking -- maybe there'd be a second chance. "Who made you kill Nate?" I asked.

"I was furious with Nate for allowing that silly wife of his to be caught in an affair with, of all people, that cowboy." James said "cowboy" with particular disdain. "Nate's bungling of his marital relations has caused our family name to be dragged through the mud."

"You killed Nate for that?"

James squinted at me. "Of course not. That sort of thing would have been forgotten in a couple of months."

"So why did you ..."

"My brother wanted to cut a deal with the District Attorney -- confess to our juggling the Wagner Savings and Loan books." James relaxed his grasp on the gun, flexed his fingers and gripped it again as tightly as before. "I ran into Nate yesterday afternoon at the Rodger's in Madeira. He said he wanted to make a clean breast of it all. A grocery store was not the place to discuss such things, so we went to my house." He looked at me as though he'd suddenly realized a truth. "You asked who made me kill Nate? Well, besides Preston, you have to take some of the responsibility, Kate."

"Me?"

"Nate voiced his fear that, with all your snooping around, *you'd* eventually uncover Preston's files. He said it'd be better for us if we turned ourselves in before that happened. Better for us? Ha! That little brother of mine was only thinking of himself. If I uncovered that can of worms, and if the Rangers got their hands on Preston's file, you can bet I'd be taking Terry Poole's place at the top of their suspect list. When I admitted to Nate what I'd done, he shocked me. He had the audacity to say he didn't want to be accused of harboring a fugitive. Fugitive? I was his older brother for God's sake. We got into a violent argument. Nate's small mind couldn't grasp the big picture -- how he was about to help Preston destroy our family's reputation. When he started to leave, I grabbed my fireplace poker and stopped him with one swing."

"And you dumped his body on the Little Miami Bike Trail?"

James nodded. "As a parting touch, I wrapped Patrick Sloane's scarf around Nate's hand. Seems I'd mixed up our scarves by mistake at church last Thursday night when I got my coat from the coat rack. Didn't realize it until I heard Patrick asking people at Sunday services if they'd found it. I don't know why I didn't tell him -- instincts I guess."

A killer's instinct. James looked like he was getting ready to make me victim number three. I had to keep him talking. "James, please. Don't do this."

"Sorry, Kate. I have to cover my trail."

"But you can't kill everyone who might know what you've done. What about the employee who initially discovered your embezzling? He might have told others. You can't possibly hope to succeed." I immediately realized that was the wrong thing to say.

James' eyes bulged in anger. "Don't *you* tell *me* what I can or can't do."

He raised his gun.

The unmistakable rumble and roar of a Harley-Davidson zooming up the driveway boomed through the windows.

"Who's that?" James said, and turned to look.

Now. His head my target, I snapped my wrist and pitched a straight, solid crystal, underhand fastball. Strike three.

The gun fired.

243

Eight days later ... *December 29th*

CHAPTER THIRTY-EIGHT ....

The sun was still soft and new on a quiet wintry morning. Boo-Kat and I trudged alongside the creek bed and through the woods surrounding my farm, both of us on a restless search -- he for sport, shoving his muzzle down every fox and rabbit hole. I was searching for perspective and closure.

As usual, the thoughts tumbling around in my brain had awakened me at three o'clock that morning. I had spent the next couple of hours, sitting up in bed, writing in my journal and re-reading newspaper clippings. Clairmont's first two murders had been *The Cincinnati Enquirer's* front page story every day for the past week.

According to Clairmont Ranger Matt Skinner, "We were finally able to identify the mystery fingerprint found on the brass candlestick used to kill Preston Schneider, as James Wagner's. We also identified the weapon used to kill Nate Wagner by matching residue samples collected from his head wound with scrapings taken from a fireplace poker found in the residence of the same James Wagner."

Yeah, Skinner -- you were hot on his trail right from the start.

The information in Preston's T-file along with my testimony was more than enough to have all charges against Terry Poole dropped.

Quotes had been gathered from everyone but me -- not that the reporters hadn't tried. I'd chosen to remain silent and avoid them, so I guess I had to take some responsibility for some of their inaccuracies.

I did not, as the paper stated, knock the gun out of James Wagner's hand just as he shot at me. I was lucky enough to bounce the crystal ball off the side of his skull, and, as he fell, the gun went off accidentally -- though I'm sure, if I hadn't taken advantage of the opportunity, James would have indeed shot me at point blank range, and I'd probably not be here to tell the story.

By the time I had filled a half-dozen journal pages with my scribbles, the gnawing in my stomach had forced me out of bed and down to the kitchen. I made myself a cup of coffee, slathered a couple of toasted bagels with cream cheese and honey, and sat at the kitchen table, watching the new day spill across the sky in a wash of burnt orange and smoky purple.

The sun was almost over the tree tops by the time Boo-Kat and I had come to the end of our patrol of the borders of my property. Well, *he* was patrolling -- I was still just trying to make sense of everything that had happened.

We came out of the woods a hundred yards from the house. I sat down on an old, bent willow garden bench. Boo jumped up and sat beside me, pushing his little body hard up against my side.

"You need a bath," I said.

Boo-Kat gave me an indignant look and snarled as I tried to

pull some of the brambles out of his fur.

It had turned out to be a pretty quiet Christmas. I don't think any of us wanted it to be any different. Cherry decided to stay another week, partly because she didn't want to miss out on the excitement of the media circus that followed the arrest of James Wagner. After all, she had played a very important part -- arriving on her motorcycle at the climactic moment in an attempt to catch up with me and not be fired from her self-appointed job as my "bodyguard". Her noisy arrival distracted James just enough to enable me to knock him out with my crystal ball. But I think Julie Ann's pleading and begging also had something to do with Cherry's change of plans. Julie Ann wanted to hear more of our travel stories and knew Cherry wouldn't leave out the wilder details of our experiences -- like I did.

I was worried about Holly and had invited her to join us for Christmas, but Terry and Marilyn had already given her the shoulders she needed to lean on, just as they had done for me. I was happy that their ordeal had ended and felt a great satisfaction in being able to help them in return.

I watched Tony drive up in his truck, park around the side of the house, and go into the commercial kitchen. A minute later, Julie Ann came out of the front door and ran down the laneway, late for her school bus. Phoebe Jo and Robert would be sitting in the family kitchen eating their porridge and discussing the schedule for the day. I watched the little world I had helped create come to life and I loved it -- even in its orderliness and predictable routines.

There was a thread running through my life right from my beginnings as a little girl following Dad around the plant learning how they made Crown Chili, and hearing the stories about my grandfather and great-grandfather. That thread continued through my time as a young girl spending hours cutting out recipes and pasting them into an old school workbook, and writing out menus for fantasy parties.

I gazed at the farmhouse and marveled at how it had all

come together -- even the rebellious phase, wandering aimlessly around the planet, collecting recipes. Everything was a stepping stone to where I was now and I wished Dad was still here to see what had become of me.

Cherry was going to jump on her motorcycle that morning and drive off to New Orleans. She would spend a few months there staying for Mardi Gras and then, "Who knows? Maybe Texas and over to visit some friends in New Mexico."

I still had that restless, rebellious spirit inside of me that wanted to go with her, but there was that thread running through my life -- the thread that tied everything together and always made sense and seemed true. I didn't want to break that connection.

A white Mercedes made its way slowly and cautiously up the gravel laneway. Mother always drove her car as if she was afraid of getting mud splashed on the compulsively cleaned white metal. I smiled to myself. She did have to make certain sacrifices -- like setting aside her mud phobia -- in order to come out here to what she called "The Wilderness" and visit me.

Boo recognized the car, jumped down off the bench, and, barking excitedly, raced alongside it to the front of the house. I didn't get there in time to keep him from jumping all over Mother. I yanked on his collar and pulled him away from her. "Hi, you're early. I don't think the rental place opens until ten o'clock."

I had agreed to accompany her to the party supply store and look for more suitable chairs for her Art Museum Women's Guild Annual New Year's bash. I was still hearing about the cheap, rickety seating I had provided for her Christmas luncheon, and, not trusting me to pick out something better, she arranged this mother-daughter outing to try to resolve the situation.

"Come inside," I said, "and have some coffee. Cherry hasn't even left yet."

"Oh? Is this the day?"

"Yes, and you're just in time to say goodbye to her."

"That's lovely. Isn't it kind of cold to be traveling around on a motorcycle this time of year?"

"She's prepared."

We walked through the front door the same time Cherry descended the staircase, looking ready to do battle with any assault on her body, clothed from the neck down in thick, black leather, except for the bright red cowboy boots on her feet. She was wrapping a heavy, red woolen scarf around her neck.

"Aren't you going to have any breakfast?" I asked.

"No. I'll stop on the road in a couple of hours. If I eat something now, it'll just make me want to lounge around for the rest of the morning."

"So ... this is it?"

Cherry wrapped her arms around my waist and gave me a bone-cruching-bodybuilder's hug. "I know I keep saying it -- but it's true -- I've had the best time." She looked up at me. "And it was great seeing you again, Katie."

I hugged her back and tears filled my eyes. I looked at Cherry through a watery veil, pulled out a handful of tissues, and dabbed my eyes as we moved together out the front door and down to the side of the house where her motorcycle was parked. Mother followed at a safe distance.

As I watched Cherry kick-start her bike, I had the feeling that something more needed to be said, but conflicting emotions kept me silent. Part of me wanted to climb on board the motorcycle with her, but it felt right to have put down roots, and some inner voice told me that staying here did not mean staying still.

Mother stepped up beside me, wearing her Cavanaugh smile.

Cherry settled into her seat, put on her helmet, and flashed me a grin.

I said, "I'm going to miss you." My voice cracked.

"I'm gonna miss you, too. But I'll be back." Cherry glanced at Mother. "'Bye, Mom."

I could see Mother's smile twitch.

Cherry revved the engine. "Katie, I'm still hooked up to

Klaus' grapevine. Don't be surprised if some friendly ghosts from the past show up on your doorstep after they hear what a good time I had." And she zoomed away.

Mother's smile had completely vanished. "That's what I'm afraid of." She shuddered, shook her head as though dismissing that unpleasant thought, and pulled a sheet of paper out of her purse. "Kathleen. I have some revisions for the New Year's menu."

If you are interested in receiving
Kate Cavanaugh's free newsletter

Thoughts at 3 A.M.

UPDATES FROM KATE
AND NEWS OF FUTURE BOOKS & EVENTS

Please complete the information below:

Name _____

Address _____

City _____ State _____ Zip _____

Mail to:

CC Publishing
PO Box 542
Loveland, Ohio 45140

To order additional copies of ADD ONE DEAD CRITIC, complete the information below.

Ship to: (Please print)

Name _____

Address _____

City _____ State _____ Zip _____

Day Phone (optional) (____) _____

_____ copies @ $12.95 each* $ _____

*Postage and handling $3.50 for first book
$1.00 @ additional copy $ _____

Ohio residents add 6% tax $ _____

*Make checks payable in U.S. funds to **CC Publishing***
Send to: CC Publishing
PO Box 542, Loveland, Ohio 45140
*Price & Postage subject to change without notice.

To order additional copies of ADD ONE DEAD CRITIC, complete the information below.

Ship to: (Please print)

Name _____

Address _____

City _____ State _____ Zip _____

Day Phone (optional) (____) _____

_____ copies @ $12.95 each* $ _____

*Postage and handling $3.50 for first book
$1.00 @ additional copy $ _____

Ohio residents add 6% tax $ _____

*Make checks payable in U.S. funds to **CC Publishing***
Send to: CC Publishing
PO Box 542, Loveland, Ohio 45140
*Price & Postage subject to change without notice.